REVELATION

JAMIE RIPP

INK STREET PRESS

ISBN: 978-1-7336261-2-5 (eBook)
ISBN: 978-1-7336261-3-2 (paperback)

Published by Ink Street Press
support@inkstreetpress.com
Edited by Alan Brown and Blair Thornburgh
Cover Design by Alexandra Purtan and Michelle Jensen
Formatted by Lorna Reid

BOOKS BY JAMIE:

Paradox Trilogy

Paradox
Revelation
Ascendance

Exclusive Bonus Chapter:

Forgotten Journal

www.jamieripp.com

I dedicate this book to my three amazing and inspiring kids,

Amber, Luke, and Lacie,
who have always believed in me.

ONE

"Are you ready?"

The door to my room slammed open. The sound pounded in my head like a jackhammer in New York City. Covering my head with the blanket, I snuggled back down into soft comfort and silently prayed for more sleep.

Michael threw open the drapes to the large windows behind the bed, which was centered against the side wall. Sun streamed through the transparent glass, bathing the room in a pool of bright early-morning light. The blankets blocked out some of it, but it was still too bright.

"For what?" I groaned as I slid my feet off the bed and looked up at the drop-dead gorgeous man who now stood next to me.

I took a few seconds to focus before I realized what today was. Then, as if transported back in time, I relived the memories of the last time I saw my parents. I saw my mom and dad standing behind me as I got into my new SUV, the day I left Las Vegas. My heart wrenched in my chest as I thought of what I would say to them now. It'd been months since I'd last seen them, and so much had changed.

I had gotten a promotion in Utah to assistant bank manager. After I moved, my whole world was turned upside down. Overnight, my life of freedom and normalcy vanished.

An attack on my life led to my abduction. I watched my best friend turn from a white werewolf to a man before my eyes. I never would have imagined that I would find myself in love with my abductor—a vampire—and living in his castle, among his coven, but here I was.

The odd thing was, there was a connection between Michael and my dad that I couldn't quite place. I knew they were both protective of me, but there was more to it than that.

Michael whispered in my ear as he brushed the hair from my face. "Your dad will be calling soon."

My dad and Michael had arranged for us to video chat so I could see and talk to my parents face-to-face. It had been almost six months since my last contact with them. But I wasn't ready. So much had happened, and they lied to me about who and what they were. Now, I balked at what we were going to talk about. I knew that Michael's coven didn't think my dad was a good guy. He alone had been the cause of most of their suffering. My dad had killed and slaughtered thousands as ordered by Nicholas, my new nemesis. Once Nicholas found out about me, he placed a price on my head, which landed me where I am now, running and fighting for my life. If that weren't bad enough, I now had nightmares that left me cringing. Whenever there was trouble or chaos on the way, my dreams warned me. With each vision, I could see what I should fear or what was to come. Vaguely, anyway.

"Yeah, I know." I ran my fingers through my hair and brushed my teeth as Michael picked out my clothes. "I'll be there in a sec."

The hallways and stairs were empty as we walked through the castle to Michael's office. It wasn't every day that I came in here, but as we approached the massive doors, awe overtook me. With an easy push, Michael opened the wooden, knot-marked doors to his upstairs office. This area was generally off-limits to the rest of the coven, only occupied during a major crisis. I shook inside as I waited for him to turn on the lights. A whiff of citrus wood polish and men's aftershave wafted through the air as I walked into the large, spacious room. While Michael's castle was traditional, his office was contemporary, in a modern, minimalist style of white and pale green. The floor was white Italian marble, giving it a sterile look that, oddly enough, fit Michael. Simplicity and masculinity were splashed throughout the room, a subtle and gentle display that only he could pull off. A soft white leather couch divided the room into a work area and a lounging space where you could kick up your feet.

Michael walked to the large, sleek, and stylish, desk that dominated the far wall, where he had his computer already set up, my parents' faces filling the screen.

"Daddy? Mama?" I asked as a tidal wave of emotions slammed against the walls of my heart. A dense and unsettling feeling of resentment and loneliness filled the emptiness around me. In all the time we lived in Vegas, the fact that they were vampires, or that I was being hunted by one of the deadliest vampires alive, never came up, and their best option had apparently been to send me away for my safety. Then they were gone. There was nothing after that. We had a few phone calls when I was living in Elsinore with Alex, but that was it. I learned more about them and their real lives from strangers than I ever did from them.

As my face appeared in the little square in the upper right-hand corner of the screen, I tried to sit still in front of the camera. The connection was not that great. A fuzzy image swayed on the screen.

"Yes, we're here, honey." Mom's voice was high-pitched and laced with tears.

"I'll see you later, luv." Michael kissed me on the cheek

and left the room. For five minutes, my parents and I talked about how I was doing, how Michael was treating me, and if Alex was still around. That was pretty much it. I had asked where they were and when I would see them again, but they gave me the same vague, random, half-answers I got in Vegas. A few minutes later, the call went static.

"What happened, luv?" Michael tried to be calm, but I knew better. The way his voice echoed the fear I felt and how his eyes met mine after the internet connection cut off was a dead giveaway.

"I don't know, it just went static." I bit my top lip as I tried not to worry too much. "Is everything okay? I mean, they are vampires, what can hurt them? It's probably just a bad connection, right?" I said, hoping to convince myself everything was as it should be.

"I'm sure they're fine, but I should check a few things out just to make sure, all right?"

"Is it that bad?"

"Nope, just a precaution."

"It's either really bad, or you're protecting me from something," I said with a smirk, knowing I had him.

"None and all of the above." Michael placed his hands on my shoulders.

Taking a deep breath, I folded my arms and shrugged my shoulders. "How long will you be gone?"

"I should only be a few days."

"Who will be here with me?" I all but yelled.

"Alex and Jonathan are never far. They'll be if you need them."

"All right, if you're sure," I said as Michael kissed my forehead then disappeared down the hall. Without looking back, Michael left the manor, and that was when I noticed how detached from everyone I felt.

4

For the last two days I'd walked aimlessly around the grounds and throughout the manor. Rumblings of broken borders and new information were whispered along the halls in hushed tones as I walked by. Members of Michael's coven were edgy, and tension cast over the corridors like a thick shadow.

Today, as I sat on one of the benches in the courtyard, something seemed amiss. Coven members greeted me when they passed, but other than that I was alone. As the dim light from the setting sun tinted the skies pink, and dusk drifted over the valley, I headed back to my room. Until now, I didn't realize how much I depended on Michael's company. I wasn't a prisoner of these walls or borders of the mansion, but I without him, I had nothing.

I was mentally and physically exhausted when I returned to my room. Even as my bed beckoned me, I was afraid to lie down and sleep. The days were long, and the nights were full of terror as I watched myself die over and over again. Night after night they trapped me like a mouse in a mouse trap. My nightmares gripped me in an intense fight of life or death. The way I died varied, but the same white-haired man was the cause each time. His hatred for me, and his determination to see me die, was resolute. Sometimes my death was fast and clean; other times it was slow and torturous. As I finally falling asleep, knowing what was going to happen, I prayed for one peaceful night's sleep.

The dark and aphotic stairway led to his white marble throne. A massive cathedra stood overlooking the men and women below him. The domineering placement demonstrated his power and authority. As I walked toward him, my shackles and chains echoed through the dim and ominous cavern. The white-haired man didn't glance in my direction or acknowledge my presence. Instead, he stood and addressed his minions, the train of his cloak trailing behind him.

"In my possession, I hold captive the daughter of Steven. The so-called prodigy the Old One spoke of, the one prophesied to overpower me." As he looked in my direction, his eyes reflected his disgust and disapproval. His gaze raked over me from head to foot, then he shook his head.

"And to think, this thing, this child, was destined to defeat me," he said, laughing. Nicholas grabbed my chains and yanked me forward. The chains dug into my skin, and blood dripped from my wrists as I fell to my knees before him. His coven laughed and jeered at me while the white-haired man yanked and shook my chains, showing his coven my defeat. Finally, his patience for me waned, and as fast as lightning, he had me by the neck, suspended in midair.

"You never had a chance of defeating me. To think, they believed I would fall at the hands of a mere child." His breath reeked of death, and his grip was suffocating. Darkness consumed me as his hands wrapped around my neck. Just as my heartbeat weakened, he dropped me. I grabbed my neck and gasped for air as he laughed at my weakness. Agony spread through my chest, leaving me writhing in pain. Slowly, my heart stopped beating entirely. I felt its last, its final beat. I could hear distant echoes, slurs from his laughing coven, and his screams of triumph.

I sat up with a start. My heart pounded, and tears rolled down my face. To my relief, I was still in bed. The nightmares left me feeling fearful and terrified that my dream was foretelling my future. I felt unsettled, like there was more to the dreams than I understood. My body shook, and my hands trembled. I took a few deep breaths and tried to shake the chills that ran up my spine. Finally, I threw off the covers. The cold and biting castle air nipped at my bare legs. I rubbed my face as the frosty air brushed my skin and I tried to forget the memory of the night. Shivering, I reluctantly got out of bed.

Things had been so different lately. It wasn't just that I lived among vampires, there was something else not right. I just couldn't figure out what it was.

I turned the squeaky, crystal knobs to the shower, and the scalding, calescent, steamy water washed over my cold and shuddering body. The water seemed to relieve most of the stress, but there was still something nagging at me. Running my hands through my hair, I took a few deep breaths and tried to relax.

As the hot fog swirled and filled the room, I wiped the mirror and stepped back to look at myself. The dark circles and bags beneath my eyes from my loss of appetite gave me a hollowed look. Reflected in the mirror was a tired and weak-looking hag. Rubbing my eyes and temples, I stared at the sad and gloomy person in front of me.

"Hello, Arri," Sara said as she bounced through the door. Sara was always so cheerful and happy. Sometimes, it was just plain annoying.

"Good morning, Sara. What are you up to today?" I asked. She was always doing something that allowed her to show off her enviable talents.

"Wow, Arri, you look terrible. What happened to you?" She came a bit closer.

"Just nightmares," I replied, and to my surprise, Sara looked shocked.

"You still have nightmares?" she asked.

"Don't werewolves have them?"

Sara looked at me strangely. "Nightmares require sleep. Something werewolves and vampires don't do. It's a complete waste of time." Sara laughed. "Come on. Get dressed and ready."

After rummaging through my closet and making myself somewhat presentable, I opened the door and Sara smiled.

"Let's get you out of here. Maybe a little sunlight and a

walk will put some color back in your cheeks." She grabbed me by the hand and led me through the castle and the busy foyer until we made it outside. "Now, tell me about your nightmares. Maybe I can help you figure out what they mean."

The weather was cool and sunny. The bright sunlight kissed my skin, and it felt good to let myself bask in the warmth for a moment. Starting off slowly, Sara and I wandered aimlessly around the yard. As we walked, I told her about my nightmares. When I was finished, Sara smirked.

"It means you will die," she said, point-blank.

"What?" I shook my head at her. "They're just dreams, Sara. Why would you say that?" Her blunt statement took me aback. Sara shrugged and looked around.

"Are you *sure* they are dreams?" Sara furrowed her brows. "Maybe they are premonitions." She sat on a nearby bench.

"Premonitions?"

"Yeah. They're like small windows in time where you can see the future." She patted the bench next to her.

"I know what premonitions are, Sara. I'm having nightmares. I'm not stupid," I said, shaking my head.

I sat down next to her, placing my hands on the bench. The seat was made of a roughly carved stone. It was nothing like the others in Michael's yard. I realized then that we were nowhere near the manor.

"Sara, where are we?"

"We are in the graveyard just outside of Michael's more prominent grounds," Sara said absently.

"Yes, I see that, but why?" I took in my surroundings. The thick trees and dense underbrush should have been a dead giveaway that we'd left the grounds, but I was so lost in my dreams that I didn't pay attention, and now here I was. In trouble and alone.

Sara let out a menacing laugh.

"I have to admit, I thought I would have to drag you here kicking and screaming, but it was easy. With your rambling and ridiculous chatter, you fell into our trap rather easily." Sara took a lingering glance behind me.

"Ah, Sara, you have done well." A woman emerged from the trees. "And with excellent timing, I might add." Her stride was slow and deliberate, her gaze was flawless and perfect, and her steps carefully measured. It wasn't long before I realized who it was.

"M-M-Mary," I stammered. I turned to Sara. "You lying, deceitful, phony little—"

Mary pushed me back, cutting me off. I tried to get to my feet, but Mary put her foot on my chest and held me down.

"It wasn't easy with you snooping through all my paperwork and asking questions, but you were easily fooled."

"And Anna?" I glared up at Mary. "Was she part of your plan too?"

Mary walked away, and I scrambled to my feet.

"Anna was of little use to me," she said. "I'm happy to say she is no longer my burden. I almost thought I would have to kill you myself, but this way I can give you to Nicholas personally. He would rather have you alive."

"I knew there was something fishy about you," I said, mustering all the courage I could. Sara stayed back the bench. I knew her casual and nonchalant mien was just a façade; she was ready to pounce if I made a move. "What do you gain from this, Mary?" I asked.

"Just the pleasure of bringing you in. Being the one who captured the prodigy is its own reward."

Sara finally stood and walked around me. As she paced, she flipped my hair and sniffed the air around me.

"I never could figure out why you thwarted my attempts several times before," Sara said, wrinkling her nose.

"She is not a pure human," Mary said.

I looked around, calculating the odds of an escape, but I was surrounded: Mary behind me and Sara to my side. They spoke of me as if I were nothing, and it infuriated me, anger forming inside me. I didn't know how I was going to make it out of this, but the hatred I felt for their betrayal was fueling my inner fire.

"Let her go!"

I startled as Jonathan emerged out of nowhere.

Sara was caught off guard and flew to Mary's side. I saw an opening where Sara once stood. Jonathan looked at me, and within a second, I understood his unvoiced thoughts.

"Two against one? Not playing fair, are we, ladies?" Jonathan said, taunting the two.

The tension ran high, and a uncomfortable silence shattered the dead air. Sara smiled a chilling grin.

"A lady should never play with her food," Jonathan said, baiting them to attack.

Mary poised herself for a fight, then reached behind her back. "You will not win, wolf. Your fighting skills are inferior." She pulled out a long, silver sword hidden in her floor-length dress. The elegant gown trailed behind her as she advanced on Jonathan, who effortlessly rounded her attack and left her turned around.

"Even with your sword, you and your sidekick haven't got a chance against me."

Mary took his jab as a challenge and charged him. Just as she reached Jonathan, he looked at me, and I understood his plan.

Sara was still here, but I paid her no mind, took my chances, and ran as fast as I could from the clearing into the forest, my heart racing.

"Sara, get her!" came Mary's barked command.

I paused only for a moment until I saw Sara running full speed straight at me. Her form phased as she became a werewolf, her red coat glistening in the mid-day sun as she closed in behind me, her face was furious and determined.

My chest hurt, and my muscles ached as I ran. I looked to the west and saw the silhouette of the castle through the trees. I was so close. I knew I had to make it. Taking a deep breath, and gathering my willpower, I focused, and pushed hard. Sara was just behind me, twenty-five yards away. The harder I tried, the faster I went. The trees blurred, and I found myself weaving in and out of the foliage as if it were second nature. I felt free. My soul was vigorous and alive. As my breathing steadied, my body felt awake and full of life. I pushed away all my barriers and ran unrestrained.

The doors to freedom were just moments away. I could hear Sara's footsteps getting closer. I had pushed as hard as I could, but it wasn't fast enough. I glanced back at my pursuer. Sara was in midair, her paw outstretched, and she caught the bottom of my jeans. I saw the ground coming, and time seemed to slow. Quickly, I tucked my head and rolled, pulling her over my head and launching her forward with my feet. She landed on her back, unprepared and shocked. Her old form returned, and she narrowed her eyes.

"I don't want to fight you, Sara," I said, landing on my feet and poising myself for more.

"Then you will die quickly." Sara lunged toward me.

I had never fought before, but I took her head-on. Adrenaline pumped through my blood as instinct and intuition took over. It was like I was fighting as someone else. I let go of all my human boundaries and limitations, allowing myself to battle willingly and purposefully. I would not be the one who dies.

"I will not surrender," I yelled as Sara charged at me

again. Her hair was stained with blood and her hands were bleeding. We circled each other. Her eyes were thoughtful as she calculated her next move, until acknowledgment shone out and a hint of a smile touched her lips.

"Sure you're ready for this?" she taunted.

"I'm ready for anything," I retorted.

Reaching behind her, she produced a thin silver sword that matched Mary's. She turned, her long blonde hair swirling around her as she flipped the hilt and charged toward me. She jabbed and swung the sword about. I tried to duck and dive, but she was faster. After one more swing, I dodged, and when I stood, Sara grabbed me by the hair, held my head back, and cut into my neck. I could feel the warm droplets of blood slowly making their way to my collarbone. Blood dripped from my hands as I tried to push the blade from my neck.

"You've been bested, so yield," she whispered.

"Never!" I yelled.

Sara scoffed. "You have lost, been beaten. Surrender now."

The grip on her sword loosened and the blade softened against my skin. Carefully, I slid my hand closer to the hilt.

"Why? Why are you doing this?" I asked.

"It's not that easy. I have lived in the shadows too long, and you are invaluable. A priceless rarity. Nicholas will pay handsomely for your apprehension. He's promised me freedom from the pack. A life of my own without the rules of the Alpha."

"You won't win," I said, as my hand finally reached the hilt. With one swift move, I pushed the sword from my neck, and just as Sara brought it back, I ducked. The blade swung behind me as I took it from her. I heard a yelp and a whine. I turned to Sara, her sword now in my hand. The bottom of her tunic slowly turned red, and the tip of the sword was stained with her blood.

"Now you see why I'm priceless," I said.

Sara, in a desperate attempt, lunged at me. Then she was lying beneath me as I towered over her fallen body. She made no effort to stand or move. She was defeated.

"You've been bested, so yield," I said, resting the sword across her neck.

I smiled within. I had actually won. The thought of Nicholas turning Sara against me chilled my heart. If he could get to her, who else could he turn against me? But as I allowed myself to reflect, Sara made her last attempt. She pushed me off her stomach and stood, weak and wobbly. As she prepared to charge again, a flash of white rushed past me, and Alex stood between Sara and me.

"Arri, I got this," Alex said. "She is my mate, and I am her Alpha. It's not your fight." He said nothing else. He glared at Sara, squared his shoulders, poised himself for a fight, and gently he pushed me back.

"She is his responsibility now. The fight is no longer your concern." Jonathan now stood behind me.

"What will happen to her?" I asked.

Jonathan turned me around to face him, then tried to cover my ears as he pulled me close to his chest. An unforgettable scream of pain and torment echoed through my ears. Now I understood what happened. Despite Jonathan's efforts, I turned myself around, and there I saw Sara's headless body, and Alex's mouth stained and dripping with her blood. He had bitten her head off for her betrayal and lost a mate in the process. My knees buckled, and I fell to the ground. When I finally looked around, I realized Sara's and my fight was not private. The entire estate had been watching.

TWO

Quiet and alone, I retreated back to the castle. As Alex and Jonathan took care of the guests outside and the mess left by Sara, I withdrew unnoticed. Shoulders hunched, my gaze focused straight ahead, I wanted to shrink from sight. As I passed through the doors, I saw nothing, heard nothing beyond my own thundering heart. I was lost and dazed as I walked into the manor. I was a hollow, empty, emotionless shell. The coven graciously bowed and moved as I passed them, each member looking startled or otherwise surprised. I was pretty amazed at myself for defeating Sara. I wasn't sure how I did it, but I did.

I stared at the long and lengthy set of stairs ahead of me. Each stair seemed to double in size the longer I stood there.

The thundering rumble of footsteps resonating through the manor echoed in the muted stairways. Alex and Jonathan were right behind me.

"Arri, are you okay?" Alex and Jonathan said in unison.

"I'll be fine," I whispered back, folding my arms and staring straight ahead. The fight had left me stunned.

Alex and Jonathan both flew around me to block my way.

"*I'll be fine* and *I am fine* are two totally different things," Jonathan said, grabbing my arm. I winced at the pain from the cut just above my elbow.

I looked at my arms and legs. My outfit was now almost immodest. Shredded strands of my tattered shirt hung off my shoulders, and my slacks were torn, exposing my bare legs.

"Fine, then. It's both." I pushed past the two of them. After a few more steps, I stopped and looked back. Finally able to feel a sliver of emotion, I rounded on them.

"You know, just once I would like someone to tell me what's going on. I'm beginning to wonder if it is any safer here than out there," I said, pointing out the window. "But right now, I just want to be left alone."

Alex and Jonathan nodded, then cautiously bowed and took a couple of steps back down the stairs.

When I entered my room, the floor-to-ceiling drapes had been drawn open, giving the room an open and airy feeling. The unlit, shaded room had undoubtedly been at the mercy of Nana. The bed was made, my evening clothes laid at the foot.

I walked to the window and tried to calm my nerves. From my view, the yard was as it should be, with no evidence of the fight anywhere. Most of the coven had gathered in small groups. A few of the men reenacted the conflict, while others engaged in some sprightly gossip. It all looked so typical, except one thing: a lone coven member looking out of place. As the others fell into lively conversation, he remained reticent, watching everyone carefully. The hair on the back of my neck stood straight on end, and chills ran up my spine. I shivered and shook my head. The feeling I got from him was just like the one I'd gotten from Sara. The same hatred that had filled her heart filled his. He looked at my window as if he knew I was there, watching him. His eyes were dark and sinful, and his smile was crooked and evil, as though he were looking right into my most feared nightmares. I tried to push my cowardice and uneasy feelings aside and backed away from the window. Goosebumps prickled my arms. I yanked the curtains shut.

I ran my hands through my hair and paced the room. The day had not gone as I had planned. As my hands reached the nape of my neck, I froze. The hair there was short and straight, as if it had been cut off. I thought back to the fight. When I ducked under the sword, Sara had my hair in her hand. I must have cut my own hair trying to escape her. A new sense of fury flared in my veins. I cursed Sara under my breath as I clenched my jaw.

She's only half-human. The phrase echoed through my mind. I paced the room again and mumbled to myself.

The ghostly sound of my steady footsteps mirrored the rhythm of my thoughts. Something tugged at my heart, something hidden deep inside that was begging to come out. Scenes of the fight flashed before me as hidden memories resurfaced. Sara's face looked excited as she chased me. The thrill of the hunt pumped through her veins as she gained on me, but when I entered the yard, her excitement faded, replaced by fear and annoyance. It was no longer a game, the fun was over, and she was about to fail. I could almost read her mind. She thought me weak and small. I remember dropping my control and freeing the inner strength that fought to the surface.

Sara's wordless thoughts haunted me. I could still see the hatred in her eyes as she lunged at me. I didn't know how I came out alive, but I gave a relieved exhaled knowing that I had.

I rubbed my face before leaning back and slouching down in the white, cushiony chair. Leaves and twigs fell from my hair and clothes, landing beside me on the chair and floor.

It seemed like only a few seconds had passed when I heard a soft knock at the door.

"Yes?" I whispered. The knob turned slowly and the door crept open.

"Can we come in?" Jonathan asked.

"Sure, why not." I looked at the door. Alex and Jonathan poked their heads in. Keeping a safe distance, they both crept into the room, their gazes analyzing me.

"Can you not linger in the doorway like that?" I cried. I knew my irritation was extreme, but it wasn't really aimed at them.

Jonathan pushed the door fully open, flipped on the light, and, hesitantly, the two of them walked in.

"Are you okay? Are you hurt?" Alex asked as his eyes scanned me.

"No, I'm fine," I said. "Just a little shaken. A few scratches, nothing that won't heal." I let my shoulders drop.

Alex kneeled before me and took my hands in his.

"I'm sorry. I didn't know she was the leak."

"Alex, how could you not know? She was your *wife*," I spat, standing up and knocking the white chair back. Startled out of his wits, Alex clambered backward, trying to regain his balance. I walked to the dresser and clenched my fists. Gritting my teeth, I placed my hands on the smooth, varnished wood. "How could this have slipped past you? It's not like Sara just changed sides overnight, Alex." My voice came out a little harsher than I expected.

"I don't know what happened," Alex said. "I don't understand how she could have betrayed us. If you haven't noticed, this didn't happen to just you." His temper rose, and I could feel his sadness and anger, each emotion fighting for dominance. And feeling that pain he was trying to suppress, I hated myself for lashing out at him. I'd thought I had some right to anger after almost dying, but that didn't excuse my behavior.

"Look, I'm sorry." He exhaled in short, calm, and controlled breaths. "It looks like Sara had fooled us all." Looking back at me, he fought to hold it together. "I never should have been that far from you." Alex took a controlled breath. Remorse, fury, and heartbreak shone in his eyes. His hands shook, and his shoulders fell. "I was asked to watch over you, and today, I failed. It is customary for you to choose my punishment." He knelt before me, his features hardening as he doubtlessly anticipated the worst, and then, slowly, he bowed his head.

"Punishment?" I said. "What are you talking about?"

Hurt flashed in Alex's eyes as Jonathan stepped beside his brother and laid a hand on his shoulder.

"Because Alex was your guardian and almost failed to protect you, and you came to great harm, it is your right to punish him as you see fit. Exile, servitude, beheading." Jonathan's pained expression on that last word made my knees weak and my stomach queasy. My heart hurt at the thought that they would even *think* that I would punish him. He had kept me alive, saved my hide on more than one occasion, even a few I'm sure I didn't get to witness.

"There is no punishment, Alex. You came to my rescue. Thank you again for saving my life." I almost broke down and cried when his shoulders sagged and a sigh of relief escaped his lips as my words sank in. "I owe you my life, Alex. There will never be a punishment."

My heart wrenched at the thought of his loss. No apology could ever make up for Alex being forced to take his own mate's life. I helped him to his feet. "I am so sorry," I said, and hugged him.

"Thank you," Alex said. "But I took a vow, and sealed myself to you. I knew the consequences that came with the job. I'm just glad you are okay." He stepped back, hollow and distant. The man before me looked like Alex, but the person reflected in his eyes had changed. Before I could say anything else, he bowed slightly, then disappeared and faded into the hallway.

Jonathan stepped forward and brushed a few leaves from my hair. With his finger, he gently caressed the tender skin under my eye.

"It's a beautiful shiner. Would you like some ice for that?"

I shook my head. "No, thank you. I'm a fast healer, remember?" I closed my eyes and dabbed my bruise. The skin felt warm and irritated. "Alex—" I started, but Jonathan butted in.

"He'll be fine. We may walk and talk like men, but our inner dog has the upper hand in the mating scene." He stared at his feet. "The man side of us grieves briefly. We feel the agony and heartache that accompanies the loss. But the inner dog moves on quickly. We don't stand around and feel sad for ourselves. Give him a day or two, and he'll be back."

Jonathan looked back up at me, took my hands, and stepped away. Then he looked at the door. "Michael is almost here. You should get cleaned up before he sees you like this." He smiled, and pulled me into a hug. "You did great. It takes a lot of courage to do what you just did."

With that, he left the room.

It took all of two minutes for Michael to barge into my room after Jonathan left. He tore through the door, letting it slam against the wall and unhook from its ancient hinges. It hung crooked, leaning against the floor as it creaked and teetered as if the last hinge was willing itself not to break. He stopped dead in his tracks when he saw me. His eyes widened, and his body tensed, each muscle stiffening. His eyes reflected sympathy, regret, and trepidation. The room was oddly silent as he stood and took in my appearance. Too late, I realized that the tattered clothing and the bruises that marred my arms, legs, and face probably looked worse than they really were; half of them were already healed, and the more serious ones were getting there, too.

In all honesty, I thought his business in town would have taken longer, and that I would've had at least enough time to take a good shower and heal up a decent amount before he came home.

"I swear, it's not as bad as it looks." I took a few tentative steps, and Michael's eyes widened at the close-up view of the injuries. I shuffled my feet, looking down and picking at a loose string on the hem of my shirt.

"You don't look fine. You look like you've been run over by a train." He pointed first to the bruises on my arms, and then to the beautiful black eye I was sporting.

"I know, but look"—I held out my arms for his examination—"I'm fine. I'm not broken or dead, I'm just a little more decoratively colored." I tried to joke, but Michael's stoic face concerned me, and my words faded into a whisper. "But Sara, well she's…" My words broke off as my heart clenched, thinking of Alex. I still couldn't bear the thought that I was to blame for his loss.

Michael chuckled softly. "If this is all you have to show after fighting a raging werewolf, I'd hate to get on your bad side." He shook his head. "It's good to see you're okay, but I'm even more relieved to see that you're alive, period." He crossed the room in three smooth strides, reached out with shaky, unsteady hands, and brushed the still-healing cut on my neck. His eyes softened, and his fingers traveled along the line of my collarbone and down my arms.

"From what the coven tells me, you put on quite a show." He took me into his arms and hugged me in relief. I tried to hide a flinch as my ribs screamed in pain. He stepped back and took my hands as he surveyed me. "Well, how bad is it?" he asked, examining my shredded clothes. Although Michael's reserved and quiet face showed no emotional signs, I could feel plenty. His heart clenched, and the unyielding fury pried at the surface, begging to be released. "What possessed you to fight her?" A hint of regret and sadness coated his words. "You should have allowed Alex and me to handle it."

"Oh, I don't know. Maybe the thought crossed my mind when I was running for my life. It didn't seem like Sara was willing to stop and chat after trying to turn me over to Mary as a reward to Nicholas. She was pretty bent on killing me."

Michael opened his mouth, but snapped it shut just as Nana came bursting through the door.

"Michael." She stopped and looked at the two of us. Her panic-stricken face sent chills down my spine. "I'm sorry to interrupt you and Miss Arri, but there has been a development downstairs." Her clothes were rumpled, and her hair was untidy. A few strands had fallen from her tight-knit bun and hung around her face.

"What kind of development?"

"The important kind, my lord." Nana's voice was strained with concern. Michael took one look at her face and nodded.

"I'll be down in a moment. Can you please set out some drinks?" Nana nodded again, but her face still showed fear and disquiet. "Thank you."

Nana didn't waste any time. Regardless of her feelings, she left immediately and closed the door behind her.

"She still gets nervous when the coven gets a little anxious. She thinks they will lose control." Michael shook his head and smiled. "I guess I can't blame her, I'm sure you did, or still do." He kissed my forehead.

"I'm not scared so much anymore. It's more like I'm inadequate and weak. So, then, I'm guessing Nana's human?"

"Yes."

"How did she come to work for you? I doubt she answered an ad in the paper."

"No. She feels like she owes me a debt. I saved her from some vampires, and for that, she offered me her services as payment. Of course, I refused, but after I found out that she was running from a forced marriage, I agreed to her request. Once we got back to the States, I offered her parents a handsome sum for her freedom and insisted they say nothing. I allowed her to work for a few months and then told her that her debt was forgiven. Since then, she has refused to leave. I always send her home for the holidays and vacations, but she keeps coming back of her own accord."

Michael pushed a few stubborn strands of hair behind my ear and kissed me softly and passionately. "I'm glad to see you are okay. You scared me. That is not an emotion I feel often, if ever. Now, why don't you get cleaned up and meet me in my office? I don't think that the issue downstairs will take long."

After I cleaned up and changed into the slacks and blouse I set out, I looked in the mirror. My new shoulder-length hair fell just below my ears and framed my thin face. The good-sized scratch where the sword had cut my neck was healing, and the deep gashes in my hands were gone. Other than my left eye, which still sported a pretty good Technicolor bruise, the rest of the evidence of the fight had healed and left no traces.

THREE

The twelve-foot oak double doors to Michael's room were smooth with occasional rough knots. They even bore some score marks from axes, and little dents from arrows. Obviously, Michael had kept them in their original shape. I stood in front of his room for what seemed like forever.

I felt Michael's presence from somewhere close by, and it ratcheted the intense beating of my heart to throbbing. Looking directly at the door, I squared my shoulders. I balled up my hand and raised my fist to knock. Then I felt him again. His presence always made my pulse skip and my stomach flutter. The draw and want I felt for him was unmistakable. I waited for a moment. Smiling to myself, I let my hand drop, and I looked down. My memories of him filled my thoughts. I would have ventured to say I loved him.

"Are you going to knock or do I need to wait here all day?" Michael's voice was playful. His hand touched my shoulder as he walked up from behind me. His warm and casual grip sent goosebumps down my spine, and my emotions stuttered.

"So why are you lingering at my door?" Placing his arms around my waist, he pulled me against him. His mouth lingered as he kissed me on the base of my neck, and the tantalizing breeze of his breath made my own breathing falter.

He pulled away and moved to stand in front of me. I could feel my cheeks flush and my knees weaken. I attempted to steady myself. Michael was always a different person when the coven was nowhere to be seen. He was mischievous, relaxed, and endearing. He wasn't afraid to be himself or show affection. Something he didn't often do in their presence.

"Art thou feeling well?" He asked in a whisper. I was still a little faint and giddy, and I knew my cheeks were blushing crimson. Michael's knowing smile told me he knew he had that effect on me.

"Better, cleaner," I said, as he touched my cheek.

"And?"

"Pardon me, my lord." Jason, a tall, thin man interrupted us. "I have a message for you." He looked sophisticated, but resembled a beatnik, with a well-pressed dark vest and light tan French beret covering his hair. He wasn't the type to be fearful or nervous with the announcement of a message, yet it appeared the mere thought of *this* message was making him tremble.

"Must you interrupt me, Jason?" Michael sounded a tad irritated and his expression hardened like steel. It seemed we were always interrupted whenever we were alone these days, and this small but simple fact irritated Michael beyond belief. Slowly, he turned to look at the gentleman. I could hear a rumble in his throat, as if he were growling.

"I'm sorry, my lord, but the message I bring needs an immediate response." There was a noticeable hesitancy in the messenger's voice. He clenched his fist, a small, rolled-up piece of paper crinkling in his hand.

"Who is the message from?" Michael's voice reeked of disdain.

"A certain Steven and Ava, sire." The man's face turned plaintive as he bowed to Michael and waited for his response.

At the mention of my father's name, I stiffened. After the attempt at seeing my parents a few days ago, I had heard nothing from them since.

"And the message, what of its contents?" Michael's tone calmed a bit, but not enough to put the man at ease.

"Now, sire?" Jason asked as he dared to allow himself a glance in my direction.

"Yes, *now*!" Michael's lack of control won. He raised his voice, and his grip on my shoulders tightened.

"Ouch." I grimaced as I shuddered in pain and tears crept into my eyes.

"Sorry, I…I…" Michael let his arms fall, and looked to the man, now standing a few steps further back than before. "What of the message?" Michael growled through his teeth.

"They are on their way, sire, and wish to meet with you before their arrival in two weeks' time, my lord." Jason bowed again. This time he took to his knee, and bowed such that his nose almost touched the floor.

"Tell them I eagerly await their arrival. The little diner by the movie theatre will do fine." There was a pause, as Michael assessed the look in my eyes. "Oh, and Jason, no one is to know what we have spoken here. The coven is to hear none of it." Jason nodded, bowed again, and turned to leave. He took a few steps and turned back to Michael.

"I beg your pardon, sire. The coven is ready when you are." Jason nodded to Michael, then to me, and disappeared around the corner. Just as Jason rounded the bend, Michael leaned down to kiss me. Our lips pressed lightly but lovingly. Michael let out a small moan before pressing harder and gripping the back of my clothes. It was only then that I heard a man clearing his throat.

Rogan stood at the corner, waiting for Michael. Rogan was a little different from the rest of the coven. He seemed suave, but something deep within him radiated a dark and esoteric temperament. He held a lighter, more familiar friendship with Michael, and they seemed to be more brothers than coven member and master. I could feel the bond they had was ancient. It was if they had been friends before they turned, and they have since faced untold hardships together that tested their character and their friendship. Yet, here they are, still loyal friends and accepting compatriots.

"Nana was on her way up to deliver a message when I met her on the stairs. I must admit, my lord, she is not looking too well. Perhaps it is time to…"

Michael took a swift step forward and gripped the front of Rogan's shirt, cutting him off.

"Old friend, watch your tongue; that is dangerous ground."

Rogan raised his hands in surrender and quickly backed off.

"You have an important call. Nana asked that you kindly take it soon." You could tell that Rogan had not only hit a sore spot with Michael, but also expected this reaction. Then, as if nothing had happened, Rogan brushed off his clothes. Michael turned to me and smiled.

"I know, duty calls," I said, looking at the toes of my shoes. "I will meet you for dinner in a minute or two." I tried to smile, but a feeble excuse of one was all I could muster.

"I will be awaiting your arrival." Michael lightly kissed the back of my hand, and turned to address Rogan. "I am warning you: keep your distance."

"Yes, sire." Rogan grinned, and Michael walked past him, offering a small smirk. After a few moments of uneasy stillness, Rogan assessed me with uncanny coolness. His gaze was stoic and stern, but his lips quirked up into a lazy smile as he met my gaze. With a quick shake of his head and not a word between us, Rogan grabbed me by the hand and offered to escort me.

"My lady, are you ready?" The look of humor and amusement danced in his eyes as he too kissed the back of my hand and offered his arm to escort me to the dining room. As we walked side by side, Rogan gently nudged me. "It seems you are quite fond of Michael, yes?"

"Yes," I replied hastily.

"It's odd he would take a liking to you. He has not shown interest in anyone, even when we were children. All he really cared about was pleasing his father. Now he wishes to please you. It is quite a turn."

"And this is bad?" I knew there had to be bad news in there somewhere.

"No, I think it is great. But do you know what you are in for?"

I stopped and looked at Rogan.

"No, what?"

Rogan grinned. "When you walk into dinner tonight, I feel I must warn you. Games are afoot. Questions as to the reason you are here, why you have been able to keep your mortality, and who you truly are…all will be asked. I want you to be prepared and keep on your toes. This is not a group to which you'll wish to show weakness."

The thought of facing the coven scared me. Who knows what they would think of me now? Judging by Nana's reaction to the development downstairs, I couldn't imagine it would be good. Sensing that I was more than a little nervous, Rogan kissed the back of my hand a second time.

"You are stronger than you think. Don't let them intimidate you." With a crooked smile and playful eyes, he shook his head. "I fear they all underestimate exactly how strong and powerful you are. It will be interesting to watch you grow." Rogan placed a reassuring hand on my shoulder. "I'll go in ahead of you. Take your time."

Rogan bowed to me and walked down the long corridor to the dining room. He slipped inside. The soft click of the doors closing behind him stopped my heart. I hesitated. Trying to calm my nerves, I reached for the knob, but paused when I heard sounds of arguing voices swelling from the other side. I wasn't going in there. I knew—or I had an idea—what the conversation was about, and there was no way I was going to get sucked into this. Just as I had made up my mind, the voices died down to only a few, and I could get a better picture of the issue.

Hearing him clear his throat, and feeling the rigid frustration saturating the air, I knew Michael was drawing the attention and calming the mass of vampires, reining in their careening thoughts.

"I told you it was dangerous for her here, and you still insisted she stay. Now look what has happened. She has brought trouble just as I said she would." A male voice burst out over the crowd's constant murmur.

"I will not be accused of holding this child hostage. I have given her her freedom. It was not by my insistence that she stay—she has asked for my protection. As for her bringing trouble, trouble would have found her sooner if it weren't for Alex's efforts. Whether or not we wanted this, it would have found us eventually." His diplomatic voice carried well, and a thin but noticeable trace of an Old English accent colored his words.

"Everything was fine until she walked through that door. There has never been an attack on any of us. Now, there have been two in less than a month." A lady with a deep Southern accent scorned. "My lord, I think what we are all asking is first, who is she, and second, why are we protecting her? Her mere presence is putting us all in grave danger. If memory serves me right, I believe Arri is being hunted down by Nicholas, and that, combined with the fact that she is a mere human, just exacerbates the situation. I think we all have the right to know why we should protect her."

I knew who she was and could envision her in her red cowboy hat and blue, jewel-studded cowboy boots. She was no older than me, and her attitude was nothing to be desired. She regularly boasted about her accomplishments and her many meals that satisfied to her every whim. It had taken me a while to understand that by meals, she meant humans. I slouched against the wall and listened to what I could.

"I understand, but Arri is only one step in Nicholas's plan. Does anyone know why she is so important to Nicholas?" Michael's voice resounded with challenge.

"To have vengeance on Steven's betrayal. Everyone knows their story," rasped a man with a leathery, rustic voice.

"Nicholas is not after her just because she is Steven's daughter, although that doesn't help the situation. His vengeance goes beyond that. The Old One told Nicholas he would be killed by a child who is only half-human. We all know Steven is a vampire—the most feared and deadly to be exact, even more so than Nicholas. But shockingly enough, Arri's mother was human upon Arri's birth, thus creating a child both vampire and human. Arri did not bring this upon us. She doesn't yet know of her importance, or of her true makings. It would have been only a matter of time before this fight reached us."

My knees went weak, and I slid down the wall until I sat on the floor with my knees to my chest. The revelation wreaked havoc in my mind. But I had kind of put two and two together a while ago. I had even almost thought about maybe being a vampire, but to hear it out loud with such assuredness rocked me. My breath came out in short spurts as I tried not to lose my head. I closed my eyes and hugged my knees even closer to my chest.

Fear and understanding enveloped everyone on the other side of the door. All I could hear, besides the quiet rustling of their clothes as they adjusted their seats, were gasps. Their reactions and their awareness scared me. I didn't know exactly what their realization was, but whatever it was, it had now stunned them all into pure, torturous silence.

"What is the plan?" An inexperienced young man broke the awkward pause. "How will we defend your mate?"

"First, we stop fighting among ourselves." Michael's voice boomed through the sturdy door and into the hall where I sat, shocked and still.

The coven members started to talk among themselves and the conversation grew steadily from a murmur to a roar.

"I see your habit of sneaking around is still intact."

I spun around and faced a petite, mouse-like face I recognized. My breath stilled in my chest.

"Catherine," I cried, and pushed myself off the floor and flew into her arms. Instead of the aloof and reserved character from the bank who would hug me briefly and step back to get some distance, she welcomed me with open arms and a soft but eager hug.

"I can't believe you're here." I pushed away for only a second. "Are Mom and Dad with you?"

Catherine pulled me back into a now not-so-soft, crushing hug. "I'm sorry, dear. They are still attending to a few loose ends. Wow, you have grown up so much since you left us." Her face lit up, and she touched my cheeks. "When your parents got word from Alex that you were attacked, and are now staying with Michael, I thought you would have been the scared little girl I knew, huddled in a corner somewhere."

Her voice and face exuded disbelief. "I didn't think you would have made such a transformation. You cut your hair!" She ran her fingers through my hair and lifted my chin to meet her gaze. "I love it."

I released her hands and tucked my hair behind my ears. "Yeah, well it wasn't my choice." I shrugged. "Sara and I got in a fight this morning, and when the sword slid behind me, it must have cut my hair." I chuckled softly and shook my head.

Catherine's eyes bugged out, fear freezing her features.

"When did this happen? Why weren't we notified?" Catherine looked at me a little closer. The shadows of the darkened corridor hid what wounds I had left, but Catherine reached behind her and flipped on a light switch. "I mean, look at you." A horrified expression contorted her face. Her eyes darted from my neck to my hands to my eyes.

"It's no big deal," I tried to assure her. "Most of the wounds are already healed and gone. There are just a few that were a little deeper. I'm fine, really."

"When did this happen?" Her words came out in slow, short bursts.

"This morning."

"Does Michael know?"

"Yes, of course. Jonathan helped me get away from Mary when Sara started to chase me…"

Catherine cut me off. "I swear, if I ever get my hands on her, she will beg for mercy…" She trailed off into mumbling.

The tiny creature standing in front of me didn't look like she would, or could, hurt a fly, but her petite form was very deceptive. Judging by anger and fury in her words, she was quite sincere.

"Jonathan took care of Mary, and Alex took care of Sara. We won't need to worry about them anymore." I bowed my head in awkward silence.

"I can't believe how nonchalant you are about all this," Catherine said. "Arri, this is not okay." She looked miffed and shocked.

We both jumped when the dining hall broke into laughter.

"So, what's going on in there?" Catherine nodded to the door.

"I don't know." I shook my head. "Apparently there was some disagreement about me. Michael was putting a stop to it."

"What kind of disagreement?"

"The kind that says Dad is a vampire and Mom was human, making me a child of two worlds and because of that, some of the members wonder if I should be allowed to stay. You know, the usual." I rolled my eyes, smiling at the odd thought.

Catherine's face drained of its color, and it was all I could do not to laugh. It was good to see that there was someone besides me that this scared.

"Oh, honey, are you okay?" As soon as she spoke, her concern made her shocked and alarmed features soften.

"Yeah, I think. I sort of suspected as much when Michael mentioned I was Steven's daughter. The others talk about him like he was a mercenary, and from what I can gather, I'm guessing he's not their equivalent to Captain America. I guess hearing it out loud took me by surprise, that's all."

Catherine shook her head, and her expression told me she was sorry. "I didn't mean to deceive you, but I didn't have a choice. When Steven gives an order, you follow, no matter what." She cringed.

"I understand. No worries." I was trying to hide my insecurities about the whole thing, but I may have failed miserably.

"Did you want to go in?" Catherine asked.

"Not re—" I jumped. The doors to the dining room flew open, and Michael stood in the doorway. His perfect silhouette made my stomach do backflips, and my heart took off into a sprint.

"There you are."

I had barely enough time to blink before he took a few smooth strides and drew next to me.

"Look who I found," I said, gesturing toward Catherine. Michael intertwined his fingers with mine.

Catherine curtsied low and bowed her head, waiting until Michael addressed her.

"Catherine, as always, it is a pleasure."

"Thank you, my lord. The pleasure is all mine." Catherine glanced at our intertwined fingers and cocked her head to one side.

Michael didn't miss a beat. "Are you here on business or pleasure?" He brought the back of my hand to his lips in a prominent show of possession.

"Both. I came to check on Arri."

"So Steven sent you," Michael said. With Catherine's quick nod, he pulled me closer to his side. I didn't understand his craving to show her our mutual adoration. It was obviously a dominance thing. Usually, around his coven, he was more discreet, but when it came to Catherine, there was a bit of tension I didn't understand. "How are they doing?"

"Good. Their replacements will be there within the week. I know they are pretty anxious to see their daughter, though." The tension around them grew until the air was tight enough to strangle.

"Do you mean to take her to them?"

"Not today. Today, I'm here to visit."

"Yes, well, I will contact her father first thing in the

morning; let him know you have arrived without harm." The silence and unspoken dismissal curled Catherine's lip into a knowing grin.

"Yes, of course, my lord." Catherine turned to me. "We'll catch up later." With that, she curtsied and left the hall.

I looked at Michael, but before I could say anything, he pulled me into an unrestrained kiss. When I opened my eyes, for a split second, there was a hint of alarm behind Michael's calm façade.

FOUR

The garden was fragrant, and its sweet aroma gently passed over us with the warm spring breeze. After Catherine and the meeting, I was grateful for what I hoped would be some uninterrupted time with Michael.

I had a few questions of my own, not to mention the fact that there was an entire meeting held to discuss me. I felt like I needed to be filled in a little. After telling Rogan that we were not to be disturbed, Michael took me by the hand and we started on a walk around the grounds.

"So, what were you doing in the old graveyard anyway?" Michael asked, and paused at my confused expression. "Jonathan filled me in." He seemed quite intrigued.

"Well…" I began. "I had another nightmare, and Sara offered to be a friend and hear me out. I didn't know she was leading me into a trap. As I talked, we walked. The next thing I knew, it was too late." I told him the rest, all about Mary and what else had happened.

"Turning Mary against us took some fancy footwork. She must have been plotting against you for a quite some time to pull this off." Michael tried to console me.

"Why did Sara take Nicholas's side?" My temper raged at the thought. I hated her for turning against me. "She said I was a rarity." I calmed my fury and shook my head. "What did she mean?" I twirled my necklace with my finger. I had an idea, but I needed to be sure.

"It means you are one of a kind." Michael smiled.

"Yes, thank you. I know the definition, and I got that, but *why*? Nicholas is going through an awful lot of trouble to kill someone he doesn't know. Why me out of millions?"

Michael stopped and took both my hands in his. "Money can corrupt the minds of those with even the best of intentions. Sara fell prey to Nicholas's greed. I'm afraid your capture has come with quite a price. I fear that his obsession with obtaining you goes well beyond a grudge."

I looked Michael right in the eyes. He knew I needed more of an explanation than just "greed."

"When Nicholas killed the Old One, he told Nicholas that he would be ruined by a child born of two worlds."

Tension grew between us. "When Nicholas heard of you, a daughter of Steven, he understood you to be the one the Old One spoke of. He is determined you are going to defeat him. This is why he is after you. If he kills you first, then the prophecy cannot come true."

I looked at Michael, stunned. I could feel the dampness of the warm night air on my skin, and I rubbed my arms involuntarily as I nodded.

"So, he will keep sending people to kill me?"

"Yes, I am afraid so."

"How do we stop him?"

"I fear the only way to stop him would be to kill him."

I was on the verge of tears. I tried as hard as I could to control myself. Lucky for me, Michael sensed my fragile state.

"It's going to be okay, luv."

With that, Michael and I walked back to the mansion in silence. Even though Michael had assured me it would be fine as if it were fact, I couldn't help but wonder if he was right. Was everything really going to be okay?

"Michael? What is the graveyard for if none of you ever

dies?" My question sounded just as awkward out loud as I felt asking it.

"Well, according to the laws of mortal civilization, the house must be owned by someone living. Thus, the castle is the creation of a foreign family and passed down to a young male member every time the previous one dies. I have died and resurfaced over four times in the last two or three hundred years. The graveyard signifies each death and rebirth." Michael pulled me closer. "Come, I have something I want to show you." His excited tone drifted over the silent yard, wiping away the strangeness that hung around his answer.

When we entered the main hall, everyone carried on as usual. No one stopped me or whispered behind my back, and when I passed, a twinge of support and acceptance flickered on the faces of even the most emotionless guests. Some of them even bowed and welcomed me as *my lady*.

My heart had yearned for acceptance, and finally, I had gained their tentative approval.

Michael pulled me past everyone and led me into the kitchen. As we walked in, I froze. Lining the counters were endless rows of gallon-sized bags of red liquid. Behind the bags were several bottles of wine. The thick contents of the bags were being heated and prepped for dinner.

"Is that…" I choked back the revolting feeling that burned my throat.

"Yes. Alain is prepping the coven's meal."

Alain looked over in our direction, and with excellent timing, he straightened before us, his face strained.

"Alain has not been in our coven long. His control around humans is not yet refined."

Alain offered me a slow bow. "What of the lady's dinner, sire?"

"Nothing, thank you. We will not be joining the coven tonight. Please, may I ask you to excuse us?"

Alain gave Michael another bow, and without further questions, left the room just as fast as he had appeared.

"We're not eating dinner with the coven?" I asked as Michael strolled toward the pantry. He opened the door and walked to the end of the shelving. The pantry was more extensive than the whole kitchen in my old house.

"No. We are going out tonight," Michael said, reappearing from the pantry. "Here, come with me." He pulled me behind him, then stopped, and reached under one of the shelves. A small clicking sound came from the far end. Michael pushed open a secret door that had been masked by the heavy shelving. A smell of rich soil drifted from the light breeze in the hallway. Packed dirt floors and more shelving gleamed in the light from behind us. Dusty, cobwebbed wine bottles lined the walls, and scattered along the floor were large, wooden crates.

I followed Michael for a few seconds when a low thudding sound trapped us in the dark and chilling cavern. The door had closed, leaving us in the pitch black. Just as my heart leaped into my throat, Michael flicked a lighter, and a soft, yellow glow gave enough brightness to see each other's faces. Michael's face turned his lips into a charming smile.

"Scared?" he teased.

All I could do was smile back, and a nervous laugh escaped my lips.

"No worries, luv." Michael grabbed my hand and pulled me along beside him.

About twenty feet into the cavern, the bottle-lined shelves went on, but we stopped, and Michael pulled a bottle from the shelf and handed it to me. "Here, hold this." He grabbed the sconce on the wall and twisted the shaft. A soft click echoed off the walls. Michael grinned.

"I'll take that." He took the bottle from me and placed it back on the shelf. "A weight-lever prevents you from opening the door unless the weight is relieved," he explained. My heart was pounding. I trusted Michael, but this was a little odd, even for him. Michael reached under one of the bottom shelves and grabbed a handle, sliding the floor away. "This is where we are going."

"I don't know, Michael." I removed my hand from his and took a few steps back. "I'm not a big fan of small, dark, confined spaces." I shuddered and cringed. "Can't I just meet you at the front door?"

Michael chuckled. "I promise, it is smaller up here than down there. I'll carry you." He jumped into the dark hole and reached up to help me in. "Trust me." He was grinning. I bit my bottom lip as I took immeasurably small steps forward. As I reached for his hands, he pulled me in and held me in his arms.

"Are you ready?" he asked. The look on my face must have mirrored the scared and unsure thudding of my heart, because he chuckled again, and the thunderous sound in his chest vibrated against my cheek. "Hold on," he whispered in my ear as he bent his head down and seized my lips with his.

Cradling me in his arms, he took off running, and I found a sort of comfort, knowing I had just placed all my trust in Michael. The cold, dark air brushed against my cheek. Pulling myself closer to his chest, I blocked the chill breeze from my face and chest.

The even tempo and gentle, rhythmic flow of his breathing lulled my erratic heartbeat. The further we ran, the more his breathing seemed to soften.

"How far are we going?"

"Twenty miles or so."

I tucked my face back against his chest. The smell of cologne and men's soap clung to his clothes.

Just minutes later, Michael slowed down. "We're here," his soft and loving voice whispered into my ear. He placed me on my feet. The darkness was absolute, with no signs of light. Michael let go of my hand and took a few steps away from me. My footsteps echoed against the cold cavern walls as I tried to follow him.

Neither the melody of his labored breathing nor his near-soundless footsteps could be heard through the darkness.

"Michael," I called after him. A small flicker of light flashed a good ten feet from me. A single torch lit up, and a flame roared to life and brought the rest of the chamber into view. As my eyes adjusted to the fire, a great stone door came into focus. When Michael lowered me into the cavern below the wine cellar, all I could see in the emptiness was a small set of stairs, but here at the end of our journey, was a large, open, and grand cavern at the base of a rather large, extravagant stone-carved door. *Ex quo defunctus sum surgam et reviviscam* was carved across the face of it.

"What does it say?" I asked, tracing a few of the letters with my fingers.

"It's Latin. It means *from whence I died, I shall rise and live again.*" The cold, smooth stone vibrated slightly with the gruff and low tone of Michael's voice.

"Are you all right?" I asked. Michael looked crestfallen.

"Yeah. I wrote that the day I brought the castle here. Your dad spoke it before he turned me..." His voice broke off, and he took the torch from the wall and used it to light another. A small, almost inconspicuous metal box was obscured within the rock wall, and the falling shadows were barely visible in the dim lighting. Michael opened the unremarkable box, and a faint green glow appeared from behind the door. Michael placed his hand on the square green screen, which lit and scanned his hand.

"Welcome back, Monsieur London." An electronic voice filled the silence between us. The massive doors gave a loud hum and clank as they swung open. Cloudy air and dust gently fell before us.

"Shall we?" Michael offered me his arm, and we walked in, side by side. After the door closed, another loud, dull thud sounded as it locked behind us. A colorful mosaic covered the floor beneath my feet. The tiles and colors blended into an unfamiliar pattern. Splashes of reds and golds bounced lightly against the gray, smooth, and polished walls.

"Shortly after I built the castle, I realized that I too would need a place to call my own. The castle may be mine, but I rarely am left in peace, as you have witnessed. I have offered my home as a refuge, asylum, vacation resort, and meeting house. I built my lair a few months after arriving here." Michael held the torch high above us, and the dim light cascaded down along the walls and stairs. The magnitude and grandeur of the room took my breath away. A circular, hollow shaft of stone rose high above the light. Spiral stairs carved from the walls encircled the entire length of pillar. Each stair had delicate scrollwork marking its edge.

"Well?" Michael asked, glancing around the height of the lit cavern around us.

"This is amazing." I smiled.

I took a deep breath through my nose, smelling the fresh and vibrant earth surrounding us.

"Come on. What I want to show you is up here." I looked up at the long spiral staircase, the stairs disappearing into the darkness above.

"Up there?" I asked.

"Yep. This is the only way up." Michael took the torch and handed it to me. "Here."

"You're serious. With the high-tech palm scanners and the all-time invention of light bulbs, you skimped on the elevator?" I asked.

"Yes, well, I didn't plan this for human use. You will be the first to ever be here." His smile was tentative, almost shy.

Giving him a break, I started up the stairs. Each carved stone was identical to the next. I climbed slowly, but finally had to stop.

"We are only a quarter of the way up. Would you like me to carry you?" Michael's offer was genuine and held no contempt for my human frailties or restrictions.

I looked at him, then shook my head. "I feel so…"

"Human," Michael finished.

"Yeah, I guess you could say that." I folded my arms and looked at the ground.

"It is nothing to be ashamed of. When I built this place, it was never designed for anyone other than me. You have outdone anyone with mortal status, and I hardly expected you to make it to the top without my assistance." His mouth settled into a thin line as he waited for my answer.

My voice seemed to have gotten lost on its way to my mouth, so I just nodded. Michael looked down at me and kissed me softly as he cradled me in his arms.

"Besides, this way, I can hold you," Michael said with a smirk, as he took off into a gentle run.

In no time at all, we made it to the top of the staircase. The brightly lit passageway before us resembled the older carved stone structure below, with the same comfort, opulence, and luxury as the castle. The entire length of the hallway was lit with cascading silver chandeliers. A burgundy Persian rug ran the extent of the lightly shaded bamboo floors.

Walking into the passageway brought a sense of formality and elegance. Michael was anything but simple. Every step he'd taken in making the tunnels, caverns, stairways, and halls, he made with purpose. Comfort was his first priority. Even here, he had made it worthy of welcoming royalty.

"Wow, this is amazing!" As we walked through the hallway and into a rather large and spacious cavern, the ambiance and elegance enveloped us, and this was quickly becoming my favorite place in the world. There was no one to interrupt us and nothing to disturb us, so it was just him and me.

FIVE

"**D**oes…" I stopped and gasped when I was abruptly halted by a guard who reminded me of a WWF wrestler. His arms were as big as my waist, and his body covered the entire entrance just in front of us. He sported a short blond military cut and a tattoo of a phoenix perched above his left ear. His nostrils were flaring like a roaring dragon when he saw me. The purpose and determination filling his brown eyes faltered when saw Michael walking close behind me.

"Let her through." Michael's voice, stern and commanding, boomed against the cavern walls.

I took a few shaky breaths before I walked past the Brock Lesnar lookalike.

As I passed the enormous man, I could feel his cold, steely gaze follow me. My uneven breathing was a dead giveaway that this man had intimidated me, and when Michael followed me with his hand at the small of my back, I heard him speak to the man in a foreign language, one that I hadn't heard before. When I glanced back at him, making sure I could continue, he gave me a reassuring nod and a genuine smile.

The dancing light from the chandeliers called my heart to its home. Walking through the warm and inviting air toward the center of a large cavern gave me goosebumps. The room seemed like it went on forever. At the opposite side, the largest painting I had ever seen hung from a gold-crested frame. A proud and dignified young man posed steadily atop a large dun Akhal-Teke horse. Although he sat tall and honorable, the soft look in his eyes told me it was Michael. The portrait showed proof of Michael's heritage.

"That was painted a year before the attack on my kingdom," Michael said, following my gaze. "My father had it painted as a gift to my mother." He twirled the ring on his finger. The thick silver band was engraved with a coat of arms. "My ancestry has been lost to the modern world. Few know of the fallen kingdom. This portrait and the castle are my only proof to my royal line." His words were solemn and reflective.

Michael walked past me and stepped behind a wet bar, where offered a glass of wine.

"I promise it's not spiked." He laughed, still holding the glass, silently asking me if I wanted a drink. I shook my head and walked further into the room. I traced my finger along a few furniture pieces and sculptures as I explored the entire space before returning to Michael. The smell of antique oil and sweet springtime floral filled the room. Freshly cut stalks of white calla lilies filled some vases; yellow and white tulips filled others. Some arrangements were almost gaudy: large gold painted vases with spray roses, spirea, jasmine, and hanging amaranthus. A sort of reverence filled me. The flame from the chandeliers gave off a soft, golden glow that permeated the entire room. Shadows frolicked with the light; the atmosphere took my breath away. Plush couches and throw pillows were scattered in small groupings, as if for conversation. Paintings from every era hung in large oversized frames, somehow making the room homier. Art that the world thought was lost was here perfectly preserved and revealed in the light of the flickering candles. Antique tapestries hung on the walls, giving the appearance of windows. Michael led me over to a couch and coffee table grouping and gestured to an overstuffed loveseat. It was comfortable—I felt as though I had sunk into a bed of roses.

Michael walked to a large stone fireplace. He placed his wine glass on the mantel, then knelt down and started a small warm fire. Michael had great taste, and even without a regular elevator, the cavern made a perfect home. Plus, the old furniture scattered about the cavern made my heart jolt. The collection Michael had hidden in the mountain would make an antique dealer jealous. Dressers, cupboards, and stands were well maintained, complete with authentic chips in the paint and everything. I leaned over to admire the end table delicately placed on a soft fluffy rug next to the couch. It was so weathered that even with my lack of antique knowledge, I would guess it was as old as Michael. A few pieces looked scorched while others looked like they were owned by Mary Tudor, the Queen of England. Everything here was ancient, and the fact that so many of these artifacts were thought to be lost to natural disasters or wars made it all the more sensible that they'd find their place among Michael's belongings.

Even with the distraction of a beautiful getaway cavern in the middle of a cliff-faced mountain, I still had the worries of today on my mind. Michael and I had a lot to discuss.

"Well?" he asked, sitting next to me and pulling me into his arms.

"What?" I knew full well what he wanted, but I was still trying to process the thoughts myself.

"I figured with the influences of my family, and the judgments you may have heard, you would want to talk about my earlier meeting."

I stared at him and carefully thought about my reply. "I don't even know where to start" I said, looking at the ground.

You don't have any questions?" Michael's face contorted into a curious, disbelieving expression.

Of course, I had questions. I knew that the members inquiries were just the tip of the iceberg, but I needed to start somewhere

"You mean to tell me out of all the things that were said tonight, you don't have anything you want to ask?" His question was honest and understandable. Why wouldn't I want to know, when I could be asking about the whole mate thing, or the *me being a vampire* thing? But in all fairness, I was not just confused, I was also lost, and above all, I felt betrayed. My parents had known that I was more than an ordinary mortal child and didn't have the gumption to tell me the truth. Instead, they tried to keep it from me and hoped it would never come up. Then, Sara decided that I needed to be given to Nicholas to be murdered. So yeah, I thought that a lair was an excellent place to start.

"Well, I'm just trying to keep it together." My voice was breaking, and my heart clenched as I tried as hard as I could to control myself. Lucky for me, Michael answered my question without any further encouragement.

"Sometimes, I forget how little you really know about my world. I have been so busy trying to protect you from the dangers outside of these walls that I didn't realize how unaware you are." He let out a chuckle.

I looked around the room and tried to avert my attention from the stinging behind my eyes. Michael's exact words in the dining room hit me again: "…making her half-human."

"You are safe here. You can ask any question you want, feel overwhelmed, even come here to just rest. There is no judgment. In a vampire's case, this, is where we are strongest, where we come to heal after a battle or when we need rest or room to think."

"I thought you were bulletproof?" I asked, with a hint of teasing in my voice.

"We are, but even a vampire can be emotional or mentally exhausted." Michael offered me a soft smile and moved closer to me, leaving just a few feet between us. "Most have their lairs under their homes, or close by. We need to have such things. In my case, I come here to get away, to think without interruption. No one knows where my lair is, not even Alex." Michael took my hands in his. "It is a vampire's most private and secret place. To openly tell someone its location is like surrendering yourself." When Michael finished, I felt his eagerness to share this rare but beautiful experience with me.

"No one?"

"No one beyond my personal bodyguards. Besides the guard outside, there are fifty or so more to protect me and this place," he bragged.

"Cool. So, out of all the girls in the world, why would you decide to bring me here?"

Michael turned to look at me directly. "I have never felt for anyone what I do for you. I am drawn to every little thing you do. When you are near me, it is all I can do not to touch your face"—Michael reached out and cupped my cheek with his palm—"push your hair behind your ear"—he pushed a stray lock of hair away from my face and secured it behind my ear—"or hold you as close as I can." A pink hue tinted his ears.

I took a deep breath and smiled at the thought. "It's just…why would you want anything to do with me when you can have your pick of the litter?" A feeling of inferiority draped over me like a heavy cloak. "Any one of those girls at the castle would bend over backward for you, and you choose me." I paused for a second to breathe, and Michael took the liberty to continue instead.

He shook his head and looked at me in awe. "You don't give yourself enough credit. Yes, you are willful and stubborn." He smiled at me. "But you are also very"—he put his finger under my chin and brought my head up to his eye level—"*very* beautiful. You have nothing and don't feel the need to prove yourself to anyone, even me, and that in itself is your biggest attraction." His eyes met mine, and neither of us let go for a while.

"There are so many other girls that are perfect and flawless." I looked at the floor. "And you choose..." The words caught in my throat. "A human." I swallowed hard.

"Arri." Michael pulled me even closer to him, and I could smell the cologne on his skin as his perfect body molded to mine. "Sweetheart, I know who you truly are, but one can argue the same about me. You have the world at your fingertips, and you chose me, a vampire who has nothing to give a human." Michael shifted under his own grip.

"Human?" I asked him, remembering what I heard through the door of their meeting.

Michael nodded knowingly. "What did you think you were?"

A shiver ran through my body and left me with goosebumps.

"I heard you tell your coven. Mom was mortal when she had me—I take it she is a vampire now—and Dad, well, I knew he was a vampire. Apparently, he was the most feared to ever walk or something—"

"Still is," Michael interrupted.

"Okay then, but that would make me half-vampire."

"Was that so hard?" Michael asked.

The words echoed in my mind as I pushed the thought around. I was never going to get used to that.

"I thought you could only be turned *into* a vampire?" My

words were hollow as I knew I was wrong. If vampires and werewolves were real in the first place, then anything was possible.

Michael shrugged.

"So, what does this make me, some sort of mutant hybrid?" Although Michael seemed to find humor in this, I was serious. "No, really, Michael, what does this make me?"

Michael paused, looked at his hands, then intertwined his fingers in mine.

"Well, this makes you special and the first of your kind. No one has ever managed to survive the blood battle between human and vampire, and that is why you carry the special sight, hearing, and speed. It also explains why you are faster than normal, but slower than us." He finished and looked at me with uncertainty.

"Blood battle?"

"Yes. When a vampire turns a human, we drain most of their blood, then the host must willingly partake of the vampire's blood in return. You see, a vampire's blood is not only poisonous, but also intoxicating. The poison kills and preserves the human body in total perfection; it also numbs the spot and promotes fast healing. A vampire bite will heal itself as soon as we let go, leaving no marks or bruising. The intoxication side of it allows us to hunt. The very blood that runs through our bodies makes us irresistible to humans. Our outward appearance is perfect, from the tone of our skin to the figure of our bodies. Once we get close enough, our smell, looks, and taste are all part of the alluring charm, but for you"—Michael brushed my cheek with the back of his hand—"it is different. You were born. It was a trial that was largely sought after when I was first turned, and when our numbers were slim. Not everyone had the power to stop once they started, so they tried to create them. When a human is pregnant with a vampire child, our blood automatically takes over and consumes the baby. It kills all traces of human blood. The baby is always frozen in time and never progressed through maturity. The mother's body eventually fails, as our blood spreads to the mother and consumes both host and child.

"How did I survive, then?"

"No one knows. After thousands of years of attempts, and countless deaths, it is impossible. There is no scientific or logical way to live through it." Michael cringed, expecting me to lose it.

"Wow. That's...a lot to take in." I was in awe. It was challenging absorb everything I just heard, and I wasn't sure what to say or ask. The thought that my entire being was not supposed to survive made sense, as did what Nicholas had said. *You were never meant to be. Half-breeds like you should not be allowed to survive.*

I didn't mean to speak the words aloud as I remembered them, but they managed to come out regardless.

"I beg your pardon?" Michael looked puzzled.

"Nicholas. The words he said in my dreams. He called me a half-breed." I looked away, and Michael said nothing. When I glanced back, he just looked at me with a grin. The questions built up as I thought about everything: the dream, the meeting, knowing that I wasn't who I thought I was. I was an imposter in my own body. But thinking on it did bring up another question.

"What is a mate?" I hesitated after asking, as the question felt more like an invitation. "I mean, I can take a guess, but what does it really entail?"

"A mate is a vampire term for a wife. Where your species has divorce, we have eternity. We mate only once. We exchange blood and a promise sealing us to each other forever.

If our mate dies, then that is it for us. We will never mate or love again."

His words hit deep. "The coven called me your mate, and you didn't correct them."

Michael looked proud and embarrassed all at once. The same pink hue tinted his cheeks, and his eyes reflected the depth of his own inner promise and truthfulness.

"Is it the same for me, since I am not really a vampire?" I asked.

"Oh, I would believe so. The bonding is so powerful that some say they can almost feel each other's presence."

"What about for you?"

"It would still mean for eternity, at least for me. It is not a decision that is made hastily." Although he kept his calm and collected composure, tried to hide his emotions from me, his feelings were beseeching and wanting.

"Do you think you are ready to be my mate?" His question was just that—a question. There was no hidden invitation or hinting; Michael and I both knew it was only a matter of time before it was truly asked. I knew the answer was yes. I was in love, not just with the man he has shown me he was, but with all of him, vampire and all.

"Do you really need to ask?".

Michael looked at me for a second, and his eyes searched me for the obvious yes. His lips curved into a precarious grin. Worry and doubt flashed across his face before he masked it with a self-assured smile.

"Is this all of it?" I asked, looking around the room.

"No," he said absently, presumably still preoccupied with my avoidance of his question. Without warning, Michael pulled me back down on the couch, holding me in his arms. There was nothing on earth that could bother me when he held me. The world disappeared, and Michael and I were the only two that existed. He tickled me playfully, then rose to his feet.

"Okay," he said. "Since I have you here, I guess I should show you around." My skin instantly cooled where he held me, and my body secretly begged for his touch.

As we exited the stateroom through a large, carved-stone archway, the hallway that appeared was much wider than I would have thought. Walking me through the endless maze of corridors and occasional sitting rooms, Michael showed me the rest of the lair. A fogged sliding glass aperture revealed a generous and unrestricted library, similar to the one in his mansion, full of books and smelling of dust and paper. Although I could have easily stayed and read for weeks without coming up for air, we didn't linger. He was much too excited to show me more of what he had created for himself, away from his coven and duties. Through another set of doors, his office gleamed with an intimidating authority. While his castle office was contemporary and sterile, this one was comfortable and elegantly traditional. The desk was simple, but stately: Four cherry-knotted, wooden legs held up a small, but exquisite, thin-boxed tabletop. The desktop itself was seamless; each piece of wood flowed perfectly and harmoniously into the next, and even with the subtle show of wear and tear, the intricacy of the carvings that decorated the sides was unmatched. I ran my fingers over the smooth and polished surface as I examined its beauty.

"I made this in my youth." Michael settled himself beside me. "I was tutored by a fine old craftsman. He settled for nothing less than the best." Michael walked to the front of the desk, took a piece of paper from his jacket pocket, and placed it in the drawer. A wooden bookcase displayed a few rare and antique books, but in general, besides the desk, everything looked new and untouched.

The third room was unconventional to say the least. Weapons were a favorite pastime of Michael's. Several antique firearms, such as a bamboo fire lance and a few scalded-metal guns made it on the wall of his one-room armory. Nothing was in a glass case or hidden behind doors; Michael kept everything in the open where he could see their history. As we walked into the room, Michael glanced over his pieces of art like they were trophies of his past.

"These are just some of the older models. I also have all the newest and up to date military and non-military weaponry. I would venture to say that I have most of the stock in the U.S." He walked to a shelf and switched two books around. The bookcase opened into yet another hidden room. "This is the only room with alternate power." Michael flicked a switch and rows and rows of track lighting endlessly lined the expansive cavern. The inner-mountain bunker was stocked full of wooden crates, one on top of the other. A few boxes lay open on the ground, displaying some high-powered laser trackers.

"Are you waiting for a war?"

"If it comes to that, yes."

"I thought you couldn't die from mortal weapons."

"We can't, but it won't stop the mortals from starting the war against us. I will not leave my family defenseless. As if mortals had a chance." Michael and I left the room shortly thereafter, and the large bookcase creaked to a slow, thudding close.

We visited a few more rooms, each furnished entirely with the same historical furniture. After we ventured further into the mountain, the tour stopped in front of a rather large set of doors. The wooden castle doors were polished and shiny. Michael was hesitant as we approached.

"This will be your bedroom." He pushed the doors open to reveal a large, well-decorated chamber.

"Where is yours?" I asked, in hopes that it wasn't too far.

"Yours conjoins with mine through that door." He said it with a hint of embarrassment. The room was well lit and had the most extravagant furniture so far. The large four-poster bed took up only a quarter of the room and was centered on a large woven wool rug. The colors were natural, designed for comfort. It was welcoming, and even with the museum-like looks, it called home to me, and I felt as if I finally belonged.

"Here," I said, wiggling till he let go of my waist. I ran over, jumped onto the oversized bed, and lay in the center. It was perfection. As soon as I laid down, I was consumed with coziness. I was so tired, and my eyelids were so heavy. With everything that had gone on tonight, I wanted to forget the world around me, forget everything. Still, with all my might, I fought to stay awake as long as I could. Michael carefully followed me to the bed. He lay on his side next to me and caressed my arm with his finger. I snuggled in closer, resting my head on his arm. The soft touch of his lips gently pressing against mine.

"I love you."

Michael's words were the last thing I remembered.

SIX

My eyes closed, and the nightmares formed. I imagined myself eating people and hunting. The images were frightening, and they appeared to be getting more and more gruesome. I could feel the panic set in as my mind raced. A loud clap snatched me out of my nightmare. Startled, I snapped awake and sat up. The room was dark, and there was no sign of light coming from anywhere. A slight rustling in the distance caught my attention. Instantly, I was aware of my unfamiliar surroundings. I looked in the direction of the sound, and a soft, careful hand grab mine. Paralyzed by fear, I froze.

"Steady, darling." Michael's voice was calm. "It's just me. Let me start some light. I'll be back in a second." His grip loosened, then disappeared. A small flicker of light in the distance roared into a fire in seconds, and Michael returned to my side.

"Nightmare?" He was concerned. He knew some of my dreams were more than just dreams. I could feel his heart ache, and uncertainty clouded his eyes. Finally, his curiosity got the better of him, and he took my hands in his.

"Yes, I think. Am I still dreaming?"

Michael studied me for a while. "Close your eyes." Skeptically, I closed them and prepared myself. "What do you feel?" Michael asked as he slipped something soft into my hands.

"Silk?" I answered.

"Yes, the sheets you were sleeping on." Michael was trying to be patient, but his voice was a little forced. "Now, what do you feel?" My cheek went warm as a soft and gentle touch caressed it. My heart raced. There was only one person in the world who could make me feel this way, and that was Michael.

"Your touch," I said, taking his hand and kissing his palm.

"How about now?" There was a pause and nothing. I was about to open my eyes when a warm, compassionate, embrace enveloped me and reached my very soul. Michael's hands cradled my face, and his perfect body molded against mine. With slow, measured movements, he pushed me back on the bed and lifted my arms above my head, holding them there against the soft silk sheets. Instinctively, I placed all my trust in him and enjoyed every second of our kiss. Time stopped. The fire seemed to slow, and the light faded to a dull dimness. When we finally released each other, I looked at Michael and gave a weak gasp.

"It was you!" I exclaimed.

"Of course it was me. Who else did you see in the room?" Michael asked in disbelief.

"No, on my way home from the fairgrounds, when I first moved here. You were the one who trapped me on the wall of the old building." I remembered his touch, and the irresistible pull he had on me. I couldn't believe I didn't see or feel it until now.

"Yes, it was." His uncertain voice betrayed his calm and collected façade.

"You knew it was me the whole time. You even asked me

where my guardian was." Michael didn't respond right away. He took his time, choosing his words carefully.

"Technically, you're right. I knew you were here before I met you. From the moment you arrived in Elsinore, I felt you. I felt your constant pull; I was drawn to you like never before. It was like you were beckoning me, and my soul did everything it could to seek you out." Michael looked away for a second and ran his hands through his hair. "I wanted you. I needed to have you. It was as if I would cease to exist if I didn't. That is why I was so mad at Alex for bringing you to me. I wasn't afraid that I would accidentally lose my self-control, and, as you put it, 'suck you dry.'" He chuckled. "But because it was hard to control myself in so many other ways."

I looked at the fire as it licked the black scorch marks on the wall. Turning to him, I smiled. "Why didn't you just tell me?"

Michael's affectionate, genuine, and deep kiss had my head spinning. Then he gave me a playful glare.

"I couldn't find the words," he said, smiling at me.

After a moment of awkward silence, Michael offered me a new set of clothing and waited patiently as I complained from the other side of the bathroom door.

"I hope I got the proper size," he said. As I came out of the bathroom, Michael let out a whistle. "It looks like I was right."

He circled around me. The grey slacks and deep blue silk shirt were a little more form-fitting than I was used to.

"Thank you."

"Anything for you." Michael offered a slight bow of his head.

Michael called in his for-all-intents-and-purposes butler and spilled out a laundry list of things to be done. After the chores and demands were noted, the butler left the room.

Within a few moments, Dominick rapped quickly on Michaels bedroom door before entering and cleared his throat behind us.

"Excuse me, my lord." Michael grabbed my hand as he gave his servant his attention.

"Yes."

"Your message has been delivered, and your car awaits you." The footman bowed slowly, and then backed out of the room.

"What car?"

"I was hoping you would join me for lunch."

"Why not eat here?"

"Well, when I built this place, I didn't think I would be entertaining such a unique individual." Michael kissed my forehead. "Something I will rectify as soon as possible."

"Rectify?" I shot him a look as my pulse tripled its pace, as though my heart was about to fall to my toes. "How so?" My voice cracked.

"By building you a kitchen." Michael shook his head and offered a smile that touched his eyes.

I let out a sigh of relief.

"Besides, I have a few errands to attend to in town, and I was hoping you would accompany me."

"Sure." My stomach gave a loud growl. I looked at the clock above the mantle. It was close to two-thirty.

"Why don't we have lunch first, then after my errands, we will retire here for the evening? I have nothing pressing to get back to till morning."

When we got back to the entrance of the lair, I saw the Brock Lesnar lookalike. His tall stance and unwavering stare filled my heart with fear. Michael picked me up and cradled me in his arms.

"Feeling human?" Michael teased, smirking at my silent

pout. I rolled my eyes and shook my head. Michael laughed loudly and took off running through the passageway tunnels until we came to a dead end. He set me down and opened a tall, thin, rough-looking door. As we walked out of the dim cavern, we entered a clearing just outside of the manor.

"I have more than one way in and out of my lair," he whispered in my ear.

From there, we walked to one of Michael's prized possessions, a sleek silver Aston Martin. It was beautiful. The red and black interior, GPS, and leather heated and cooled seats were only a few of the many finishing touches that accentuated the car. The Aston Martin was running and waiting in the driveway. With characteristic elegance and sophistication, Michael opened the door for me before getting in and reaching for my hand. Nothing but the heavenly and intoxicating purr of the engine sounded as we left the circular driveway on our way to town.

When we arrived in Richfield, Michael and I walked side by side. He had one arm around my waist and the other in his pocket. Walking down the streets of a town I only knew for a short while brought back many memories. I remembered when I first met Michael, when my life seemed simple. Now, things seemed different. When I first moved in, no one in town noticed me or knew I existed. Now, everyone stopped and stared. I was on the arm of the most desired man in Richfield.

"Why are they all staring at you?" I asked in a low voice.

"They are not staring at me. They are staring at you." His words came out quietly as we walked through the doors of a modern Chinese restaurant, and waited in line to be seated. The establishment was reasonably packed. The simple lines of modern Chinese décor, the white and red color motif, and the elegant imitation marble floors put this place over the top. It was one of the town's newer and more expensive restaurants. The longer we waited, the more and more apparent the stares became and the more the conversation quieted.

"Why don't you start your errands, and when I'm done, I'll call you. I know you don't eat"—I lowered my voice further—"like me, and I would hate to make you wait on me." Everyone staring at me was making me uncomfortable.

Michael leaned down to ear level. "To wait on you would be a pleasure, and I would never ask you to dine alone. Besides, just because I have a special diet doesn't mean I don't eat food." His lips brushed my cheek when the maître d' came up to the front.

"Table or booth?" he asked. He didn't bother looking up at us as he busied himself with menus and silverware.

"Table, please," Michael answered and intertwined his fingers in mine. The gentleman looked up, his eyebrows raised.

"Two?" he echoed.

"Yes, thank you," Michael looked at me, and then to the host, who stood still, staring at the two of us. "Is there a problem?"

"No, sir," the host said as his eyes lingered on me, then forcibly returned to Michael. "Right this way, please."

He led us through the restaurant and past a few tables. As we passed each one, the patrons' eyes followed us. The only exception was a gangly, red-haired man at a table near the far end of the restaurant. I knew him. That disheveled, unkempt, miserable-looking little man was Seth—the slimy, slick-haired guy who always bugged me at the credit union, asking me out. He'd been so upset when I declined his offers over and over again. Now, his squinty, dark brown, almost black eyes glowered in our direction. He looked at us as if we had personally wronged him and held us in contempt. After we were seated at a small table in the center of the restaurant, away from Seth, I let out a sigh of relief.

"Will this be okay?" the maître d' asked.

"Yes, thank you." Michael clearly found it quite amusing that the host was so enamored with me and grinned. He seemed utterly oblivious to the stalker in the corner.

"Your waiter will be Treven; may I get your drinks while you wait?" The host never took his eyes off me, and my face felt warmer by the second.

"Thank you; we will have a bottle of Chardonnay and a Coke." While Michael ordered, I took a small, casual glance in Seth's direction, and there he was, foodless and scowling as he drank from a brown bottle. His undivided attention was making me nervous. With our order in hand, the host left, and my concern lifted somewhat when Michael's voice drew my attention.

"So, why here, out of all the places to move to?" Michael asked. It took me a moment to respond, seeing as this question came from nowhere.

"I was trying to get away from my parents. Believe it or not, they suffocated me. They watched every move I made. I wanted my freedom." I shrugged and took another glance around the restaurant. Everyone was trying to peer at us casually, but they all failed miserably at hiding their curiosity.

"What is it with everyone here?" I asked, leaning over the table, and lowering my voice to a level only he could hear.

Michael chuckled and looked around. "You have managed to capture everyone's eyes."

I fidgeted in my seat and rolled my shoulders, trying to relax.

"Good evening, have you decided on your meal?" The waiter, Treven, looked down at his order sheet and did his best to avert his attention away from me. He was an attractive man with bleach white teeth, blond spikey hair, and soft brown eyes. Like all the waiters, his white apron was tied around his waist with a few straws and pencils sticking out of the front pockets, but his slightly oversized slacks and white button-up shirt was enough to show he was more of a relaxed sort of guy.

"The lady will have Sesame chicken, and I will have the Kung Pao beef." Michael looked at me, folded his menu, and thanked the waiter, who accepted our menus without thought.

"Yes, sir." The waiter immediately left and attended to our order.

After the waiter brought our meals, I ate until I was stuffed. After I'd finished, Michael and I lingered a little while longer and talked.

"Arri, is that you?" a small voice asked from a neighboring table. Claire, an old coworker of mine, came and stood in front of me. She was tall and thin, with her brunette hair haphazardly pinned back and a fake grin.

"Claire, how are you?" I stood to accept a superficial hug.

"Fine, how are you? Mary said you couldn't take it and quit." Claire fought back an impolite laugh.

"I'm afraid it was my fault," Michael said. He offered no further explanation. He just stood and offered a polite bow.

"Oh, and you are…?" Claire tried to look confused, as if she didn't know him, but the gleam in her eyes and the light pink hue that tinted her cheeks gave her away.

"I'm sorry. Claire, this is Michael. Michael, this is Claire. She worked with me at the bank," I said, introducing them as if they were strangers.

"It's a pleasure," Michael said. "Would you like to join us, Claire?" Michael gestured to an empty chair as he returned to his seat.

"No, thank you. I am here with some friends," Claire gestured to a table of five or six girls near the window, then turned back to us. "Are you coming back to work now that you are back? We could use a good manager."

"No, I'm afraid not. Right now I'm sort of…taking a break for a while."

Claire didn't look like she believed me. "Where did you go, anyway?"

Michael looked back at Claire. "Her family and I have been traveling; I don't think work would fit into her chaotic schedule."

Claire bit her lip, trying to cover up a knowing smile.

"What happened to Mary?" I asked, as if I didn't know.

"After you left, Anna was reported missing, and about a week or two ago, Mary didn't show up at work." Claire threw her hands in the air then placed them back on her hips. "Her apartment looked as if it had been deserted for months. There was no furniture, food, or anything, just a few clothes in a dresser and a fridge. Weird, huh? It's like she just up and left." Claire's eyes were wide, and her mouth dropped open. As always, Claire spoke with her hands, swiping, clapping, and snapping to emphasis her story. It was no surprise that she and many of the other girls would have been shocked by what happened.

"Yes, well, I'm sorry about both Anna and Mary. I hope you get a good manager to replace them." I smiled and tried to think of a friendly but firm way to excuse Michael and me. Michael could clearly sense my unease.

"Well, it was a pleasure to meet you, Claire. If you will excuse us, we are late for a meeting." Michael stood again as Claire left our table.

"A friend?" he asked after she was out of earshot, and sat once again. He signaled the waiter for the check.

"No. No one there liked me." I shook my head.

"I find that hard to believe." Michael placed his card in

the small black folder, and the waiter disappeared behind the kitchen doors.

"Yeah, well, Mary made it seem like I was sent by the credit union to fill Anna's place against her will. They turned against me. I was surprised they didn't tar and feather me in the parking lot after work." I laughed absently. "I know now it was a planned entrapment by Sara and Mary to make me feel rejected." I shook the memories from my head and smiled back at Michael. The waiter returned with a receipt and Michael's card.

"I, for one, am pleased that you ended up with me." Michael reached across the table and brought my hand to his lips. The girls with Claire, still watching, were awed at the gesture. I blushed and turned my head.

"Come," Michael said, helping me from my seat. He signed the thin slip of paper, retrieved his card, and slipped it in his wallet. As we left the restaurant, I looked to Seth's table. But some time during Claire's visit to us, he had left.

As we stopped in front of a vintage, red-brick building, I had a flashback. An old, black and white newspaper, picturing a girl covered in a white sheet, clouded my thoughts. My hands shook, and my breathing trembled, knowing that I was the reason Maggie died.

"What is it?" Michael asked as he squeezed my hand gently.

"Maggie Cartmen. This is where she was pictured." The memory of the event haunted me.

"Would you like to wait in the car? This shouldn't take long. I need to talk to the mayor for a moment."

"No, I'm okay." I shook my head. "What business would you have with the mayor?" Michael didn't answer, but his expression changed, and he looked determined as we entered the mayor's office.

"Oh, Mr. London," said a redheaded woman of medium height and build. She stood and fumbled around her desk, knocking almost everything over. "The mayor is expecting you." She gave a wide, pleasant grin.

Michael nodded to the young girl and crossed the room to the mayor's office. Without knocking, Michael walked in, held the door open for me, and closed it behind us. The click of the lock echoed throughout the office.

"Ah, Mr. London, how are you?" Behind the large mahogany desk Mayor Calhaine stood and shook Michael's hand, then reached out to me. As he leaned over his desk, his plaid short-sleeved button-up stretched and strained as his large stomach brushed up against his computer and moved it back a few inches. His short graying hair gleamed in the sun from the window beside him. The worried and slightly panicked expression in his gentle blue eyes as he searched mine spiked my curiosity. Looking around his large but stuffed and crowded office several bookshelves lined the walls, but dust outlining all except a few. I was guessing they were more for show than for reading.

"Mayor Calhaine, this is Arri Stone, the young woman I have spoken to you about."

"Yes, of course." The mayor's large and pudgy hand shook mine.

"Arri, this is Mayor Angus Calhaine."

"Hello."

After the pleasantries, Michael held out a slightly worn burgundy chair across from the mayor's desk for me.

As the mayor sat down, he tried to look calm, but the small twitch of his mouth as he concentrated on every word Michael said, and the subtle physical jerk of his shoulders as Michael's voice rose, betrayed his fear.

Did he know how different Michael was from us, or was

it the natural fear of predator and prey? Looking out the window, I saw a nest cradled in the fork of a thick tree branch just outside. A mother bluebird and her fledglings stood frozen and scared as they looked at Michael. Just like the mayor, the birds recognized something unnatural, predatory. It was almost as if they were instinctively wired to flee from him.

Why didn't I feel the same way? Human and animal alike had the same reaction. But not me. Michael's very presence was alluring. I thought of this small but vital information. Michael said everything about him is meant to invite you in. If so, why did the mayor seem so different? Did he know of Michael's true nature?

As the meeting came to a close, Michael pulled a manila envelope out of his jacket and offered it to the mayor.

"As we have discussed," Michael's voice was calm but unnerving, "I know this matter will not go unseen and the locals are likely to inquire about Anna and Mary, but I'm sure you are aware how vital it is to keep this information from ever surfacing."

Sweat beaded above the mayor's brow, and his breath quickened.

The redhead was just finishing her lunch as we left, and all but choked as she shoved the last of her granola bar in her mouth. She stood to see us out. Michael just waved a dismissive hand and held the door open for me.

"Wow, you really have a way with the ladies. Please tell me I don't act like her."

Michael shook his head. "No, you made me work for it." He smiled and kissed the top of my head as we made our way through town. There were a few times when I thought I saw Seth watching us and following us, but I never chanced a look. I feared if I did, he would be there with the same scrunched scowl on his face. He had it in for me, but boy was I happy to know at least he was human. It was the vampires that I feared.

With each and every errand, everyone eagerly greeted Michael. After all the constant, unyielding attention, as bad as a paparazzi attack, Michael and I eventually wound our way back to the Aston Martin. Michael helped me in first then got in and started the engine. It roared to life, then gently lulled and hummed in the background as Michael checked his phone before we left the small town and headed back home. I was pleased to know that the purring of the engine was all I was going to hear for a few minutes. I quietly thought back through the day and tried to sort out what Michael's errands really were. Whatever was in the manila envelopes that he passed to everyone had something to do with Mary and Anna. Some, like the mayor, were nervous, but most seemed to recognize the manila envelopes and seemed to know what was going on. Were those people like Michael? Had I been living among vampires before I met Michael and just not known? Before I knew it and before I could ask Michael, we arrived in front of the manor. As we pulled into the drive, Michael's tall and stern looking chauffeur, Nolan, waited for us by the door. When we came to a stop, Nolan bent down and opened my door helping me out before meeting Michael by his door.

"Thank you, Nolan," Michael told the chauffeur as he got out of the car. "We won't need the car for the rest of the evening." After he said this, I drew a deep inhale in relief, knowing that we were home and away from the onlookers. I was even more relieved when Michael took me back to the quiet seclusion of his lair instead of the manor.

SEVEN

I searched the empty space next to me. Michael was not there like I'd expected he would be. I knew I was safe here—Fort Knox had nothing on Michael's lair—but I still felt a little abandoned and vulnerable. Michael was normally next to me when I woke up, or at least in the same room. But not today.

Maybe he needed to hunt; he'd eaten the last of his meals before we went to town. The thought of Michael hunting turned to the thought of him pinning me to the bed yesterday, his body and scent melding with mine. Even though that moment was short lived, the way he held my hands, and the desperate longing I felt for him, tortured me.

After getting dressed, I wandered through the endless maze of hallways. Finally, I managed to find his office. It was neat and tidy; there were no stray papers, no waste in the waste bin, and even the pens and pencils were in order, organized by height and size. The chandeliers looked like they had just been lit; no wax was dripping or pooled in the candle bases. I opened the book that lay on the desk. A bookmark in the center opened to a map of Egypt, Morocco, and Nigeria. Morocco was circled and an arrow pointed to Egypt. It looked like Michael was planning a trip or at least plotting one. I didn't want to think of him leaving, since I would probably be here alone and closed the book and left his office. Finding my way back to the bedroom, I cleaned it up and made the bed. When I picked Michael's pillow up from the floor, there was a note beneath it.

Arri my love,

I would like to thank you for spending the week's end with me. I have truly enjoyed your company. With my family around and watching the two of us, I was rather surprised to find you just as adorable and loving as when we first met. Your impact and significance has made me realize just how much I love you.

I blushed. It was nice to read that, even though I felt I was just an ordinary girl, Michael—a vampire, no less—saw me as something more. Just as I finished the note, Michael walked through the door.

"The pink in your cheeks looks good on you." His patient and loving smile greeted me at the door. "I was wondering when you were going to wake up."

"What time is it?" I asked, looking around the walls for a clock.

"About six-thirty."

"In the morning?"

"Yes." In four swift steps he was in front of me, hands on my waist.

"Well, sorry I slept in," I said sarcastically, shaking my head.

Michael leaned into me with a smirk on his face. As I opened my mouth to ask what was so funny, he gave me a feverish kiss. One hand wrapped around the nape of my neck and the other made its way to the small of my back, tugging at my shirt. His body was crushed against mine and his grip tightened until I heard fabric ripping. Breaking the kiss and taking slow, measured breaths, Michael smiled. "I can't get too carried away with you. You are still too fragile." He let go of my waist and turned me around to see the rip in my shirt.

"Here." Michael disappeared for a fraction of a second and returned with a navy blue blouse. "Put this on." He kissed me on the cheek. After he left the room, I changed, then met up with him in the hallway. Hand in hand, we walked to the long underground corridor.

I crawled through the small opening in the pantry floor followed closely by Michael. He took no time in opening the pantry door, and the two of us walked out as if there were nothing strange about it. We stopped at the bottom of the stairs.

"I need to address my coven and inform them of Phoenix's arrival. Their reactions are bound to be less than warm wishes. Are you okay by yourself for a moment?"

"Of course. I think I will get something to eat while I wait."

Michael kissed me on the cheek and bid me farewell. As soon as he walked through the door to the dining room, which now I figured was just a fancy name for meeting room, the room went stagnant.

The mansion was quiet. There was a definite tension in the air. I looked around the house on my way to the kitchen. The silence rattled my bones, and the atmosphere was icy and unnerving. It was the calm before a storm. Mustering up all the bravery I had, I picked up speed and almost ran to the kitchen. The main hall was empty, and the house looked deserted. No one was in sight. Michael's beautiful mansion was dark, forsaken, and felt eerie, haunted. I furrowed my brows and took a few deep breaths, rubbing my arms, hoping it would calm my nerves. I choked down a fast breakfast of dry cereal with my back against the wall. Something was wrong, but what? The tension seemed to ease a little as I walked back down the hall and up the spiral staircase. When I reached my room, Nana was just leaving.

"Oh, Miss Arri, how are you?" Her weary and sunken eyes were dull and almost lifeless.

"Nana, are you okay? You look tired."

Her worn expression didn't change as she tried to straighten her shoulders and hold her head high. She was a woman of dignity and character, but today, she looked more like an overworked housemaid.

"I'm fine, dearie; just a few more hours of sleep should do the trick," she said in a hollow and morose voice.

"Are you sure, Nana?" I asked, grabbing her tiny, frail arm and walking her back into my room. Just as I shut the door, her composure faltered. She dropped her shoulders and hung her head. It looked like all the life had been sucked out of her. For the last week, Nana had not looked like herself. Her general fun and loving character had been lost and a shell of what she once was had taken over.

"I'm fine." Her words were blank.

"Nana, tell me."

Nana took her cold, clammy hand and grabbed my shoulder to steady herself.

"No worries, luv. It takes a little more than a cold to stop stubborn old me." She attempted a grin. Her touch sent chills down my spine and my eyes closed.

In the far depths of my mind, shadows appeared in a dim pool of light. I could see the vague outline of a man's frame clouding a doorway. My heart pulsed like I was running laps. The man kicked the door closed behind him and the light in the room vanished. The moonlit windows brought the room back into view, and the light barely glimmered on him as he walked to the bed and sat, still and unmoving. His dark, shadowed face leaned down closer to me. I felt scared, and dizziness consumed me, then darkness and nothing.

"Arri? Arri?" a distant voice beckoned me.

Jamie Ripp

I opened my eyes and saw Nana staring back at me, visibly worried. Her hand stayed on my cheek, but now, her other hand was cool against mine. I snapped awake, fully aware.

"Sorry, Nana. I was lost in thought."

Nana nodded. "Is there anything I can do for you, dearie?"

"No, thank you. You should get some rest if you have a cold. I'm sure Michael will be okay with you taking a few days for yourself."

Nana and I were about to leave when a knock at the door rang through the room. Nana jumped and her balance faltered slightly before she gained her composure.

I let her hands go and walked to the door. When I opened it, the hallway was crowded as members passed through with their luggage. I paused. Nana made her way to the door and pushed past me.

"I'll be leaving you to your orders. Thank you, dearie." Nana grabbed my arm in gratitude and I cringed inside. I didn't want to see that again.

"Ethan," I greeted after Nana left.

"Morning, my lady. Michael has requested your company in his chambers at your leisure."

I closed my eyes and calmed my breathing. Michael's room was no more than a few corridors over.

A few minutes later, I knocked on his door.

"Yes?" Michael answered wearing just his jeans. His ripped chest and abs disappearing into the waistband caught my undivided attention. I took in a breath as a smile touched my lips, and my eyes lingered on the gorgeous and tempting man in front of me. He ran his finger up and down my arm, sending shivers through my body.

"Is this what you came here for?" Michael's voice was

playful as he placed his hand under my chin and pulled me up to meet his gaze. There was a hint of something mischievous in his eyes as his head leaned down to meet mine.

The kiss was sensuous and alluring, but before I got enough, he broke away and stepped back.

My face flushed, heat pricking at my cheeks. I couldn't take my eyes off of him. I closed my eyes and breathed as calmly as I could. When I looked back at him, he had already dressed and stood in front of me with an artful and devilish grin on his face.

"Did you like the view?" His words were taunting and all I could do was nod. I couldn't find my voice as I just gaped at him. Embarrassed, I smiled and turned my head. "What can I do for you, my love?" He stepped closer and held my waist. The pressure was strong and firm. Pulling my hips to his, he kissed my neck.

With little effort, Michael tugged me into his room. He kicked the door closed and turned me around, holding me from behind. His lips brushed the base of my neck as his arms wrapped around me, protective and possessive. When he let go, and I finally managed to open my eyes, I was taken aback. For all the luxuries he offered elsewhere, his own room was spartan and stark. There were no frills or trinkets. A lone dresser and armoire adorned one wall, while a mirror and a large king-sized bed lay along the other. A stack of old books half-covered by the shirt he wore yesterday sat on the floor at the base of a record player, which seemed to be substituting for a nightstand.

"I'm not in here much. At times, I barely remember I have a room." He pushed a hand through his damp hair. The smell of cologne and soap permeated the room. Michael turned me around to face him and held my hands.

"Nana," I started, as Michael searched my eyes. I let out

a breath and shook my head. "Do you remember when I told you I could feel others' thoughts?" I looked up through my eyelashes at Michael. He was stern, but a hint of concern gleamed behind his eyes. I opened my mouth to explain what I saw, but I couldn't. I couldn't be sure of what I really saw—although I was pretty sure. Changing tactics at the last moment, I finally managed to find my voice.

"No, I'm afraid not. What do you mean?" His words were careful.

"I, well…" I didn't quite know how to explain it. *Oh, by the way, I can feel your thoughts.* Probably wasn't the best idea.

"Arri?" Michael's voice broke through my thoughts. Blinking to bring myself back to the present, I stared into his perfect green eyes. My heart plummeted. Michael had been scared to tell me he was a vampire, and yet, here I was, in the same situation: afraid to confess my true self.

"You know those odd abilities I have that aren't quite up to vampire standards?" Michael nodded and raised a single, curious eyebrow. "Well…" I paused and looked down at my shoes hoping a moment to collect myself would make it easier. It didn't. "One of those wonderful little talents I have makes it so I can also feel your thoughts. Those of envy, malicious intent, love, even confusion—I can feel them." I stopped and bit my lip, waiting for him to bolt.

"My envy? My malicious intent?" Michael's hands gripped mine a little tighter.

"No, I didn't mean you in particular, just emotions and thoughts in general. Happy, sad, it doesn't matter." I let go of Michael's hands, folded my arms and took a few steps back, still refusing to look at him. Maybe if I didn't look him in the eye, the blow might hurt less. Not likely, but just maybe.

Michael didn't say anything. I couldn't see it, but I could feel him staring at me, gauging me, deciding whether or not to trust me. I could feel his inner battle. The conflict between what he knew to be true and how much he trusted me raged inside him. Finally, with a heavy sigh, and a large step forward, Michael pulled me into a hug and kissed the top of my head.

"I believe you." Those three little words meant the world to me, but I could still feel his uncertainty.

"Well." Pulling out of his arms, and regaining a little personal space, I continued before I had a chance to analyze his thoughts. "Nana is looking quite ill. I tried to get her to tell me if anything was wrong, but you know how stubborn she can be."

Michael nodded. "I have noticed a change in her as well. I was hoping it was just a tired spell, but I fear I am wrong. Do you know anything else?" He eyed me, looking for anything that would give me away, and I tried my best not to flinch under his intense gaze.

A knock at the door drew his attention.

"Yes?" Michael said, taking a few steps away from me and opened the door.

"A Ms. Phoenix has passed the perimeter." The beatnik-looking gentleman said, bowing and backing from the door.

"This is not over, luv." Michael said, crossing the room to where I sat on his bed. I shrugged and smiled at him. Seeing my simple but obvious challenge, Michael carefully laid me back on the bed. His mouth teased the skin of my neck and his fingers teased the skin between my pants and the rim of my shirt. Sucking in a shallow breath, I pushed him back as I sat up. A look of triumph shone on his face.

"Don't be so cocky, my sweet. You haven't won yet." Michael laughed, then helped me to my feet. "My willingness to let you go is only due to us having a guest to greet." Walking hand in hand, we left the room and as we passed, a few members in the hallway and in the foyer whispered murmurs of the elusive Phoenix. As we walked through the castle doors, the bright sun warmed my face, and we waited to greet our guest.

EIGHT

Pounding hooves shook the ground. I threw a frightened look at Michael, but a smile curved his lips. At the tree line, a streak of black peeked through the trunks surrounding the castle. A team of black Belgian horses thundered out and down the drive in a cloud of dust, with a large white coupe drawn behind in their wake. The carriage pulled up and stopped in front of the manor. The design and detailing was so intricate and extensive I could hardly believe it. Even through the dust cloud, I could see carvings, scroll work, and paintings that adorned the carriage. A lot of effort had gone into maintaining and keeping the coupe in its original style. It was pulled directly from the Victorian days. I couldn't see who was inside, but I was guessing that the infamous Phoenix was seated behind the thick burgundy velvet drapes.

A tall but ordinary-looking man stepped off his leather covered seat. His short black hair, basic black slacks and white button-up shirt were nothing spectacular. He pulled out the stool, then unfolded a red carpet that rolled about twenty feet from the carriage. After dusting off the carpet and the stairs, he straightened to his full height and opened the door. The interior of the coupe was just as highly decorated as the exterior. The seats were facing each other with plush cushions lined with red velvet and satin. The carpeted floors extended to the foot stool used to help the passenger in and out of the carriage.

When the passenger emerged from the shadows of the carriage, my mouth fell open. I could not believe my eyes. When she stepped out from the carriage, as she hiked up her skirt a bit to step down, her black, knee-high boots, laced to the top, peeked out from beneath. A creature so delicate and meek stepped onto the carpeted drive. She was beautiful. Her hair was raven black with bluish-green low-lights gleaming in places and two streaks of white framing her face. Her eyes were almost pastel blue and she had the figure of a Barbie doll. I was sure that no woman—besides my mother—could top her beauty. It was a little depressing living among vampires; they were always so flawless, which made me feel like a troll. I leaned against Michael, folded my arms, and stared for a moment longer. She was breathtaking. A silk-lined black corset held snug against her skin, showing a little more than I was used to seeing; subtle frills lined the top and bottom. Silver buttons ran up the front of the corset, and a maroon-purple, slightly form-fitting floor-length skirt finished the outfit. She fiddled with a maroon silk drawstring bag, then stopped suddenly. Her eyes closed, then opened, and she looked at me with a faint smile. She held my gaze, and then turned to the driver.

"That would be all, Colijn. I think I can take it from here." Her words were laced with propriety. The driver gave her one exaggerated nod, then mounted the driver's seat and drove off.

Across the yard, a few of the members watched the guest arrive and looked at her in awe and fear. As soon as she picked up her bags, the small group retreated from view. My heart skipped a few beats as I watched her scrutinize me.

Looking reluctant to release me from her thrall, she turned her head to Michael. I was surprised when Michael let go of my waist and stepped away from me and toward the delicate creature. As he approached her, she curtsied low and bowed her head. Michael stopped in front of her, and with his finger, lifted her chin up, and as he did, she rose.

"Hello, old friend. It is good to see you are still well and as ravishing as ever."

I felt a pang of jealousy. Of course she was ravishing.

"Thank you, my lord. I see that you are the same."

I fought the urge to cringe. Why was I jealous, anyway? I never got jealous.

"You have my gratitude for your efficient reply to my summons. There is a lot that needs to be done, and I'm afraid I am on unfamiliar grounds." Michael offered her his arm, and they turned me.

"Is that the child?" The woman's voice was whimsical.

Michael looked at me. He offered a reassuring smile as they approached, and offered me his other arm. I politely shook my head and fell in step behind them. "Yes it is," he cooed.

When we reached the threshold, the old knotted doors swung open. The grand hall was packed as everyone waited for us to enter. The crowd split and murmured as she approached. This petite, perfect goddess had somehow commanded a respect that showed on everyone's face. When the room saw Michael standing just behind her, everyone quieted and bowed at his very appearance.

I took the last few steps behind them and stood behind the crowd, peering through the small spaces between people. Staring at the back of their heads, a small smile touched my lips and I shook my head. Why would I have ever believed that I could have held his attention for long?

"Arri?" Michael's voice rang out over the crowd as they instantly quieted. I tried to stay tucked behind everyone, but

Jamie Ripp

the cluster of people nearest me parted, and the rest of the crowd followed suit. Plastering a half-smile on my face, I stepped forward.

"Michael," I replied as I allowed him a small respectful bow of my head. He leaned over and kissed me on the cheek, whispering in my ear.

"You look pale."

My appearance was more or less reflecting my usual self. "I'm fine."

"This is Phoenix. She has been a friend since the beginning. Phoenix, it is a pleasure to introduce you to Arri. She is my special guest." Just as the formalities ended, Nana pushed her way through everyone.

"Michael, there is an urgent matter from Egypt." Her proper English voice cracked with uncertainty and sounded a little congested.

"Thank you, Nana." He turned to the two of us. "If you will excuse me." With that, he kissed the back of my hand and left Phoenix and me alone.

I didn't know what to do or say. Phoenix's modern approach to the corset gave her quite the intimidating appearance, but she seemed to pull it off nicely.

"So, you are the world-famous Arri," she said, her voice chiming.

"I don't know about the world-famous part, but my name is Arri." I looked down at my feet and fiddled with my shirt hem.

"Well, either way, it is an honor to meet you." She bowed her head and curtsied to me.

As she addressed me, everyone around us paused in disbelief.

"You know, I am a bit thirsty, if you wouldn't mind?" Phoenix's voice carried over the vast expanse of the foyer. "The day trip was less than appetizing."

Her words hit me. "Day?" I asked in confusion.

"Yes. The sun may not burn us to ashes, but the dark provides less suspicion when it comes to feeding." She snickered a little, but other than that she seemed serious.

"Sorry, I meant to ask…where did you travel from?" I assumed she came from a more exotic location that would have extended her travel.

"Ah…Greece. At least for now."

"I can get that drink for you. What would be your flavor?" A smooth and icy voice sounded from behind us. A member of Michael's coven stepped forth. He was tall and lanky. His blond hair was slicked back and he had the whole *007* look down to a T. He was the same blond that had looked at me through the window the other day, and the only member to approach the house without his hood up—Gavin. There was something about him that gave me the creeps. I shivered at his unusual, hostile look.

Phoenix glanced at me, and with careful steps, I backed away from her.

"It was a pleasure to meet you," I said as Gavin approached her, and then, turned to walk upstairs when she caught my arm and pulled me gently back to her side.

"It's all right," she said to Gavin. "I believe Arri could use a drink as well." With careful but attentive firmness in her grip, she led me away by the arm.

"So, I take it you've been here before?" I asked, as she guided us through the maze of hallways until we made to the kitchen doors.

"Yes. Michael had invited me here a few hundred years ago, to one of his astounding centennial balls. His receptions are wonderful; have you been?"

I yanked my arm free from her grip. "No, I only met Michael this last fall. He helped me out of a small situation." I left the details out, not sure how much she already knew.

"Living through one of Nicholas's henchman attacking you in the dead of night is no small situation." Phoenix rounded on me and shot me a skeptical glare.

"I guess not."

"So, are you going?" Phoenix asked as we sat down to a small table in the corner of the kitchen.

"Going?" I inquired as she threw me a Coke and snapped her fingers at Alain, who had appeared out of nowhere.

"A drink, please," she said, unfolding a napkin in her lap.

"Yes, Ms. Phoenix. Which flavor would you like?"

"O is fine."

My stomach turned at the notion of thinking of blood types as flavors, but I supposed it was no different than humans labeling our wine.

Alain left the two of us for a split second and returned with a large, polished thin metal goblet filled to a half-inch below the rim. The bold, dark red liquid sloshed slightly as he set it down. Without hesitation, Phoenix grabbed the goblet and brought it to her lips. She drank the entire contents and set it down with a light clink on the tabletop.

"Another!" She snapped in the air, and Alain appeared out of nowhere once again with a second drink in his hand.

"The centennial ball," she went on. "It will be held in a month."

"I'm afraid I haven't been invited." I was only guessing, only because Michael hadn't brought it up.

"Oh pish posh, with everything Michael has said about you, I'm surprised that you and he are not mates yet. He adores you. I'm sure it was just an oversight on his part."

"Yeah, I guess." To keep myself from overanalyzing the issue, I changed topics. "So, how was your journey?" I tried to bring us into normal conversation.

"Long, but fair. Travel is always hard." Her answer was short and to the point.

There was another round of silence until Phoenix downed her second, third, and then fourth goblet of blood. The color had returned to her cheeks, her lips filled to a deep red, and her temperament became more relaxed and calm.

"You said world-famous. How else did you hear about me?" I asked, looking around the kitchen at all the meticulously hung stainless steel pots and pans that had no use that I was aware of.

"Mostly from rumor. Mention of you has touch every corner of the planet, but I got the details from Michael. He is taken by you, as I said." Her eyes wandered over me from head to toe then back again. Her gaze lingered on my face and then over my thin, petite physique. I shrugged and fidgeted as I felt her appraise me.

"I can see why Michael is so"—her features scrunched and she looked deep in thought—"captured by you. You are a great specimen." She smiled as though she had given me the praise of a lifetime.

"Thank you, I think." I smiled back.

"In the letter Michael sent me, he told me how you fought with a werewolf. Is that correct?"

"Yes, unfortunately." I looked anywhere but at her.

"You seem embarrassed by this."

"Well, that too. Sara, the werewolf I fought, was a friend, or so I thought. I am sad about the consequences of the fight, but a little unnerved on how I did it." I played with the rim of my Coke and took another sip.

"Is it that hard for you to see?"

"See what?"

"Your uniqueness is unprecedented. Your ability to hold human and vampire blood within you and not give into either side is exceptional."

I nodded. I was still debating on how much blood from

each I had in me. My human side was obviously the more dominant side; otherwise, I would act a little more like them. "So, where are you coming from locally? There is no way that you and a team of Belgian horses rode all the way from Greece."

"How did you know they were Belgians?"

"I love horses. I had a few books growing up on types and breeds. It kind of stuck with me."

Phoenix took a sideways glance at me then laughed, a sound like echoing chimes bouncing off the sterile countertops.

"I acquired them in Colorado yesterday. Utah is only a hop skip and a jump from there." She spoke as if this was common knowledge.

"Nice. So…what did Michael bring you here for?" I was being a little bold, as if she would ever answer me, but I could hope.

"To meet you. He has been hinting to the fact that you are in need of a little friendship. Apparently Sara was not what she seemed."

"And what makes you think you are a good friend? How do I know I can trust you?" I quipped back.

"Nice. You have a little sass behind that timid façade." Phoenix beamed at me. "Well, I guess that is enough pleasantries. It seems Michael and you have some plans for this afternoon. I'm sure he will come looking for you soon enough." Phoenix laughed. "See?" She nodded at the door. Just as I looked back, Michael came sauntering in.

"Ah, I see you have been getting acquainted." He walked to my side and leaned to kiss my cheek. "I know I have promised you lunch in town, but there has been an issue with getting your pa—" Michael paused, then looked to Phoenix. "Would you mind taking Arri into town?" His expression held no emotion, but there was something rigid in his voice.

"Yes, of course, my lord." Phoenix stood and left the room without a second glance in my direction.

"What's wrong? I thought you and I were going to lunch." A hint of disappointment strained my voice in spite of myself. I was looking forward to having a non-coven lunch.

"I know I promised, but there is some business that I need to take care of." He offered no further explanation.

"I don't care. There is always business." I couldn't keep the miffed tone out of my voice.

"I need you to understand this." His eyes were pleading, but my temper didn't care.

"Yeah, but I want to know what this business is. Nana said there was something from Egypt. You had a book open to Egypt on your desk this morning. What's up?"

Michael narrowed his eyes at me and spoke carefully, evenly, as though restraining his temper.

"I'm not going to ask you what you were doing in my office, but if you must know, your parents are having a time getting back into the states. It seems some of the political colleagues I have there have been approached by Nicholas's men. They were bribed to keep your parents there until Nicholas says go. They were also threatened that if they do allow them to leave the country, then their families, friends, and any acquaintances will be killed." There was more, I could tell, and Michael cringed as he spoke.

"So now what? How will we got them home?" I asked. My chest tightened in fear for my parents.

"I have to call an emergency meeting and hope to rectify this situation without any bloodshed."

"I thought most of the coven left this morning?"

"They did, but there is still time."

"Can I help?" I knew I couldn't, but in the off chance that I could, I had to offer.

"No." He caressed my cheek with the back of his hand. "And I don't need you snooping." He gave me a playful, skeptical look.

"I don't snoop," I whispered.

"All the same, I need you to go with Phoenix; she can protect you better than anyone." With that, he pulled me up from the chair, kissed the back of my hand, and swept me into his arms, kissing me. His lips were soft but restrained. I knew he wanted more, but he kept himself in control. He broke off the kiss, and I felt the absence of his heat like a storm without rain.

"Now go." He set me back down on the floor and pushed me through the door of the kitchen. When we went outside, Phoenix was already waiting for me in the driveway.

"Really, Phoenix?" Michael asked. Behind the wheel, Phoenix just grinned. The red Bugatti Veyron Super Sport was a stunning and ostentatious roadster. The red and black exterior was intimidating and flawless, and the light gray leather interior was immaculate and polished, much like its driver.

"You don't mind, do you?" Phoenix smiled.

Michael growled and pinned her with a contemptuous glare. "Do not harm even one hair on her head. She'll be safe with you, right, Phoenix?" he warned Phoenix, then turned to me. The scornful look he gave Phoenix was gone and a loving pair of emerald eyes looked back at me.

"Yes, sir. Of course." There was a small twinge of nervousness in her voice.

"All right, I'll see you tonight. Stay out of trouble, okay?" Michael kissed me goodbye, and I slipped into the car next to Phoenix.

NINE

O n the way to town, the car was quiet. Phoenix was reaching impossible speeds and I cringed in the corner of my seat, hanging on to the door handle.

"Are we in a hurry?" I asked, noticing the speedometer.

Phoenix gripped the steering wheel and let out an excited cry of delight. The wind flew past us as she rushed through the trees. For an hour, we sat in silence, just the sound of the gravel road beneath us as we swerved and weaved on the road. The hollow absence pricked the back of my neck. I was hoping we would go to town and not a little shack on the side of the street. I cursed myself for leaving the castle, but even more so, for trusting her. There was something about her. I wanted to trust her; I thought I could. But still, I thought I could trust Sara too, and that didn't end well. My posture stiffened when Phoenix turned to look at me.

"Where would you like to go first? I'm afraid there is nothing in town that I would especially prefer." Phoenix had no problem stating the obvious.

"Do you eat nothing besides…" I couldn't say it. Phoenix laughed and shook her head.

"Okay, how about the diner?"

"And where would that diner be?"

"It's on Main Street, just past the movie theater."

I was getting carsick watching the trees pass one by one.

"Why did Michael send for you?"

"He was hoping I could help him with your training, but mostly for your protection from Nicholas and his minions. Apparently, you have been attacked twice in his home."

"Yeah, but where do you fit in?"

Phoenix let out a full, hearty laugh.

"Calm yourself. There is no need to raise your blood pressure. I'm only a failsafe to help you prepare if ever you're in a fight." I looked at Phoenix. Her expression shifted to one of intrigue. "Don't worry. I won't allow anything to happen to you."

Phoenix continued to weave in and out of the trees then turned onto a paved road. The speed limit was seventy-five, but she managed to overlook that little detail, and settle the speedometer at a mere one hundred.

Minutes later, as we pulled in front of the diner, people paused to see such an exquisite automobile in real life. The other vehicles on the road slowed down and crept past. Without a second glance, Phoenix hopped out of the car, then assisted me with my door, paying them no attention. The car was one thing, but Phoenix herself made the men swoon just as much. I could feel everyone's attention shift from the car to the amazing creature standing next to me.

As we approached the diner, I stopped at the entrance. My legs froze. I knew Michael trusted her, and I knew the coven revered and venerated her, but did I? Michael must have trusted her enough to send for her and then turn around and have her take me to town. But I didn't know if I did. She seemed okay, but I guess only time would tell.

"They don't serve on the sidewalk; you need to enter the facility," Phoenix joked. I laughed nervously. "Come on. Trust me, you have nothing to fear." Her self-confidence irritated me.

As Phoenix and I entered, the patrons quieted, and the waitresses stilled. The entire establishment stopped and stared.

"Table or booth?" The woman behind the host stand asked.

"Booth, please," Phoenix said with ease and elegance. Everyone gawked at the two of us as we were seated. Phoenix took the empty seat facing the entrance, and I sat on the other side. The window was warm as the sun shone in and heated our seats.

The diner was an old-fashioned restaurant. It had the original 1960s furniture mixed with western and semi-contemporary pictures. There was no real theme, just a hodgepodge of quaint and scattered items. I felt right at home. There was something about small-town diners and cafés that spoke home to my heart. I loved the castle, but the polished, sterile environment was too much for me.

"Thank you," I said as the waitress handed us our menus. I had been here several times before I went to live at the castle, so I kind of knew the menu by heart.

"So." Phoenix interlaced her fingers and leaned forward. "How did you defeat Sara?" The intensity of the question was scary.

"I don't know. I guess instinct took over."

"Instinct? You're just going to chalk it up to instinct?"

"No," I admitted. "I guess I could say it was my vampire side, but I'm not too sure that side of me is prominent enough to defeat a werewolf."

"It could easily be your fight-or-flight response. There was no way to flee, so you fought. You know, your vampire side would explain the ability to fight and win. Have you ever considered that with your background and parents, the reason for the constant attempts on your life is that you are..." She stopped and smiled.

"What are you trying to say?" I shook my head.

"I think you're more vampire than you want to admit."

"For the attacks, a grudge maybe. But the vampire thing, I know. I'm just not sure I like the idea. I mean, just a few months ago, I was living a normal life. Now, I'm just supposed to be okay with the fact that there are people trying to kill me and things like vampires and werewolves are more than things you read in books." Even as I spoke, I knew what she was saying, though. She was saying that my vampire side saved my hide, and she was right. I just wanted to pretend that none of this was real and live in my bubblegum world of butterflies and bunnies, but it was too late for that. "I am only half-vampire, Phoenix. Nothing more."

"Sure, I'll let you believe that for now." Phoenix's voice was oddly high-pitched and upbeat.

"Yay for you."

"And what is wrong with being like me?" Her eyes narrowed and she folded her arms. "In my opinion, I would rather be like me than you. We've all been forced into this world, and you are no different."

The waitress came back. "Have you had enough time to look over the menu?"

Phoenix looked at the folded menu in front of her and picked it up.

"You know, Arri, I'm not really hungry. I ate on the trip here, but why don't you order?" I knew what she meant by *ate* and my stomach turned.

The waitress glanced at a group of men waiting patiently by the door.

"Excuse me, I'll be back to take your order in a moment."

"Phoenix?" I said.

"Hmm?" she answered without looking up. She was trying a little too hard to fit in. She intently read the menu as if it had some hidden message.

"It's Gav—ouch!" I whispered. Phoenix kicked me in the shins. She didn't say anything else. She just nodded that she knew, then continued to read.

The men at the door were a few of the coven members, but not just any coven members. It was Gavin, the *007* lookalike, and three of his henchmen. The waitress seated him and his men on the other side of the room, near the window.

When the waitress returned, I ordered my usual turkey sandwich, and Phoenix opted out of eating.

The room returned to its normal lively murmuring of conversation after a few moments, undoubtedly about our visit. A few glassy-eyed, twentysomething girls with disheveled hair and wrinkled clothes came in and walked right to Gavin's table. Gavin and his men, though oddly out of place, managed to fit in with the ladies. The men exuded trouble. An edgy and dangerous vibe danced off them in waves. Their perfect porcelain skin and their self-confidence made them a magnet to anyone within walking distance. Even though they lived and walked in the vampire world, Gavin and his men didn't dress like the others. They dressed down with jeans and loose fitted shirts, but what seemed to catch Phoenix's attention was the women that accompanied them. The women were obviously enthralled, their eyes were glossed over, the way their skin had faded to a grayish hue, and the slight unbalance of their walk showed the obvious signs: Gavin and his motley crew were up to no good.

When the waitress served me, Gavin rose to meet us. "Ladies," he greeted us.

"To what do we owe the pleasure?" Phoenix's cavalier approach to his question infuriated him.

"Careful, sister. I only came to see the girl. It's interesting."

"What is interesting, Gavin, is your complete disregard for the rules." I glanced behind him, indicating the two girls that waiting for them at their table. I didn't know what came over me—maybe it was Phoenix's presence—but I stood my ground.

"If you're not careful, Arri, I might be tempted to do what we were meant to do, and that is hunt you down and drain you," he seethed through gritted teeth. His words were dark, and his expression was even darker. I was not surprised. To him I was just a mortal, but given that he knew of my relationship with Michael, to be this open and brutal was gutsy. What if I told Michael of his ill-mannered behavior? Of course, I would be signing my own death certificate if I did. I ignored him and turned my attention to Phoenix who was watching everything unfold. Then, Mr. *007* grabbed my fork and tossed it behind him.

"I think it's time for you to leave. I hear Nicholas is still waiting for you company. You don't belong among the rest of us. You never did. You are an abomination and have tainted our blood." The diner went quiet. His voice was low but venomous. I doubted anyone but us vampires could even hear him. "I do not appreciate the way you treat us, and frankly the way you treat most humans…you think you are better than us, than everyone. That you know everything. But in reality, you know very little." Snap—just like that, his voice returned to normal. "I would prefer if you left. I have no desire to see you nor be around you. You come in and out of the conversations not knowing what's been said, but seem to find the time to judge me and who I am. *I know who I am—who are you?*"

"This is not the time or place to discuss th—" Before I had the chance to finish, he grabbed me by the neck and pulled me out of my seat. My feet kicked helplessly above the ground. Patrons screamed and yelled but the other two men blocked the doors. I was shocked, but it only took me a minute to regain my composure and fight back. I grabbed his hands, fighting his grip, and managed to pull him off of me and fall free to the ground. I clutched my neck and stood gasping for air. Instinct took over and I turned around and yanked at his arm. With one small tug, I sent him flying through the air. Gavin landed on his back a few tables away with a crashing thud. More yelling and screaming echoed through the small space, but I ignored everyone else and I walked toward him. I could feel everyone watching us with surprise and awe. Passing a table, I reached over and grabbed a steak knife from a young man's hand. When Gavin landed, he scampered to his feet. I pushed him back down, kneeling over him on one knee and pressed the blade against his neck.

"Do not talk to me that way," I said through my teeth. "I may be human, but I pack quite a punch." I felt my eyes burn with anger while Gavin's flashed with uncertainty and fear. Throwing the knife to the side, I slowly rose to my feet. Behind me, I could feel Gavin's anger rise until he snapped.

"Why you—"

His words were cut short when Phoenix soundlessly leaped before him, swords crossing his throat.

"I am not afraid to use these." Her tone was even, but her words were deliberate and full of purpose. "Arri may have used restraint, but I have been told I have no such control. Speak that way to her one more time, and I will personally make sure you never drink again." She lowered her swords and with a simple swing of her blades, his clothes were shredded. Gavin fell to his knees and backed away from her at a crawl. I walked to the door and left without even looking back. When I got to the corner of the street, I finally allowed myself to stop and breathe. I felt Phoenix's presence.

"I'm impressed." She said from behind me. I turned to

see her bow to me with evident admiration. "I thought you said you were weak."

"No, just half-human." I smiled back at her.

TEN

I ran my hands through my hair as Phoenix and I walked down the crowded town street. Passersby watched me. Their stares were intense, and they were not even trying to hide them. People looked at me with open confusion; the men gawked and the women glared. The men felt pleased and lustful while the women were jealous and resentful. I myself felt uneasy. I had not changed since I first arrived, but they were looking at me like I was brand new.

I tried to turn my attention back to my current issue as I watched the people celebrating the start of spring. The storefronts were full of newly blossomed flowers, yearling trees, and colorful arrays of home and garden decorations. For the most part, the townspeople seemed happy and care-free. Their lives were packed full of mundane stresses like bills, traffic, the occasional worry of an illness. They didn't have to look over their shoulders every time they sneezed. Then there was me. I was a freak who happened to be strong enough to survive the battle between human and vampire blood. It was strange. Everyone in Michael's coven, including a few outsiders, had already accepted me. They knew I was going to be attacked every minute of every day, and still chose to protect me, even at the cost of their own lives. My so-called weakness had debilitated me. Made me fearful I could not protect myself...

There was the answer to my problem. I needed to learn to fight for myself. A smile touched my lips.

"I can hear you thinking from over here," Phoenix piped up.

"Oh, sorry." I paused to look over at her. She finished her text, then placed her phone back in her bag. "I was just wondering," I went on. "Why would Gavin attack me with you right beside me? I mean, everyone seems to fear you, and yet Gavin didn't." I couldn't remember what Gavin felt, but whatever it was didn't stop him from making his thoughts known. As I shook the memory from my head, Phoenix stepped in front of me.

"Whatever he felt is irrelevant. His actions spoke loud enough. Gavin was obviously working for Nicholas, and regardless of who was at your side, he would have acted in the same manner." Phoenix placed her hands on my shoulders. "Now that we solved this, let's move onto more pressing matters like world hunger." That made me smile. The seriousness had left her voice and the conversation was over. Nodding at the people on the street, Phoenix let out a laugh. "You guys really do celebrate everything, don't you?"

I nodded as we sauntered past the several decorated shops. As we passed a not-so-conservative bridal store, Phoenix let out a hoot.

"Oh my! Wow!" At this, everyone within a one-block radius turned to look at her, and of course, she didn't notice, or care. "This corset is amazing. It's a shame no one wears them anymore. Come on, you have to try it on."

She grabbed me by the arm and started to drag me to the store entrance.

"No way," I protested. "Besides, shouldn't we be getting back to the manor to tell Michael what happened?"

"I already texted him, and this will only take a moment."

"No. Way." I pulled my arm free from her grip. "I'm not going to wear a corset, Phoenix." I gave an incredulous chuckle. Although Phoenix had the style for a corset, I was more inclined to dress with a conservative flair.

"Oh really? What is so wrong with wearing a corset?" She placed her hands on her hips. The current corset she wore more than effectively accentuated her figure and flaunted her perfect body; it was a statement of superiority.

"Well, it would be nice to be as self-assured as you, but I am sorely lacking in the confidence department." I shook my head, and Phoenix laughed.

"You are underestimating yourself."

That was it. No lecture, no long drawn out excuse for my being timid or hesitant, just that *you underestimate yourself.*

As the midafternoon sun hid behind some adverse and aggressive clouds, the darkening skies soon unveiled their hidden agenda, and the heavens opened, and rain poured down like an open faucet. I found myself standing on the sidewalk staring off into the distance. The road was drenched, and mini-rivers swept the dirt off the streets. As the people ran for cover, screaming like the rain might kill them, and the store clerks rushed to gather all the outside sale items, Phoenix and I remained out in the open. The water drenched us as we looked up at the skies. Although I felt the rain, I didn't feel the cold splash of water. It was like the rain had no temperature. Or maybe it was me. Since Michael brought me into his home, I had learned more about myself than I ever had at home, and though I may walk and talk like a human, I was finding I was less and less like one, no matter how hard I tried to ignore it.

Phoenix looked over at me as I burst into a fit of laughter. The events of today vanished into a surreal moment. It was funny when I thought about it. I watched mindlessly as a leaf drifted its way down the gutter and danced in front of me. Until today, I wanted to hide from the problem I now faced, but I had a feeling, that no matter where I went, my problem would follow me. Now, I realized that no matter how much I wanted normal, my life would always be anything but ordinary. I was going to have to fight this if I wanted to live any life at all. My mind felt like mush and my heart began to hurt, knowing there was no other way.

"Arri?" Phoenix was in front of me, cupping my cheeks as she forced me to look at her. Another leaf drifted from a nearby tree and surfed along the water. It looked so delicate; even with rain pounding and the winds raging, the leaf just took things as they came and soared through the storm with ease.

"Why can't I be more like that?" I said, pointing to the leaf. "Why am I so afraid to make a mistake or do something wrong? I have been suffocated all my life, and now I have the opportunity to be free and spread my wings, but I feel like my wings are clipped and flying is just a tease. I can feel the change, but I'm afraid. Phoenix, I don't know if I am ready to be one of you. Who in their right mind would give their self up so easily to become a vampire? To bear the weight of something of this magnitude is terrifying." As I said it, I was absently looking in the distance. No matter how brave I wanted to be, I was terrified, and even with the support of Phoenix, I felt alone. I wanted my mom and my dad. I needed Michael. I needed the ones I trusted the most, the ones I looked to for advice when I was scared or unsure.

"And you do carry a heavy burden, a burden I am sad to see you have to deal with, but you also have support." Phoenix grabbed my hand. "We are in this together. I am here for you."

"Thank you, Phoenix, but you look at me like I am the

Holy Grail and in reality I feel like nothing more than a dinged-up tin cup."

"Arri, you have to have faith in yourself."

"Thanks, but I have as much faith in myself to beat Nicholas as I do walking down the center of town in pounding rain and not get pelted by one drop." I turned to look at Phoenix. "I don't know what I'm doing, or if I can even learn to fight like you. But if I am going to do this, there is no time like the present." I stepped off the sidewalk and into a puddle. "How do you suggest we start?"

"That depends. Where you are going?"

I looked at her, confused.

"If you are heading to France, I would go west, but if you are going to Denmark, I would head north." There was little humor in her voice, but I could tell that internally she was laughing.

"I'm being serious, Phoenix! I have a feeling I'm going to regret this. So, if I'm going to fight Nicholas, I need to learn how." I shook my head and folded my arms.

"We start now," she said. "Are you sure you want to do this?"

I hesitated. "Yes." I finally nodded.

"Okay then, let's get the car and we'll start at Michael's. I doubt the wonderful citizens of Richfield want to see me teach you to fight."

I was confronting my bleak outlook on my future like it was the barren road in front of me. By the time I had accepted the idea of I had to do and decided to actually take action, the rain had stopped. Going back to basics and putting one foot in front of the other was going to be harder than it looked. As I got into the car with Phoenix, I looked back to see the world I was leaving behind. Normalcy would be replaced by fear. I was consciously putting myself in harm's way, but hopefully, when this was all over, I would gain a life I had only dreamed of. A life I could call my own. Was my freedom worth my life? I pondered the thought, but I had already made up my mind. There was no other choice. If I turned back now, I would always be running, and Nicholas's threats would never stop.

As we headed out of town, I was convinced now more than ever. I would fight for my freedom.

We didn't get too far out of town when a car pulled out in front of us, forcing us to stop.

"So, I see you're still alive?" It was Mark, behind the cracked tinted window of a black Rolls Royce. The car door opened, and he stepped out and approached us. He looked like a mob boss, all decked out in a pin-striped suit and white leather shoes.

Phoenix froze, and my heart dropped to the floor.

Really? I thought. What was he doing here? Didn't I just do this? Wasn't I just fighting?

Just then, Mark's minions stepped out of the car alongside him. I looked over to Phoenix who gave him an exaggerated look of irritation and shook her head in frustration.

"What do you want?" she asked.

"It's easy really. I want what belongs to me." Mark responded as he gave me a pointed look.

"You think she belongs to you?"

"Of course she does. I wasted a year of my life proving myself to her parents. And after being saddled with her for several months, I figure I'm owed a lot. You have no idea the suffering I went through for this freak, this human."

Phoenix narrowed her eyes at Mark, then growled as she bared her teeth.

"I'll give you until the count of three to leave, or I will be forced to take matters into my own hands," she bit out.

"I'm sorry. Who are you?" Mark asked as his men surrounded the car. "I don't think I have made your acquaintance."

Phoenix laughed. "I'm sorry. I usually don't associate with the likes of you. But I am Phoenix."

A shadow of doubt and fear crossed his face before he hid it behind his arrogant mask. "I don't believe you. Phoenix is a myth." The waver in his voice betrayed his cocky appearance.

"Yes, well, don't say I didn't warn you." Phoenix took a quick glance in my direction while she strapped her swords around her waist, and I knew she was about to try something—I just didn't know what. With a pleading look, Phoenix tugged my arm and pulled me into the driver's seat.

"Stay put," she ordered.

Then, after locking the doors, she exited the car.

Where did she think she was going? There were at least eight men out there, and only one of her.

I felt like I was targeted by a red, flashing, neon sign that pointed me out to every Tom, Dick, and Harry that wanted to make a name for himself, and Mark was just one of many that got the memo. With one last look, Phoenix withdrew her swords from their sheaths and swung them in invitation.

"All right, who's first?"

The first to join the party was a blond who looked almost as if he had painted his jeans on. He was tall, and built, and the look on his face was comical as he approached Phoenix in a mock fight stance. It took just one swipe of her swords for him to fall to the ground.

"I did warn you," she said plainly as she moved to take on her next victim. One after the other, they fell at her feet, and she wasn't even breaking a sweat. With only two men standing between Phoenix and Mark, Mark's fear became physically evident. With a quick glance at Phoenix as she busied herself with the last remaining minion, Mark bolted toward town and disappeared.

As I peered out of the window, I shook my head. Then, three more SUVs pulled up, each full of what looked like about seven or eight men. Without even glancing at Phoenix, I could feel her thoughts. It wasn't fear of the men she felt; it was the fear of them getting me. I didn't know if she could take on all of them, but when I reached for the door handle, Phoenix shook her head and glared at me, telling me not to move.

Wham, wham, wham. I jumped in my seat. Three of Nicholas's men were hitting the car door, teasing and taunting me. I doubted that the door, or the glass window would hold them off at all if they really wanted to get me.

As fear and panic started to build, I closed my eyes and bit my bottom lip. I debated whether or not to get out and help Phoenix, or let her deal with it. After what she'd done with the last eight men, I doubted there was anything I could do to help her, but I felt so useless stuck in the car like a sitting duck—a soon-to-be-*dead* duck if the men on the outside decided to hit the window any harder.

With no time to think or plan, and knowing I couldn't just sit here, I fastened my seatbelt. From the corner of her eye, Phoenix saw me. A smile curled her lips and she simply nodded.

As soon as Phoenix was ready, I slammed the car into gear and right into one of the SUVs. The men scattered and the SUV moved enough for my car to squeeze by. Just as I sped off, Phoenix jumped behind me and took on the men as she gave me a head start. I just had to make it to the castle—or at least its border—and Michael and his men would help me.

Merging onto the freeway, I jammed my foot on the gas. The tires screeched, and the car jolted sideways, but I just kept on going. I cut people off in every direction. Finally, I was home free. I didn't know if I was being followed, but the chances were far greater than I was willing to take.

What was Mark up to? He never ran from a fight. Now it was safe to say that Mark was a permanent part of Nicholas' evil plan to kill me. So what was he thinking?

The exit to Elsinore was only a mile away, and I knew there was a back way to Michael's. I looked down and saw that Phoenix had left her phone. It was only for a second, but when I looked back up, I saw it—a flash of black cross the road ahead. I was alert and on edge. Once again, I could feel the panicked emotions of someone afraid to fail. The same emotions I felt when Mark found out who Phoenix was, when she disposed of his men one by one. I was scared and nervous, but I was also annoyed.

Then, from out of nowhere, a man, perfect and porcelain, stood in the center of the road and stared at me through the window. He was glaring, taunting, and gesturing me to hit him. Options ran through my head: hitting him, swerving and trying to dodge him, or making an immediate stop. I knew I couldn't stop until I got home, but what was I supposed to do in a situation like this?

If I hit him, I might not damage him, but I would damage myself. If I dodged him, I'd give him an opening while I was swerving and he would be able to jump at my car. Stopping was just insane, leaving me stuck in the middle of the freeway with nowhere to run. I was still debating the best course of action when I ran out of time and I was headed for a full-impact collision with the vampire.

I picked up Phoenix's phone and dialed Jonathan's number, yelling, "help!" as loud as I could in the hopes that he could make it here before I ended up dead.

As I got closer, time appeared to slow down. I saw his

menacing grin stretch across his face, as he had thought he had won. The breeze running through his ash-colored hair, that perfect face, a face I knew so well. A face I would see almost every day. My hatred surged to the surface. I fought myself trying to control it, but I was too furious. My blood boiled. I wanted nothing more than to get revenge.

My vampire side was in control and time changed again. It was slower and delayed. Hoping I could use that to my advantage and stall Mark long enough for Jonathan and Alex to come, I would need to plan my next move carefully; it needed to be perfect to the last half-second. I knew how fast vampires were and how fast I wasn't.

Just as the car hit Mark, I saw him brace for the impact.

The car whined in pain as the hood buckled, and the metal rippled toward me. I waited for the right timing as the car that once looked strong and priceless now looked fluid and sad. The windows cracked, then shattered, and small bits of glass flew around me and cut me. The accessories flew everywhere. I could feel the warm blood dripping down my cheek and neck. I looked Mark in the eyes, then smiled. I knew something he did not. I could see everything happening in slow motion and he was now in the middle of metal, wrapping around him, encompassing him. I jumped out of the window just as the warping impact if the crumpling metal reached the driver's seat and landed softly and gracefully in the middle of the road. I started to run, but heard a loud growl and the whistling of air as the car few in my direction. I quickly ducked as the whooshed over my head. Mark stood there, unaffected by my plan, and stared at me.

I stood up, tall and unafraid of him. I was focused and I could feel my anger surface again. My eyes narrowed, ready for the fight. My devious smile beckoned him to battle. I was waiting for even the slightest move. I wasn't just fighting for the vampires. I was fighting for me, for my life. Mark's undying devotion and loyalty to Nicholas and his want to destroy or capture me died quickly when his eyes met mine and he saw my fearless advance. I was not just beckoning him; I was walking toward him, showing him I had no fear.

I hoped that Alex and Jonathan would be close. Their speed was far beyond any car. I just prayed it would be sooner rather than too late. As I silently hoped for their help, a rustling sound came from behind me, and movement from the hills to the side of Mark were the answer to my plea. I would have been happy with just Alex and Jonathan, but I couldn't help but smile when eight or ten close members of the pack slowly emerged from the darkness. They emerged from every direction, enclosing Mark. Alex and Jonathan came to stand next to me with their hackles up and a low, menacing rumble reverberating in their throats. The packs' bared white teeth and slow, deliberate pace clearly sent chills to Mark's heart. Mark's stance never changed, but fear and anger glimmered in his narrowed eyes. Cars that passed us honked and swerved, as if we cared. Mark glanced around at the wolves, and I could feel his excitement and courage plummet. He was outnumbered. He knew he had no chance, but his pride won as he took a desperate lunge at me. I braced for the hit—I was ready to take him.

Alex jumped in front of me, blocking Mark. Jonathan nudged me toward the side of the road and kept me there. Alex and Mark fought, tumbling around the road, each trying to stay on top. Mark was no match for Alex, but he took good advantage of Alex's weaknesses. Although Alex was trained and skilled, Mark was more agile. Even as some of the pack tried to divert the traffic from the fight, a few made it through their perimeter. A large roaring Harley Davidson rounded the corner and veered to miss Mark, but Mark grabbed the bike's front wheel and threw both bike and rider toward Alex. With little to no effort, Alex dodged the bike. An ancient blue pickup truck slammed on his brakes as he saw Mark, trying to stop, but it was too late. Alex took advantage and hit the truck's broad side, shoving hard it in Mark's direction. The pickup knocked Mark back, but not enough to stop the fight. Mark was quick to rebound and ducked the next vehicle that Alex hurled in his direction. As Alex reached for the poor unknowing black Audi that was unfortunate enough to be driving tonight, Mark rammed Alex in the side, rolling the two over and over again. They bounced off oncoming traffic and tumbled through the dividing cement partitions until a loud yell came from somewhere within their struggle.

For a moment, their bodies lay motionless in the center of the road as the rest of the pack carefully approached their Alpha. It looked as if the fight was over, but who had won? A whimper came from Jonathan. Moving away from me, his form slowly phased, as if he had just walked through a wave of smoke and heat. I cringed, not knowing the result. Was Alex okay? I tried to walk toward him, but Jonathan glared at me, telling me to stay put. Seconds passed as Alex lay there. Then, with a gasp of air, Alex rolled over and whined. Just like Jonathan, his body wavered as if from the heat of a flame until he was lying on the cold asphalt in his human form. It was easy to see now who had won. Alex slowly got up while holding his arm and Mark's lifeless body lay off to the side. As I ran to Alex, it was clear how Mark had died: Alex had removed his head in the struggle. That must have been the yell I heard.

"Where's Phoenix?" Alex asked.

I wrapped my arms around my waist. "Phoenix stayed behind and fought the rest of the men—"

"The rest of them?" He sliced his hand through the air

to cut me off. "Let's back up. Are there any broken bones, cuts, bruises, anything?" I shook my head, and Alex looked less than convinced.

"Alex, really, I'm fine," I insisted.

"Good. Now what were you thinking trying to take him on?" Alex's emotions ran between frustration and concern. He looked me over for injuries through narrowed and furious eyes. "He could have killed you, Arri." Alex yelled and pointed his finger in my direction. With what looked like a great deal of restraint, he forced himself to take a breath and lower his finger.

"I know, but there wasn't anywhere to hide, either," I snapped back. "I may not have given a stellar performance or saved Michael's car, but I stalled him long enough for you to get here. It was the best I could do," I said as I placed my hands on my hips. Jonathan put his arm around my shoulders and pulled me away from Alex.

"Yes, we know," Jonathan piped up, "but did you really want to deprive Alex of his fun?" Jonathan chuckled and looked away, listening. Honking car horns from the stopped traffic and crescendoing sirens filled the air. "Unless you want to explain to the police that you hit a vampire in the middle of the road and totaled your car, we'd best get moving." He elbowed me lightly in the side.

Knowing Jonathan was right, and we couldn't get caught, we jumped the freeway bridge rail and landed in the desert just a few feet below the road. I looked back to the wreckage and smoking cars we left behind, and anger boiled inside me. I prayed the innocent people that were hurt because of Mark and Nicholas got help before it was too late. I hated leaving them, but what was the alternative?

"You might want to calm down. If they didn't believe you hit a vampire, they would think you *were* the vampire, and your eyes would prove it. Red," he said, noting my confusion, and pointed to my eyes.

"Sorry, I didn't realize," I said, trying to tamp down my temper.

"Let's go, everyone. We need to get a move on." Jonathan commanded the rest of the pack as he and Alex signaled them in. Smiling down at me, Jonathan playfully tugged my arm.

Just off the freeway, in the shadows of the bridge, we passed the ball of metal that used to be Michael's car. The boys cringed and shook their heads. I had a feeling they would have stopped and paid their condolences, if not perform a eulogy, if we had the time.

"Ouch. Michael will be less than pleased to hear one of his prized cars was totaled." Jonathan winced. "Who was that guy, anyway?" he asked.

"Mark," Alex answered for me. "He was Arri's boyfriend in Las Vegas. He was the same man that we fought at the movie theater."

ELEVEN

G uilt coated my heart as I thought about Phoenix. I'd abandoned her. She could be dead, hurt, maybe even captured, and I wouldn't know. As we came to the outskirts of Elsinore, tension filled the air. Even the wolves perked up when they sensed it. It was undeniable, and got thicker and heavier as we walked into the small little town I used to live in. Stopping dead in his tracks, Alex looked up at the night sky.

"We need to find her shelter. The rain will be upon us before we can get her to the mansion," Alex said, commanding his pack.

"How about the old house? No one lives there yet, right?" Jonathan asked with definite hesitancy in his voice.

"You don't mean there?" I said.

Alex nodded and took out his phone.

"No, no, no, no, no. I won't!" I shouted. "Do you remember what happened the last time I was there? A crazy man broke in and attacked me. And not just talking a minor break-in where a few of my things were stolen. I'm talking the kind where he tried to *kill* me!" It started to drizzle, and the temperature dropped a few degrees.

"No one is going to kill you," Alex said, tucking his phone back in his pocket. "We need to get you out of this rain, and just until we can get you to the manor. Michael is already on his way. He will be here soon." Alex seemed a bit uneasy, but just as he spoke, the light drizzle turned into a downpour and the wind picked up speed, emphasizing our need to seek shelter.

"I'll go on ahead and scout out the house," Alex said, pointing to Jonathan and to me to stay put until he returned. It was only a few blocks away, but I would have rather it been a few miles. I didn't want to go. When Alex came back, he smiled.

"I did recon, and I assured you the house was empty and abandoned. It will be fine until Michael gets here."

I trusted Alex, but the prickles on the back of my neck made me nervous.

As we approached the house, I stilled. My heart sank. The house looked sad and lonely. My beautiful yard was overgrown, and all my bucolic, manicured plants were dead. The grass looked ready for a safari and grew into the planters unchecked. Dirt and debris covered the entrance.

"Arri, you go inside, while we keep watch from out here." Alex said as the pack took off in different directions. Jonathan and Alex both smiled back at me before phasing. Their human forms slowly waved and transformed to their werewolf form.

I had flashbacks as I approached the house. The door was basic, though new and sturdy, but when I left this house another life and time ago, the door was half off its hinges and most of the windows were broken. Now, the house looked better than when I'd left it and far more eerie. Tears threatened my eyes as I felt the same fear from before that horrible night grip me.

"Something is wrong," I muttered and stepped onto the driveway. My breath shook. Tension tightened my shoulders and I gritted my teeth as my hands covered my trembling mouth. I stared at the house in disbelief. I didn't anticipate ever setting foot here again. I wanted to fall to my knees. Shaking my head, I walked toward the door as it clattered in protest against the strong winds. It seemed like Michael had made some repairs to the outside, but I was even more afraid of what I might find inside. Opening the door unlocked all my old memories. As I pulled it open, it creaked and moaned before crashing against the wall with a loud slam. Slowly and cautiously, I walked through the mudroom and into the kitchen. My breath caught as I remembered the last time I saw this place. It was a mess; the windows were broken and shattered. The sound of broken glass and rubble on the floor when Michael picked me up echoed in my mind. The cupboards had been smashed. There were a few moments after the wolves showed up that I don't really remember, but I remembered enough.

I forced my way through the new kitchen, looking at the new cabinets and new countertops. A new fridge and new microwave occupied the small corner where the phone used to hang. When I finally made it into the living room, I took a steadying breath. This is where it had all happened, but with the freshly painted walls, new drapes and pictures, the house seemed unfamiliar and foreboding. There had been a bloodstain in the corner where I broke my leg, but the new floors erased all evidence of it. The light and fan were new, as was the furniture and other fixtures.

With the house so clean and ordinary, everything that happened felt like nothing but a bad dream.

On the floor in front of me was a book—the same book I was reading before the attack. I even remembered the last sentence I read. "And the war began, making a room for a new leader."

I shook my head. Just minutes ago, in the diner with

Phoenix, I'd tried not to accept the new world around me. I wanted to ignore the attacks, the signs, and the changes I noticed within myself, but now I saw that I had never been normal. Normalcy was the fairytale. Silent tears streaked my face as I fell to my knees. This was so unbelievable. I was at a loss for words.

A moment of clarity surfaced in my inner chaos. The fear faded and I felt strong—strong and angry. Taking a few breaths, I walked to my old bedroom. It, too, looked like it had just been built. The new décor looked nothing like it had when I was here. The bed was neatly made and the nightstand was arranged with a small lamp, an alarm clock, and a vase for cut flowers. It looked like it was ready for guests, but a single piece of paper neatly folded and pinned to a dead rose stood out against the contrast of my new reality and the fresh new setting. I stared at it.

My curiosity took over, and I opened the letter.

Arri,

I was going to kill you painlessly and fast, but now I won't give you the pleasure. Your death will be long, painful, and drawn out. Every step you've taken today was planned, and you have followed instruction well. By the end of tonight, you will be begging and pleading for your worthless life.

Until we meet again!

N.

My insides recoiled. I knew the fight wasn't over. My false sense of strength and security melted into fear and hopelessness. Turning to the door, I took one last look at my surroundings. The damage the vampire caused a few brief months ago had been well beyond repair, or so I thought, but Michael managed to do it. Still, what this place needed was a wrecking ball, not a renovation.

Still, I felt little better about being here, with Alex and

the pack making perimeter sweeps, and a maybe little safer than if I had walked back to the manor in this driving rain. Although Jonathan hid his talents well, he was an excellent handyman and a great cook, and if the world were coming to an end, I would want him on my side. He was a survivor, a trained military operative, and he never let anything get in his way. I was praying for his diligence tonight.

Sitting down on the large hard sofa, I leaned my head back and closed my eyes. I tried to calm my erratic fears as I considered how tonight could end. It felt like the voices in my head would never stop, but then, my thoughts went blank, and my mind pushed and pulled at me until I was sucked into oblivion. Shadows started to take form and I found myself in a forest.

The trees were so thick I couldn't see through them. I knew there was someone out here just baiting me, but I couldn't find whoever it was. The further I went, the stronger the emotions got. The blind hatred stung my inner core. I couldn't go any further. I was far enough as it was, and whoever it was pursuing me was hoping I would get lost. I stopped. The presence I felt was an unfriendly one. I spun around. The man in front of me looked like he'd been a catch back in his day. Now, his eyes were sunken. The hair on his head was a translucent white. His face was bony and his pale skin glowed in the light of the full moon. But the sense of power and evil told me he was more than a skinny, harmless man. He was harboring much more.

"Nicholas," I said.

He pulled back his lips to reveal his extended fangs. I cringed, trying to hold back the scream that threatened to escape my lips. When he lunged to sink his fangs into my neck, I started to run, but it was no use. He pinned me to the damp earth and a scream poured out of me at last. I fought with all I had, and with one final yell, I tapped into a hidden strength. Before I knew

114

it, I was summoning a demon from within, and Nicholas flew back and into a tree, branches snapping as he left his imprint in the trunk.

"Arri!" he yelled. I paused—just enough time for him to tackle me to the ground. Something pinched my wrist and—

I snapped awake.

Pins and needles pricked my skin as I struggled to tame the emotions swarming in my heart.

Looking around the barren room, I could sense something was off. How long had I been passed out, and where was the pack? Except for the sounds of the raging storm outside, an odd silence seeped through the room like fog. Lightning crackled, and thunder followed. In the gleam of the flashing light, I saw it, perfectly poised and grinning—the face of my current nemesis.

"Gavin!" I cursed. I looked for the wolves, but they were gone. Where were they? Seeing my confused and searching gaze, Gavin laughed.

"Oh, are you looking for the pathetic excuses for wolves that were here trying to protect you? They're out hunting the decoys. Like throwing steaks to a dog, really. It was the perfect timing for a storm, if I do say so myself. Made my job a little easier. And now here I am." He gave me a mocking bow and walked to my side.

"What do you want, Gavin?" I asked. "What do you have to gain?"

"I have everything to gain. Prestige, power, reputation. Your precious Michael has become weak with your presence, and blinded by his love for you. I was able to slip through the cracks and he never suspected a thing. Nicholas was right. Michael is just as weak as your father. Steven could have had everything, but instead he defied Nicholas and his rule to be with a mongrel. A female, a *human*, no less."

His words were venomous, and he paced as he revealed his thoughts. "I won't make that same mistake. It was I that attacked you the night you were here alone, but somehow you managed to escape with the help of your dogs. I must say, I never thought Michael would take a human into a house of vampires. We have all been careful around humans, even managed to teach ourselves control, but to bring you into the lion's den was pure genius. Even I never would have thought that you were dumb enough to fall for a vampire. You are one stubborn little girl. Now here you are, right where I want you. Defenseless."

His words were foul, but I felt less intimidation than I'd expected. He had just called my dad weak, but if I learned anything from the vampires, it was that my dad was just as feared, if not a little more, than Nicholas. Plus, Michael was master over the largest coven in the world, and that was supposed to be *weak*?

"You now have three options. One, you can run and make it a little more sporting. Two, you can just come with me and let Nicholas kill you himself, which I think is most fitting. Or three, you can try to fight us, which I would love to see."

At that, two of his minions rushed in through the front door leading right to the living room, foaming at the mouth as if imagining the sport and fun if I chose to run or fight, their fingers twitching.

I should have been terrified, but I was calm, hoping more than anything that Jonathan and Alex would figure out the ruse and come to my rescue.

Gavin grabbed for my arm, but I dodged him.

"Oh, so you are going to run?" Gavin, obviously pleased, grinned at my effort.

Breathing tightly, and hoping I had a plan up my sleeve,

I bit my lip. Gavin saw my nervousness and I could tell he was waiting for me to make even the slightest move. But my heart was racing and panic pounded in my chest.

"What if we make a deal?" It took me a moment to recognize my own voice. But it was mine, no matter how shaky or squeaky it was. I didn't mean or think to say anything—I was still working on a plan and I went and interrupted myself. I was shocked, and so, it seemed, was Gavin. He laughed.

"It's gutsy, a human making a deal with a vampire, especially when you don't hold any cards. But I will consider it your last request," Gavin said, mocking me.

Even if I had no plan, and had no idea what deal I was going to make, I was mad that he'd insulted me.

That was it. I didn't want to be cocky, but I had beaten him before. Maybe I could beat him now. But I didn't have a chance if I fought all of them at once.

"Yes, a deal. I will fight you, but I will fight you one at a time." It was insanity speaking, but if I could hold them off long enough for my trusty backups to come, then I might live through this. Gavin looked skeptical, but agreed, and sent in the smaller of his two sidekicks. I recognized him—Mr. Creepy. The pasty-faced guy who always seemed to follow Gavin. He had been watching me, following my every move.

My renovated living room was now a dangerous fighting ring. Gavin would obviously take pleasure in seeing me fight to my death; he was sinister and crazy like that. I was in fact fighting, hopefully not to the death, but at least enough to keep myself alive.

Like a referee in a cage match, Gavin lifted his hand and signaled the start of our fight. His face was unfeeling and blank; it was hard to read what he was thinking. My opponent, on the other hand, was cocky and unrestrained. A smug grin creased his perfect cheeks. His furrowed brows and narrowed eyes flaunted his anger and superiority well. He felt he was beyond me.

Still, I was afraid. I was a goner unless someone came and saved the day, or I was somehow able to summon that inner demon, the strength that I'd tapped into when I fought Gavin before, that roaring emotional tide that gave me force and courage.

Mr. Creepy stalked in a circle around me, taunting me with his hands. Asking me to come and get him. As he lunged, I darted around the room in any and all directions to get away. I was not as skilled in fighting, and I knew not engaging was my best strategy.

This guy was a little smaller than Gavin, but he was built and toned. I could see his flexed muscle through the tight, worn T-shirt he was wearing. Maybe my plan was not so bright after all. All I'd managed to do was create an environment where I had no chance.

Finally, he grew visibly annoyed at my running, and he struck out. His first blow was strong and hard, landing right in my stomach. I gasped for air and hit the ground in a fetal position, and through great effort managed to suck in a breath. The air hit my lungs and a small spurt of energy jolted my core. I sat up and stared down my enemy, who was laughing and imitating me as he grabbed his stomach and mockingly fell to the ground himself. Maybe I was outclassed as a fighter, but I was not willing to give up this easy. I stumbled to my feet and took another breath. Each inhale was getting easier and the tide of strength was rising. Mr. Creepy cocked his head and grinned.

"Are you ready for round two?" he jeered. *Yes.* I could do better than a single blow. I realized this whole thing was a game to the both of us. To him, it was a game to see how long he could play with his food. To me, it was a game of staying alive. He cracked his neck and bounced around on the balls of his feet like he was a boxer in a fight. But this time, I was the one to advance. I looked down and tried to summon that inner demon, the strength I needed. It always seemed to come when I needed it most, or when my life depended on it, and hopefully, it heard my plea now and would come to my aid. With concentration, with focus on my unyielding will to live, a wave of strength and confidence flooded my body. It was more than adrenaline; it was determination to survive. My inner force was awakening. When I looked back up, my eyes were narrow and burning in anger. I turned my mouth up in a taunting smile. If I was going to be taken out, I was not going to go without a fight.

A growl grew in my throat and I snarled at the man. I had no fangs, but I bit my bottom lip for a good toothy smile. The game had changed; now I was a tiger and he was my prey. I braced myself, then, like a cat, I sprang at him. I was barely off the ground when his cocky attitude dwindled, and fear began to fill his heart. He was no longer sure of his kill. Fear shone in his eyes as he evaded me. He hunched his shoulders as he cowered on the outer rink. He wanted nothing to do with the failure of losing to a human. The mumbles and cries in the background of his fellow men yelling for him to fight fell silent, and there was nothing in the air but agitation and fear. His eyes widened, and in his last effort, he ran from the house with the second minion in tow. I turned to the only person left in the ring: Gavin. He didn't look too confident now, but I knew he was still sure he could defeat me.

Suddenly I was wary of my instincts. I didn't feel as if I was in charge of my own body, like I was an amenable host to the fighting will inside. I fought to keep my wits about me and have the courage to at least control the unyielding force.

All I could do was hold the demon back, but only enough from allowing it to show its true colors.

Gavin stepped closer, baiting me to advance. I took the opportunity and growled again. I jumped for a kick, but he blocked me, and I landed on my feet, crouched, waiting for his defense. My only hope was to catch him off guard. But, like the coward I knew he was, he backed away and again I was the one to advance. Then, in an instant, I was on the ground. He'd tackled me, raining down endless blows, hit after hit, enjoying himself. Pain slammed into me with the waving force of his swings. I could feel my skin split and blood drip down my cheeks.

Gavin swung his fist back for the ending blow. *No.* Somehow, I summoned enough strength to throw him off me. I stumbled and crawled to my feet. There on the ground was a piece of broken metal from the coffee table that Gavin threw to the side. I grabbed it on my way up as he lunged at me again. I dodged, Gavin landing on his knees, just long enough for me to run behind him. Now he was at my mercy. I didn't know how to kill a vampire. I didn't want to kill anyone, period, but I was determined to stay alive. And because I was pretty sure any living thing needed a head to survive, I placed the makeshift knife to his neck.

"I don't want to hurt you," I uttered. "But why couldn't you just leave me alone and pick on someone of your own kind?" My voice was quivery and I had tears in my eyes. I was reeling from what just happened, afraid of what I might have to do. "I don't want to kill you, Gavin, but I won't let you kill me either." My hands shook as I knew I held his life in my hands. If I let him go he would only try to kill me again, but I was too afraid to kill him myself. I wasn't ready to make the call. As I tried to decide his fate, Gavin nudged me hard to one side and that small awkward movement pushed me off balance just enough for me to stumble. My grip against Gavin's neck loosened and Gavin looked back at me with a winning smile and a gleam in his eye before I fell forward slightly and suddenly, Gavin was gone, like the coward he was.

Whatever had just happened, I knew it wasn't good. I stepped backward shakily, breathing in a final inhale as reality sank in. Warm blood soaked my shirt and through stabbing pain I looked down to see the scrap of metal stuck in my side. I took a deep breath, dizzy and foggy. Breathing was hard. And my strength and willpower were running out.

TWELVE

Stabbed? How?

The blade sticking out of my side was a reminder of my mortality. The demon inside of me was gone, and I was back to the weak human I wanted to be before all of this, the human I was when I was not fighting for my life. I had no idea what to do. I didn't know where to go. I was wounded and I had no one here to help me. I closed my eyes to block out the sight of the metal lodged inside me.

"Michael," I whimpered. I needed him now more than anything. I wanted him to be here with me. To be the last one I saw. To show me his loving face, the sweet smile that I fell in love with, and the touch I would never forget. I knew he was the only one I wanted and needed.

I gritted my teeth. I could feel the burning growing strong and fast. Michael was on his way, and I was not about to die before I saw him again. My heart and soul cried out to him.

"Ahhh!" The pain surged. Tears filled my eyes. With one final plea to see him again, I collected every ounce of energy and courage I had left. I took a deep quivering breath, grabbed the metal shard, and staggered to the door. With each step, the blade plunged further into my side, and I was barely able to stay conscious. I made my way, but the agony was more than I could bear. I tried to fight it, but I couldn't.

I had always wanted a life of adventure. I realized too late that with adventure came peril and possibly death.

As I stepped down into the sunroom, I felt overwhelmed, unprepared, but I couldn't stop now. Numbness washed over me, my vision blurring. Each blink was getting longer as it got harder to open my eyes. Shaking my head, I allowed myself to cry. My efforts were failing.

I pleaded for Michael. I could almost feel him. The butterflies in my stomach, the gentle race of my heart, and the feeling of home washed over me. It felt like he was close by. I couldn't see him, but I could feel him, feel his soul. With a weak smile, I thought *this is it*. This was my end. Accepting this, knowing I was not going to make it, knowing I would not live, I closed my eyes and allowed myself to hear Michael's voice one last time. It was like he was right beside me. His smell filled my memories, his touch, his soft kiss. I remembered the way he caressed my skin. How his name would linger on my lips, and how my heart would dance when I felt his presence. But most of all, I remembered the way my soul would ache the moment he left my side.

There was a connection between Michael and me that I couldn't explain. From the moment we met, there was that spark that lit the two of us. Even when I was alone, I could feel his very existence, and that was enough for me to finally let go.

It was a strange feeling, dying. It was like drowning. My lungs fought for air, and breathing hurt. I was suffocating. The continuous dripping of warm liquid scorched my throat with each metallic drop. The copper taste made me want to gag, but I had no choice but to swallow, one drip after another. Even as my foggy mind seemed to slowly clear and come back alive, my arms and legs lay still, cold, and frozen. The slow and lethargic beat of my heart felt like a pounding hammer, and with each agonizing beat, a burning fire slowly replaced my cold and lifeless body. What was this? Had I passed death and was I now in hell? What have I done?

The pain was too great. I could not run from it. With my sweat-soaked hair plastered to my face and neck, I closed out the world like I was simply closing my eyes. I heard nothing. I thought nothing. All I felt was the endless ache as my heart beat too hard and fast. And though dying was painful, and even scary, it was also deeply sad. I wept for the ones I was leaving behind. I was losing the battle; with one last thought of Michael, I surrendered to my ultimate death.

Then, a sound rang out, as though from the end of a long tunnel.

"Arri? Arri?" I heard a pleading voice. "Arri? Arri?" There it was again.

Arri? That sounds familiar. Wait, that's…me.

The voice was familiar, too. Then, as if the tunnel I was stuck in had shrunk, the voice sharpened and cleared.

"Arri." *I know that voice; I know that sweet voice, that caring voice, it's Michael.*

Loud, thundering footsteps that seemed to echo in my head.

"Michael, what have you done?" another voice asked in disbelief. There was something about that voice too. I knew it—Alex.

"I saved her life." The sound of Michael's loving voice comforted me.

"But you have no idea how that is going to affect her."

"But she was too close to death. I had no choice."

As if pulling myself from an endless void, I fought to open my eyes, I fought to feel again. Just as I opened my eyes, a blurred figure loomed over me, the tanned skin, the brown hair, the bright emerald-green eyes…I knew at once it was Michael. My throat was so dry. I tried to say his name.

"Shh, it's okay." His soft hand caressed my cheek. At his touch, I knew I was safe. I knew everything was going to be fine.

Images flashed through my mind, barely discernable before they disappeared: men running through a courtyard, arrows flying at a castle wall, my dad's face appearing through the shadows of a doorway, worldwide adventures, even people, some I knew, and some I didn't. Mostly, they were images of me. Me, scared but intrigued, as I was pressed against a stone wall. Me at the bank. Me when I tried to make my final stand in Michael's foyer. Each image of myself triggered an emotion—love, protectiveness, fear, admiration, vulnerability. These were not my feelings. When I saw myself, I saw a frightened, fragile, unworthy little girl. But that image was from someone who saw me differently than I saw myself. When I was scared, they saw courage. They felt protectiveness and admiration when I felt fear and weakness. Then, just as fast as the images pounded through my head, they stopped.

"Agh…" I tried to yell, but any attempt at violent cries fell silent. Just as my mind went blank, my arm burned with unforgiving pain, like fire seared across my skin, branding me. It etched its way from my wrist to my forearm, only to stop suddenly. Then, everything went black once more.

I was calm and at peace. Breathing was a steady effort, but it was getting easier. My body felt rested, and although I fought to wake up, my eyes would not budge. I wasn't sure if I was dead, but I could hear voices in the distance. With each passing moment, they were getting closer and clearer.

"Has she woken?" a man's voice whispered.

"No, not yet. She is trying, though." A second voice, luring and seductive, rang in my ears.

"You need nourishment, sire. You cannot help her if you are weak." The first man spoke again.

"When she wakes," the velvet voice purred.

It was good to hear Michael's voice. Tears filled my eyes, and slowly I opened them.

The figures before me were shadowed and faded. I closed my eyes, opened them again. Although it was bright, my view was coming into focus. I tried to lift my hand to block the blinding light, but I was too tired. Still, my surroundings sharpened, and I found myself lying on a plush, silken comforter. After everything I went through, and all the pain I suffered, I was surprised I made it through alive.

"Good evening." The voice was gentle.

Taking a deep breath, I winced a little in pain. The room around me was coming into focus and I was not sure where I was. I inhaled and winced again. I was still fatigued, but I was too afraid to close my eyes. I didn't know if they would open again.

"Don't fear, my love. I've got you." I felt a slight touch on my hand. A light, caressing kiss lingered on my cheek. My heart practically stopped. Slowly, I looked over to see Michael and his soft green eyes, loosely tousled brown waves, and the loving smile I remembered gazing down upon me.

"Michael," I managed to whisper. I wanted to reach up and hug him to be sure it was really him, but weakness and exhaustion weighed me down like a hundred-pound anvil. I looked to Michael for help, but he just sat there, his head hung and his eyes were sad.

"What's wrong?" I asked.

He looked away. Firelight lit his face, shadows of worry and doubt across his features.

"You never should have fought him." Michael tried to hide it, but regret suffused his words.

"If I didn't fight him, he would have killed me." I thought back to the fight. Something was missing. "Oh no, the pack. And Phoenix."

"No worries. They are all here and accounted for. Alex and Jonathan are beside themselves, and Phoenix is pacing, waiting for you.

I closed my eyes and gritted my teeth. With weak and uneven breaths, I attempted to pull myself up. In one swift movement, Michael's gentle hands helped me maneuver until I was sitting up and resting against several white pillows. The blankets fell to just above my waist. I should have been mortified, but in place of a shirt, I was wrapped from the chest to my waist in bandages, which were new and clean except for the small bloodstain at my side where the metal piece had been.

"Apparently my healing powers don't work anymore." My words were playful, but my heart remembered the fight, the pain it had caused. Michael carefully touched my cheek and pulled my chin to face him.

"You scared me. I thought I had lost you." His heart seemed to be breaking as he looked down at me. I could see his thoughts as he ran through the trees and to the house, pulled me from the blood-soaked floor, held me in his arms. As I saw this, his thoughts and fear of losing me filled the air.

"I thought I was gone too. I started to black out. The next thing I remember was a burning pain, and then…I woke up here." There was a lump in my throat when I swallowed.

"You had us all worried. But what I don't know is who attacked you, and how you got away." His face turned serious.

"It was Gavin," I said, defeated. "He doesn't give up easily. He somehow tricked Alex and Jonathan into following some decoys. When I was alone, three of them came after me—Gavin and his henchman. I magically scared the first two, and then only pure luck helped me with Gavin. I don't know how, but I had him. I had him by his neck and I was debating on whether or not I wanted to kill him when I hesitated too long. He grabbed that metal piece and stabbed me before I knew what had happened. Then he ran from the house and disappeared. I thought I was gone."

Michael's soul was filled with anger. He planned to get even with Gavin by whatever means necessary. He tried to hide it, but I could feel his every thought.

"Why did he run?" I asked. "He could have just killed me and got it over with, but he didn't."

"He probably thought you were dead. Normally, a human cannot live through that. You lost a lot of blood. It was a miracle you made it."

"I would have expected him to take me to Nicholas."

"I'm guessing he panicked, or Alex and I were too close. We got there just after it happened. Alex and Jonathan chased him, and I came in to find you."

I could feel Michael was hiding something, that would have to wait until later. There was knock on my bedroom door. George, the coven doctor, slowly pushed the door open and stood awkwardly just inside my room. A slight smile touched his pristine features as his left foot rubbed the back of his right leg and he itched the back of his neck. I had met him once before when Michael first brought me here and my ankle was broken. Here I was again laying in the same bed, with Michael sitting next to me, and the nice doctor tending to my mortal wounds. George didn't wear a white coat or anything, just jeans and a partially tucked-in blue shirt. His brown leather shoes were untied, but his hair was neat and immaculate.

"I'm sorry to interrupt, but I just need to check your bandages."

"Hi George," I fidgeted until I was comfortable. "It's good to see you again." I laughed and waved him in.

He walked to the side of the bed and placed his fingers on my wrist. "Your heart rate is back up and strong. Now, I need you to tell me if you have any pain and how much it hurts, okay?" He pressed around my side, but I was fine. Then he pressed the spot where Gavin stabbed me and I jumped.

"Okay! That hurts!" I yelled. "Er, sorry."

"Good, good. It means you are healing. But it may take a few days. You will need to take it easy until you are completely recovered, or you may reopen the wound." He looked at Michael. "She was lucky you found her when you did. You took a great risk. Fortunately for you, she seems to be doing well. Without your—"

Michael shot him a pointed glare.

"Well, I guess everything seems to be in order," the doctor finished nervously. "I'll just leave the two of you alone." The doctor gestured with his thumb over his shoulder and toward the door. "I'll be back in a bit with your meal." George's voice quivered as he backed out of the room and closed the door with a resounding click.

I turned to look at Michael.

"Are you hungry? Thirsty?" Michael looked at the floor then back up to me. I adjusted myself.

"Whoa, where are you going?" Michael asked.

"Nowhere. I'm just uncomfortable." I moved to rest more comfortably, with no pain, but Michael was on pins and needles. I rubbed my face and yawned. My tired and aching body won out, and I grabbed Michael's hand to pull him carefully to lie next to me. I hadn't forgotten about what the doctor said, but I would have to confront Michael later. Right now, I wanted to sleep. Cuddling in his arms, I could smell his scent and feel his steady breathing on my skin. With one last, intoxicating breath, I fell asleep knowing I was back in his arms.

THIRTEEN

F or the remainder of the night, my mind ran in circles. Men frantically scurried away from me down ancient streets. People with bloodstained lips hunted and chased me through abandoned mine shafts. But most confusing was the wave of emotions that flooded through me. Unbreakable love, devotion, protectiveness…these were just a few, but with them came comfort and contentment. Then, as if with the flip of a switch, the dreams started again. I could have sworn that I was really there, being attacked by my own dad. It was as if I could feel the bite against my throat, the pain and burning spread through my body, the feel of his strong and rough grip as he held me still.

I sat up suddenly, cold sweat coating my face and neck.

"Wow," I grumbled. Putting my palms to my temples and closing my eyes, I tried to relieve the pain. Opening my eyes again, slower this time, I glanced around the room. The drapes were open, and a steady beam of light cascaded through the space, illuminating my room. My heart slowed in relief as I realized everything had just been a dream. I was safe.

Stretching, I looked down and saw I had acquired a new set of clothing beyond the bandages I was wearing before.

The new shirt was a men's long-sleeved sweater I recognized as Michael's. His intoxicating scent still drenched the fabric. Under a trance from his scent, I let the nightmares fade into the recesses of my mind, and let myself bask in the comfort of knowing I was home, and still alive.

After a while, wanting to test out my healing abilities, and wanting to get out of bed for a change, I carefully moved around the room, testing for any discomfort. I was relieved to be somewhat, even mostly, pain-free. Physically it was like nothing happened—well, kind of—and the injury from the attack was almost nonexistent.

Perfect, I thought. I hated it when I was hurt. It wasn't the pain that really bothered me, although I wasn't a fan of it. It was the fact I felt so human, different from the ones I lived with. But I also felt like a vampire, which was different from what I thought I was. It was all another reminder that I was a neither—not vampire nor human.

As I rummaged through the dresser and closet for my clothes, nervousness and trepidation seeped through my thoughts, but I didn't think the thoughts were mine. I felt happy and a little carefree, which was a nice change. I was content. Brushing the emotions aside, I headed for the shower.

After I turned on the water, I looked in the mirror, and barely recognized the person looking back at me. My complexion was smooth and refined, and my face was thin and taut. With a satisfied smile, I ran my hands under the hot stream of the shower, and started to feel a little better. After adjusting the temperature, I stepped in, allowing it to fall down my back. I closed my eyes and relaxed. This was perfection, I thought. *It doesn't get much better than this.*

But I should have known that the perfection would be short lived. As soon as I reached out my left arm to grab the loofah, I froze. On the inside of my wrist, scored in crimson, was an intricately laced scroll mark. I blinked. The euphoric feeling I'd had just moments ago faded, and uncertainty took its place. I closed my eyes and shook my head, and then looked back at my wrist. *Yep, it's still there.* Pulling my wrist back, I stared at the mark more closely. If I took my mind away from the fact that it wasn't normal to have this shiny tattoo on my wrist, and that it was just more proof that I was some sort of walking paranormal freak, it really was beautiful. It sparkled in the water, like it was made of glitter. Tracing the score mark, I was surprised that it was neither raised nor indented, but smooth as my normal skin, as if it were projected or drawn. The color was strong and vibrant, and the shape was rich and sophisticated, but oddly enough, the mark in general was simple. If it hadn't magically appeared out of nowhere, I could maybe appreciate its beauty.

As I finished my shower, I kept looking at the mark like it had a secret. Like it was about to tell me the cryptic code to life's unanswered questions. Unfortunately, all it did was sit there, doing nothing. After drying off and putting on my clothes, I looked in the mirror and it hit me. What would Michael think? I stared at myself, and like a beacon in the dead of night, the mark stood out.

"Now what?" I thought aloud. Biting my lip, and thinking of my nonexistent options, I paced the room. Until I figured this out, I had to hide it. No one could know, especially Michael. I stopped to look in a few drawers in the nightstand like it would hold my solution, but all I found was some stationery and a photo of my parents. Another reality I would eventually have to face, as they were on their way.

The closet was filled to the brim with anything a girl could want, except something to cover a magical tattoo. But in the dresser, I saw a few light and airy long-sleeved shirts. Hoping I could pull one off, I quickly changed. Reexamining myself in the mirror, I smiled.

"It just might work," I said. The sleeve reached just past my wrist. "No one will be the wiser," I thought aloud.

Smiling to myself, I sat in contentment as I looked out of the window. The weather looked warm and inviting. The leaves were swaying in a light breeze. Men from Michael's coven meandered through the yard. The sun was bright, beckoning me. It was the perfect spring day. Just as I was about to turn away from the window, a slight movement at the treeline caught my eye. It was so subtle that no one in the yard saw it. Everyone talked among themselves, wandered about, and in a few cases, sat on benches, doing nothing in particular.

But it felt like something was out there. I closed my eyes and focused. *Whatever it is, it's familiar.* Shaking my head, I looked back at the tree line. There it was again. The movement was so slight, it was almost nonexistent. Folding my arms, I glared at the spot. Whoever—or whatever—it was, was out there. I just knew it. I stared at the trees, biting my thumbnail. Then, as if a shield was lifted, I could see the outline of two forms. Two people hiding among the shadows.

"Mom? Dad?" I muttered.

My parents had been missing in action since our attempt at a Skype call a few weeks ago. The last I heard, Michael was having trouble getting them out of Egypt. That was the same day that I went to town. If I didn't know any better, Nicholas didn't want them here while his evil accomplices carried out their attempt at my capture, which they should have pulled off successfully. I still didn't know why Gavin left me for dead. I thought the idea was to obtain me either dead or alive.

Something in Nicholas's plans has changed.

But what? I wondered, still focused on the statue-like figures in the trees.

What are they waiting for? I know my dad's not the most loved vampire to ever walk, but why hide if he has all the power?

As if they had enough of playing a game of hide and seek, they slowly entered the clearing, their movements slow and calculated. It was strange. No one noticed them: not a flinch, not a glance, nothing, no reactions. It was as if they weren't there. They made it further into the yard, and it wasn't until they reached the fountain, only feet from the doors, that anyone noticed them. I stared in amazement. It was like a veil had hidden them until they were ready to be revealed, and then everyone saw them at once. Even from behind my bedroom window, I could see the gasps and almost hear the murmuring as people stepped back and away from my parents. Their reactions all came at the same time, The men carefully nudged their mates behind them shielding them. The same fear permeating their very essence. They were terrified. My dad was the most feared; some said he held more power than Nicholas. I didn't know why they would hide. My only guess would be to cause the least amount of panic possible.

Then, just like that, my parents disappeared into the castle.

Two minutes later, I descended the stairs, searching for my parents and Michael. Muted and muffled voices drifted through the halls. I followed the sound and came face-to-face with the dreaded dining-meeting room once again. It would seem that eventually, they would figure out that these doors didn't stop me from snooping or eavesdropping. But until they discovered my secret to hearing everything they said, I could pause to listen for a few moments before making my appearance.

"I understand your concern, but Arri is fine." Michael was trying to keep his calm. I could feel his need to control his anger.

"But how—" My dad, as usual, tried to be the commanding voice in the room.

"It was my mistake," Michael interjected. "I left her alone with Phoenix while I dealt with your issue." His voice reverberated through the door and into the halls.

"I thought I made it clear that she was to be protected, not babysat by those who can't follow the simplest of instructions." My dad's voice raised a few decibels.

"Phoenix is perfectly capable of protecting Arri. It is because of Phoenix that she survived at all." Michael's voice was just under a yell.

"I believe Alex made a mistake by asking for your assistance. It is because of your negligence that my daughter was hurt at all. You were supposed to keep her safe. Ava and I will take it from here." My dad's words rung with finality.

"I understand your concern, old friend," Michael's tone turned soft and familiar, "but your daughter has become a member of this coven since arriving here. I apply the same rules to her as I do to all my members. She has the right to decide on her own."

"Let her decide? I don't believe it is her decision. Ava and I have sacrificed everything to keep her safe. I will not allow our plans to be ruined by the decision of a child."

At this, my temper flared. I had heard enough. He had no right. They *both* gave up the right to decide for me when they started lying to me. Seething with anger, I barged through the doors and into the dining room. The wooden doors slammed against the wall.

"Yes, Dad. The decision is mine." I looked my dad right in the eyes.

"Oh, Arri," my mom said as she ran to hug me. Instantly, my anger melted. Seeing the look of love and concern in her eyes showed me how much she really missed me. I had missed her just as much. "It feels like ages. Look at you," she said, cupping my chin and admiring me. "You look great. Living here agrees with you." My mom was, as usual, the mediator.

"Oh? What makes you think that?" My dad's demeaning tone stunned me for a moment. Then my wits were back.

"No, Dad. You lost the right to decide for me the moment you and Mom lied to me, the moment you kept the truth from me." It felt good to stand up for myself, even if it felt like I was disrespecting them as well. "You guys abandoned me when I needed protection the most, leaving Alex to take over your role. It should have been *you* who accompanied me. You and Mom have been manipulating me my whole life. Making me think I was normal, but I never was. I think it is safe to say that I have done just fine without you. I am staying." As the words left my mouth, my mom deflated, her shoulders dropping and her head bowing. I knew what I said was harsh, but I'd done my best to forget the past. It never belonged to me in the first place.

"I believe you are out of place, daughter. I will not tolerate insubordination." My dad never spoke to me like this; he was always the strong but silent type. For some unknown reason, though, his words didn't faze me. Although his presence was strong, I refused to back down. It was hard to stand up to him, but I needed to. If I didn't, then I would always live his life, not mine.

"No. I am not out of place. You, Dad, are the one who is wrong. Since I got here, I have grown more than you think. I have made friends here in the coven, and I have no intention of leaving. If you and Mom want to protect me, then fine, stay here and protect me. But as for me, I'm staying and that is not negotiable."

With the snap of a finger, my dad was beside me, holding me by the arm. His strong, rough grip pressed into my arm, allowing no escape.

"You *will* come with your mother and me." His demanding voice almost had me reconsidering. But I closed my eyes, gathered my strength, and whipped my arm from his grasp. It took me a second to realize what had happened, but one moment, I was staring at my dad, showing him I was not going to be hauled out of here without a fight, and the next, Michael had pulled me behind him, placing himself between my dad and me.

"What is the meaning of this?" My dad's cold, hard tone was nothing less than frightening, but Michael didn't flinch and stepped to my side.

"I warn you," he said. "Although you may be her father, you are only a guest on my land, and in my home. Arri is a member of this coven, and until she decides to leave voluntarily, she is under my protection. Have I made myself clear?"

My dad pushed me to Michael. Without delay, Michael wrapped his arms around me and pulled me to him. After that, my mom and dad exchanged a knowing glance. I never thought about how my parents would see my relationship with Michael. Being with him was second nature. Luckily for me, my parents didn't press the issue.

With the matter of my safety settled, and the power struggle between Michael and my dad ripping through the air like a lightning storm, my mom and I left the meeting.

As I showed my mom to their quarters, I realized she had yet to speak since the argument between my dad and me. I knew she was hurt because I stood my ground and defied my dad. Either way, this was not going to be the family reunion any of us was expecting.

FOURTEEN

The silence stretched between us, and it felt like we were more different and distant than ever before. My mom didn't know what to say about her absence, and I didn't know what to say about the independence I had found during my stay here.

"This is it. This will be your quarters while you are here," I said as awkwardness permeated the space. "Well, I better get back downstairs."

I smiled casually and started to leave the room, but as I reached the door, my mom stopped me.

"It's good to see you, honey," she said with wistfulness.

I nodded.

"You too, Mom," I said as a bit of longing and heartbreak flittered through me. Then I closed the door behind me and left her with her thoughts.

As I headed back downstairs, I passed my dad in the hall.

"How long?" he asked, stopping.

"How long?" I repeated.

"Yes. How long have you been seeing each other?" His words were hollow and forlorn.

"Since he kidnapped me. But I met him at the bank first."

"Kidnapped?" he asked, shocked and confused.

"Yeah." I tilted my head to the side. It never dawned on

me that my parents may not have been as well informed as I thought they were. Continuing past me, he started mumbling something in Aramaic. I called out to him, "Dad!"

"Yes?"

"Don't get me wrong. I am happy to see you both, you and Mom. But why are you here? There was no way that you could have heard about the accident and gotten here so fast."

My dad considered.

"Your mother and I got wind that Nicholas was up to something big. We took advantage of the lapse in their security to get through. When we got here, you had already been hurt. Although no one would tell us what happened." He looked at me for an explanation, but that discussion would have to wait. This wasn't the place to have this conversation. Understanding, my dad nodded and continued up the stairs.

"Oh, hun?" he called out.

"Yeah, Dad?"

"It's good to see you." Dad was never affectionate, but these words were as close to a hug as he got.

It was strange having my parents here; it was even odder that I was not accompanied by Michael. Actually, I'd expected Michael to be with me when I woke up. I thought he would have been afraid to leave my side. I didn't expect to have to go looking for him.

As I descended the stairs, I saw Alex huffing through the foyer, making his way to the back of the house. Following his hasty footsteps, I came to a halt when I heard him yelling from behind the library door.

"That's enough, Alex." Michael growled. "We will not speak of this here. The consequences are too high if we're overheard."

"Yeah, but what of the—"

"I said *enough*!" Michael's voice reverberated through the door and into the halls. "I thought I made my position clear."

"But there is no telling what the side effects of what you have done will do to her will be. What effects it will have on her…" Alex's voice carried obvious concern.

"Yes I know. The side effects are still undetermined"— Michael lowered his voice—"but you understand that I had no choice. It was the only way I could save her. You and I both know that a mortal hospital would have been too dangerous. I acted on impulse, but I felt I had *no choice.*"

Alex's words echoed in my head. *There is no telling what the side effects of what you have done will do to her. What effects it will have on her.* But just as I thought of his words, the world disappeared. Darkness closed in on me, and in the slightest bit of light, I was thrown back to that night. I remembered hearing those exact words. *Michael, what have you done?* It was Alex's voice. He was close and I was in pain. I remember hearing Michael's voice calling out to me, and the sensation of drowning. *You don't know the effects it will have on her.* Alex's voice again. This time, I saw the world though Michael's eyes as he held me, and looked down upon my lifeless body. The scene around me unfolded as I saw Michael tipping my head back. I couldn't make out what he was doing. The world was too out of focus to see any detail, but I knew this moment was pivotal.

With a gasp of air, I flew back to reality. The hallway came into focus, and the continuous chanting of my name rang out again.

"Arri?" Michael was holding me by the shoulders. A look of fear and confusion marked his brow. "Arri, are you okay? Can you hear me?" I stared at Michael. For a split second, I felt nothing. There were no residual emotions. I was left with nothing. All I had was the memory. "Arri?" I was pulled out of my thoughts as Michael's voice pierced my mind. Staring at him blankly, I blinked several times.

"Yeah?" I answered with no emotion.

"Arri," Michael repeated. Looking around, I found myself sitting in a chair in the hallway. The table next to me was in disarray. The delicate doily was amiss and hanging off the end, and the vase of flowers that sat atop was on the floor, broken: glass littered the hardwood, water pooling, and flowers scattered everywhere. "Are you feeling okay? Maybe you should go back to bed and I'll retrieve the doctor." Michael's concerned voice brought my attention back to him. Finally, my emotions came flooding through me as it all sunk in. "Arri."

"Yeah, sorry, what?" A crowd surrounded me, and as I looked around, I noticed that everyone had the same concerned and cautious look on their faces. "What's going on?"

Alex, standing next to me, took my hand. "You feel like ice." I pulled my hand back. The crowd murmured.

"I'm fine."

"What happened?" Michael asked.

"What do you mean?" I didn't know what to tell them.

"You knocked over the table, fell into the chair, then you stared ahead, unblinking, for the last twenty minutes." Alex's voice rose as he spoke and his concern was turning into panic.

"I...I don't know. I was... and then... it doesn't matter."

"Oh, yes it does." Alex's voice was stern.

"No, it doesn't," I repeated through my teeth. Folding my arms, I stared him down. Alex put his hands up in surrender.

"Okay, I give up." Alex rose to his feet. To my relief, most of my admirers nodded and went on their way, but Alex and Michael eyed each other with suspicion—and something else. I felt uncertain. They knew something.

"So, what brought you downstairs?" Michael asked, taking my hands and helping me up.

"You." I smiled, but Michael saw right through it.

"Are you sure you're feeling okay?" Michael wrapped his arms around me and rested his chin on my head.

"Yeah, I guess. It's just seeing my parents, and arguing with my dad, you know. I wasn't prepared. I hadn't expected them to be here so soon." Pulling out of his arms, I took his hand in mine and led him to the kitchen.

"You don't want them here?" he asked.

"No, it's not that. It's just…for the last year, I've been somewhat independent. Now that they're here, it will be like taking a huge jump backward. They will have me where they used to have me, quiet and submissive with no opinion. I love my parents, but I don't think they really believe in me." The fullness of my honesty weighed on my heart. Deep down, part of me knew it was true, but superficially, I had hoped that they would see me for the person I could be, and not as the person they'd like me to be.

"Oh, come on. It can't be that bad. From what I saw in the dining room, you held your ground pretty well."

"Yeah, but for how long? It's only a matter of time before they get their way. If there's one thing I've learned about them, it's that they have more patience than the two of us put together." I shook my head as Michael and I entered the kitchen.

"Alain?" Michael said.

"Yes, my lord." Alain magically appeared out of nowhere as he so often did.

"Arri, what would you like?"

For some odd reason, my mind shot back to the metallic taste I'd sensed when I was dying, and I gave a slight shudder. Michael placed his hand on my shoulder. Just as I knew there was something he hadn't told me, he knew there was something I wasn't telling him. Although Michael kept distantly observant, something was different. While I could only feel Alex's emotions, it was like I could feel Michael's thoughts. It was different than reading them; it was like taking a small peek, a glimpse, of what he thought. A window of what was going on in Michael's head. Something happened the night I almost died, and Michael was paranoid that it had changed me. But changed me how? I couldn't be sure, but I was pretty certain that the vision had something to do with it. Looking back, I tried to remember the words that triggered the memory.

"Arri, are you sure you don't want to go back to bed and lie down for a while? You're looking awfully pale." Michael gave me a skeptical look.

"No, I'm fine, just a little spacey."

"Sir?" Alain asked. I had almost forgotten he was there. He was like a walking empty shell—no emotion. Michael didn't miss a beat.

"Sorry, Alain," I said. "May I have some toast?" Alain said nothing.

"Arri, you look sick. I would feel better if you went back to bed," Michael insisted. He turned his head and glared at Alain, who seemed more involved in our little conversation than he should have been, and snapped his fingers for Alain to resume his duties.

"No, I'm fine. I just, I feel a little off. That's all."

"Off? How?" Michael asked as he pulled out a chair for me.

"I don't know. I can feel it, but I can't describe it. You know?"

Michael studied me for a moment, then gestured for me to sit.

As I grabbed the back of the chair, Michael's and my fingers touched, and *zap*! I was flying through a movie in

143

reverse. Images flashed before me. The loving face of a woman as she wiped dirt from my brow, a room filled with people seated at a table looking to me in anticipation…just random pictures flashing in strobe light, one after the other. Then *zoom*! It was like I was hurled back until the images stretched from view, and I was sucked back to the present.

Breathing a little heavily, I looked at Michael who was ready for bear. His shoulders were tense, and his body was frozen.

"What is it?" Michael asked as I snatched my hand away from his.

"What was that?" I asked, as my hand prickled like it had been asleep. I could still feel the electricity running through my fingers.

"What was what? You just froze." Michael took a deep breath. "Arri, I can't help you unless you tell me what's wrong." He felt annoyed with my behavior, but until I knew what was going on, I was going to have to keep it to myself. Who knew what trouble would ensue if being a half-vampire brought death knocking at my door?

"Nothing's wrong. Like I said, I'm just feeling a little off. My mind keeps flashing through images and memories. I think I'm just trying to sort out what happened. I guess I didn't realize exactly how much I've been through in the last week."

Without hesitation, Michael nodded.

"For everything you have been through, you have taken it better than I would have expected. I'm starting to wonder if there is anything you can't do." Michael's chest rumbled as he chuckled, but I sensed he was hiding something with that laugh.

FIFTEEN

"So what now?" Michael asked as he stood behind me and pulled me back against him. His arms snaked around me, and his chin rested on my shoulder as he kissed my cheek.

"Nothing. Just don't make me go back to bed." I gave him a playful glare. After being in bed for the last few days, I had enough energy to light up the town. It was amazing, really. It felt like I just had a good rest, and now, I felt on top of the world.

"Wouldn't dare," Michael teased as we left the kitchen and walked down the hallway. When we came to the foyer, we saw a few of the coven members deep in conversation. With casual ease, Michael let go of my waist and stepped beside me as he took my hand.

"I know Phoenix and Catherine are around here somewhere. I'm sure they are eager to see you."

"Catherine? I thought she left." I was excited, although I wasn't sure exactly how to act. We always had a manager-employee relationship, and now that things were different, I didn't know where that left us.

"She did," Michael brought my hand up to his lips, "but when we ran into a few snags getting your parents back, she came back to be with you. She was very displeased when she heard you were hurt." He chuckled. "Catherine can be quite the dramatic."

"Catherine? Are you sure? I was barely able to get an emotion out of her. Between her and my mother, she was always the logical one. It was her idea to send me to Jessie's after the first attack in Vegas."

Michael snapped his attention from my mouth to my eyes. "Jessie?"

"Yeah, I think he was in London. Why? Do you know him?"

"He is one of the oldest members of my coven." His words were absent, and the flash of images started again. But this time, they came a little slower. I could see them like the reel of an old black-and-white movie. My dad's face as he introduced a young man, no older than twenty. The man's searching eyes were confused and weary. His long, black hair was pulled into a ponytail, and his features were soft and angelic. He was the perfect lure. As my dad left, the man pledged his life to me, and then I was back in the present. This time Michael only observed me quietly. He was afraid that if he pushed too hard, I would run. I hated withholding things from him, but I was scared. Somehow these visions were connected to the mark on my wrist. I hadn't noticed it until now, but every time I had one of these visions, it tingled and felt warm. Worst yet, what if the mark was a sign that he needed to kill me? What if it meant that I was turning into Nicholas? I needed to know what it was, and what it meant, before I shared it with Michael.

Michael's skeptical look implored me to trust him, but my heart was not ready for me to say anything yet. I was afraid I'd lose him. I think that part of me was hoping that when I woke tomorrow, it would all be gone.

"Are you sure that you don't want to change into something a little cooler? It's a little warm out here." Michael suggested as we left the castle. The outside air was just as I had imagined it would be. The inviting scene beckoned me to be out here and enjoy. I looked up to the sun and closed my eyes, letting the heat warm my face. It felt great. I felt alive.

"No, I'm okay. I still have a bit of a chill; I think my body is still recuperating," I said, knowing I had not only lied, but also kept something from Michael. I needed these long sleeves to keep the mark hidden.

Off into the distance, I heard loud cracks, as if wood hit wood. Searching the yard, I saw two people sword fighting, but with wooden sticks.

Phoenix? Catherine?

The two of them made unyielding advances as they attacked each other and hit with purpose.

"You can't beat me!" Phoenix yelled as she swung the stick at Catherine's head.

"And why do you say that?" Catherine replied as she ducked a forceful blow.

"Because, I am a goddess. No one can beat me."

I looked to Michael and he just nodded.

"No one has ever beaten her that has tried. She is definitely one that I am grateful is on my side. There are some that would compare her to Athena, the Greek goddess of war."

"You only think that, but you are no goddess," Catherine said as the stick came at her again. This time, she was not as fast, and was knocked to the ground.

"Ha ha, another victory!" Phoenix exclaimed, pointing at Catherine, who was lying on the grass, mumbling beneath her breath.

"Would you like to go say hi?" Michael nudged me in their direction as Phoenix helped Catherine up off the ground.

"So, how about seven out of thirteen?"

"No thanks, Phoenix. I think I'm done."

"So you concede? Ha, told you I was Athena." Phoenix started to do a victory dance until she looked up and saw me.

"Arri!" Her cry was more of a musical shriek than a yell as she sprinted in our direction. It was all of a half-second before she appeared before me with a loud crack. "You're awake!" she squealed.

"Yes, I guess I am," I said, smiling in embarrassment. Phoenix took no time to pull me into a hug. Her strength was fierce as she squeezed.

"Agh!" I whimpered as I reached down and held my side, biting my lip as I smiled through the pain.

"Oh, Arri. I am so sorry!" Phoenix said.

"No need to apologize. I guess I'm still a little fragile."

"How do you feel?" Catherine asked as she shot a glare at Phoenix.

"I feel good, but…restless, I guess." *Good, if you don't count the strange visions, and the mark on my wrist*, I thought.

"How are you? Are you okay?" I asked Phoenix, remembering that I bailed on her when Mark and his men surrounded us.

"Who, me? I'm fine! What would be wrong with little ol' me?" Phoenix looked confused.

"I feel horrible for leaving you alone with all of Mark's men. There were way too many of them. I should have stayed."

Phoenix let out a whimsical laugh. "It is going to take more than a few dozen men to defeat me. You never should have had to face Mark and Gavin alone. I am truly sorry for that. I am in your debt." Phoenix knelt before me and bowed her head.

"Phoenix…" I was about to decline her debt, but Michael and Catherine both shook their heads. "Thank you."

She rose. Her normal self-assured nature and confidence had faded and she seemed more humbled, chastened. I still didn't like the idea of someone being in my debt, though.

"My lord," Catherine spoke, "if I may have a word." She looked at me with concern in her eyes, seeming rather disturbed.

"Arri, will you be okay on your own?" Michael looked deep into my eyes. He was still worried about me. He was reluctant to leave me on my own, but there was something that told me he needed to hear what Catherine had to say.

"I'll be fine. I've got Phoenix," I said gesturing to Phoenix, who stood with her head still lowered.

"Yes," he agreed. A hint of uncertainty tinged his heart. There was something major I was missing. Something that all of them knew. But being totally immersed in my own thoughts, I missed out on the rest of the conversation. When I looked back up, Michael and Catherine were headed toward the castle.

"So, are you up for a sparring round?" Phoenix asked.

"Sparring round? You've got to be kidding me, right?" The idea sounded insane. Sparring with Phoenix was like volunteering for a death match with the titans.

"No, but this will tell me where you are on your training."

"Training? Are we still doing that?"

"Of course we are. Why wouldn't we?" She was totally confused. I was about to point out that besides the fact that just a few days ago I was almost gutted like a fish, I didn't stand a chance against her.

"Okay," I reluctantly agreed. "I guess I can try. Are you going to take it easy on me?" Hopefully she'd at least *try* not to kill me in the first round.

"Take it easy? Not on your life. Do I look like the kind of person who would tread lightly?" She cocked her head.

"No, I guess not," I said nervously, biting my lip.

"How about this—I'll take it easy, but only until you get the hang of it. Okay?"

"Fine, deal."

Phoenix tossed the stick at me, but before it hit me, I reached out and snagged it with blinding speed. The stick cracked against my palm as I grabbed it, startling not only me, but also Phoenix. The feel of the hilt felt familiar. Something about the leather braiding awoke a hidden memory. The weight and the balance triggered something inside me, almost like an instinct.

As we walked to the center of the courtyard, several of the coven members gathered. The cement circle acted as a ring, and our crowd seated themselves around us. Phoenix and I rounded each other a few times before her hand twitched, and she grabbed the wooden stick like a sword.

As the onlookers hushed, my footsteps echoed throughout the courtyard. With each passing second, Phoenix grew visibly more anxious. She watched me with determination, and she waited for me to make the first move. Slowly, I gripped the makeshift sword, and took a careful step forward. This was it—the move that Phoenix was waiting for. With precision footwork, she swung the sword around her and advanced.

My heart raced and panic surged through my veins. Just as she hurled the wood in my direction, I matched her hit for hit. Phoenix's eyebrows furrowed in wonderment, and she took no time in driving me back. I tried to match her level and speed as I defended myself. Her strikes started off slowly, but her speed and strength increased as I was driven back. Finally, just as Phoenix's sword came at me one last time, I lost my balance. From the corner of my eye, I saw two familiar people exiting the castle. For a split second, my attention was drawn away—*my parents*. The next thing I knew, my feet left the concrete, and I was airborne. With a vibrating thud, my back hit the ground, and the wind was knocked out of me.

"Never lose focus on your enemy," Phoenix said as she pointed the sword in my direction.

As I gasped for air, the world spun and several of the coven members' faces, including Phoenix's, appeared above me.

"Arri?"

I heard my name, but it sounded distant and garbled. Sucking in another breath, I looked for the two people who had distracted me.

"Mom? Dad?" I called out in confusion.

"Phoenix!" Michael yelled. "What is the meaning of this?"

There was little or no time to react before my dad's voice cut through the silence. "Is this how you have been treating my daughter?"

Michael appeared beside me and helped me to my feet. "I will talk to you later," he told Phoenix, who dropped to her knees in submission.

"No," I said through labored breathing. "I volunteered. Phoenix was honoring my request. The fight was my idea," I lied. "She is supposed to train me, isn't she?" I held my hand to my chest and took several deep breaths. The last thing I needed was my parents coming in and ruining things. As I looked around and saw the many people who bowed to them, my sudden anger returned.

"Yes, but not before you have healed from the last one."

"Nicholas won't wait for me to heal any more than I have the power to control the sun."

As I dusted myself off, I picked up the fighting stick and handed it to Phoenix.

My mom took my arm to escort me to the castle. I looked back at Phoenix. She was stock-still and nodding as my dad spoke to her. His voice was too low for me make it out, but whatever he said to her had her scared.

Yanking my arm from my mom, I stood back and looked at her.

"Thanks, Mom, but I got it." My mom's face fell, and

hurt filled her eyes. I knew it was mean of me to be so short with them, but there was so much I was still angry over. They were wrong to conceal something as important as being half-vampire, not to mention the fact that I was being hunted. This was something that never should have been kept from me. It should have been something that I was told from birth so that I would have been more capable of protecting myself.

"Honey, I wanted to be there." Her words were soft.

"I know you did, but why *weren't* you? You had plenty of opportunities. When you found out that Nicholas was behind the attacks at the bank, you should have told me everything then. Not leaving the country right after I moved. You should have been here to help and guide me. Instead—"

My dad interrupted. "Arri, that's enough. You have no idea what we have gone through knowing you were out here alone."

"But I wasn't alone. I had friends. People who cared enough about me to help me through all the chaos. Alex and Jonathan have been invaluable. And even though I just met Phoenix, she has taught me that no good will come from hiding. She even saved my life." My dad looked over at Phoenix and a little bit of repentance filled his eyes.

"And Michael?" My dad's words were forced.

"Yes," Michael said as he placed himself between my dad and me.

"What role do you play in my daughter's life?"

Michael looked from my dad to me. His eyes softened. A smile curved his lips, and there was a look of obvious adoration in his eyes.

"Please, if I may, we have a lot to discuss. May we take this inside?" Although everyone, including Michael, felt fear in my dad's presence, Michael still held authority, even over the mighty Steven.

As my dad——grabbed my mom's arm and escorted her to the castle, Michael leaned over and kissed my cheek.

"Just give us a few moments." He winked at me, and with that, the three of them departed for the castle.

"Are you crazy?!" Phoenix asked as she pointed a slim finger in my direction. "Do you know who that is?"

"Yeah, that's my mom and dad. I thought that was obvious."

"I know *that*, but hasn't anyone told you?"

"Told me what?" I knew everyone and everything was fearful of my dad—even the humans, although they didn't know why. I, on the other hand, didn't see my dad with such fear. I would have to agree that he was beyond intimidating, but there was something I sensed within him that no one else did. He felt unease, despair, and pain. He felt like it was his fault that I was in danger.

"Steven has no tolerance for disrespect, Arri. He was responsible for the 1483 massacre. He killed over four thousand men because of their perceived disrespect. I doubt that he will show restraint even for his daughter." Phoenix meant every word. She was scared for me. "See, vampires hold respect to be the upmost form of loyalty. To disrespect another is to show that they places no value on your life." There was nothing for me to say. All I could do was nod. The relationship was different between my dad and me. In some ways, he almost feared me.

"My dad has my respect," I said. "There are still many things that he needs to earn back from me. Both my parents have a lot to make up for, in fact."

Phoenix thought about it as she placed her hands on her hips, cocking her head to one side then the other before deciding not to push the issue.

Accepting that for now, I grinned then held the sword

up by the hilt. Phoenix hesitated as she looked at the sword and back at me again several times before narrowing her eyes at me. Shaking her head, she took the shaft of the weapon from me.

"Are you sure you want to do this? I fear we will both be in trouble if you get hurt again."

"I wasn't hurt," I argued. "It was a minor reminder that I need to fight harder." My voice was filled with false courage.

Satisfied that she got her point across, Phoenix held her sword in front of her face, and then whipped it off to the side to show she was ready for battle.

In this round, it was harder to focus. I could feel the frustration from Michael seeping from the house, the worry from Phoenix, and the hesitation and fear from the coven in response to my parents' arrival. I myself felt anger from my parents' random pop in and their indifference toward what their absence had meant.

Putting the sword in front of my face, I took a deep breath and focused all the emotions, to center myself. Bringing the sword off to the side, I waited for Phoenix to start.

"Your move, you lost," she taunted.

I nodded. This time, instead of taking a step, I lunged at her with the sword. The crack of wood echoed through the empty courtyard as she deflected my attack. Our swords smacked over and over as we charged and bounded at each other. Phoenix darted back as she tried to regain control, but I didn't give in. Fair or not, that opening move showed I was winning. The anger, frustration, fear, and worry all fed into my strength. Each emotion added that much more power behind my focus and speed. In an instant, I had summoned the demon within. My moves were more controlled. My steps mimicked hers. My motions were fluid as I recalled Phoenix's technique. Even my rhythmic breathing showed no signs of strain. I felt alive. I felt free. Now, more than ever, I felt like I was one of them.

Drawing on my strength, I hit with power and purpose. Strike after strike, I was relentless until finally, with one last blow, I knocked the sword from Phoenix's hand. In awe, she knelt before me. It took me a moment to realize that she never got a hit in. The whole fight, she was on the defensive.

SIXTEEN

I stared in disbelief at my hands and the wooden sword as I held it against her neck. *I think I beat Phoenix. She has been bested by no one, and I think I did it.* I looked from my hands to her face, but she wasn't looking back at me. She was focused on my left arm.

In the whirl of the fight, I had forgotten about the mark. I was so bent on letting out my frustrations that I lost track of my sleeve movement. Dropping the sword, I stepped back and tugged down the hem to cover the mark. But Phoenix was quick. She was up off her knees and in front of me, shoving my sleeve back up, faster than lightning. With palpable fear, her heart sank, and her face paled. If I didn't know she was a vampire, I would have thought she was having a heart attack.

I pulled free of her grip and readjusted my sleeve as quickly as I could. I didn't mean for her to see it. This was my secret. She was not supposed to know. No one was. The pained expression on her face had me scared. With the calmest voice I could muster, I looked Phoenix in the eyes.

"What? Are you all right?" I tried to play it off like it was nothing.

"How long have you had that mark?" she asked, never taking her eyes off my covered wrist.

"I noticed it this morning. Why, what is it?" I didn't know if I really wanted to know the answer. Instead of the calm and casual Phoenix who took everything as it came, this Phoenix was physically trembling. "Phoenix?" I said, confusion and anticipation lacing my voice.

"Does Michael know?"

"No, he doesn't. I know I am already a paranormal weirdo, but I don't want Michael to think I am even weirder."

Phoenix chuckled, clearly nervous.

"I was hoping to keep it a secret," I said, shrugging. "At least for a while, anyway. At least until I knew what it was. Do you know?" My voice betrayed my false courage.

"Come on," she said. She took me by the wrist and pulled me to the castle.

"So, I guess you're not going to keep my secret for me?" I tried to joke as I tugged at her grip to free my arm. Her fingers tightened even harder. Just as she opened the door, mom passed through the entrance. It looked like she was on her way outside to pay us a visit.

"What's going on? Is everything all right?" In another context, my mom's——well-polished and sophisticated voice would come off as overly regal and proud, but here, it matched the setting. Her hushed tone and raised eyebrows revealed her suspicion as she glanced between the two of us.

"Pardon me, my lady." Phoenix paused before she bowed to her waist, never letting up her concentration or the grip she had on me. "It is urgent that I speak with Michael immediately." Mom looked at me and saw the fear in my eyes. I was not scared of seeing Michael. I just didn't want him to know that I was tainted with this mark, whatever it was.

"Of course, but Messieurs Steven and Michael are in a meeting. Is everything all right?" my mom repeated.

"I don't know. It is not my place to discuss." With that, Phoenix pulled me down the hallway toward the library, and my mom followed in tow.

"Phoenix, I don't think it is a good idea for you to interrupt them." My mom's voice barely reached us down the empty hallway before she turned and followed us.

"What I do not understand is...*how*?"

My dad's voice seeped out as we neared the office.

"I'm not really sure," Michael's voice admitted. "The boundaries are set, and the rules are clear, but the old ones never really did care to follow them."

"Careful. I may be in an agreeable mood, but I will not be insulted."

"My apologies. My intention was not to insult you, but this fight is being played not by our rules, but by yours. I was only pointing out the differences." Frustration varnished Michael's every word.

"You're right. In our time, we fought for what we wanted. It was never a matter of diplomacy." Before I heard any more, we arrived at the library doors. Without even the slightest hesitation, Phoenix barged through them with my mom behind us. The wood splintered and crashed against the wall as though she had just ripped the doors off its hinges. With remarkable speed, Michael rushed to our side.

"Are you out of your mind?" he growled. Phoenix stopped and knelt at Michael's feet.

"Is this how you run your coven?" My dad's outraged voice boomed across the room thundering off the walls. "By letting them run amok and disrespecting the sanctity of a private meeting?" His eyes narrowed on the kneeling Phoenix, and then at me, burning with fury and disgust.

"Have I not taught you better, or have you forgotten the rules while gaining your independence?" he seethed at me.

"That was not my intention, my lord. I come to you with something that requires your immediate attention. It is dire that it be addressed right away," Phoenix explained, keeping her head down and her voice soft and repentant.

"You may rise," Michael said, and turned to me, his eyes filled with questions. I tried to pull my arm free of Phoenix's death grip, but my attempts were futile. "This is rather unusual. It had better be crucial," he warned.

With a simple nod, Phoenix looked to my dad, and then back to Michael. As she tried to push up my sleeve to bare my mark, I growled in anger.

"Enough!" I yelled. My temper roiled. The ground shook slightly, and the air vibrated as I gritted my teeth. Looking at Phoenix, I yanked on my arm one last time, and she stumbled back in shock.

"This is *my* secret to confess, not yours." My temper still evident in my voice, I glared at my stunned and shaken friend. This *was* mine. I would not be outed, or allow another to tell on me. Surveying Phoenix and my parents, as my mom now held my dad's arm, I stood tall and without fear. As Michael met looked at me, my bravery softened, and fear and uncertainty filled my heart.

"I need to talk to Michael alone," I said, not taking my eyes off Michael. I was hoping that if I could tell him from my point of view, he might be a little more understanding. Michael nodded.

"You may leave us now." Michael said to my parents and Phoenix, gesturing to the doors.

"I don't think..." my dad stood in anger.

"I do," Michael interrupted. "This is not a matter for you or Lady Ava. If there is something that Arri wishes to say, then her wish must be carried through."

"You are going to honor the wish of a child over the rights we have as parents?" My dad reached for my hand, but I dodged. Carefully, I studied my parents' resolute expressions. It was obvious that my dad was not in a negotiating mood. Still, this was between Michael and me.

"Yes, Steven, I am. Although, she may be your daughter, she is still a member of my coven, anointed or not. And Arri is no longer a child."

My dad searched my face, looking for any admission of the truth. Michael pulled me back behind him.

"Now that we are here, she is no longer your responsibility. I'm sure Ava and I can take it from here." My dad's words were more like a warning or a threat than a suggestion.

"No, Dad. Michael's right." I walked out from behind Michael. "From the moment I arrived here, I became a member of this coven. Even if I weren't, I would still choose him."

"But Arri...surely, you can tell us anything that you wish to tell Michael," my mom pleaded from beside my dad.

"I'm sorry, but I still must ask you to leave. Arri and I will be out when we are done." Michael's words were strong and adamant. He was in a very uncompromising mood. With one last hard glance, Michael gestured to the door once more.

"Just remember who gave you your position," my dad said as he, my mom, and Phoenix left the room.

With my parents gone, it was easier to think. I walked to the window and opened the thick, heavy curtains. The day was winding down, but the last bit of sunlight was still rich in the sky. The mountains were painted red and orange, as if they glowed from within.

"You know, it's amazing really..." I started. "It seems that every day gets weirder and weirder."

Michael eyed me with concern. "Oh, and how so?"

"Well, just a few days ago, I was semi-normal. Yeah, I was half-vampire, but then...something changed when I almost died."

"And what was that?" Michael asked evenly, but it was obvious he was struggling to maintain his calm.

"Well…" I turned from the window. His emerald eyes offered me courage and reassurance to tell him the truth. Biting my lip, I lowered my head with contrition and held up my arm. My sleeve was up just far enough that he could see a hint of the crimson mark peeking from underneath the thin fabric.

With a slight gasp, Michael took my arm, and gently pushed up the rest of my sleeve. His eyes searched me for any sign of regret.

"Are you okay with this?" His concern, fear, and pride were palpable. He felt responsible, and yet, somehow, *proud* of the mark.

"I don't know." I shook my head and looked down at my shoes.

"What do you mean you don't know?" Michael asked, wiping a single tear from my cheek.

"That's just it. I don't know if I'm okay, because I don't know what it is. I don't know how it happened. I don't know how I got it, but most of all, I don't know what it means." As I finally made eye contact with him, his gaze softened. Silent tears were now pouring down my cheeks. Through quivering breaths, I strained for air. "What is this, Michael?" I asked, and held a hand to my aching chest.

"Hey." Michael cupped my cheeks and looked in my eyes. "It's all right." He shook his head. "Come here." He pulled me into his arms, holding me close. When my hysterics calmed and reason crept to the surface, I pulled back and looked up at him. "Here, let's sit down." He took my hand and I followed him to the couch.

I'd seen Michael with the other coven members, with my parents, when he seemed to hold himself tall and with power. But with me, he showed his softer side. With a gentle touch, Michael took my arm and pulled my left sleeve up to my elbow a second time. The glistening mark shone in the light of the late afternoon sun.

My mind raced, and tears resurfaced in my eyes.

"Michael, I'm sorry. I didn't know about the mark—"

Michael interrupted. "Are you under the impression that I am upset with you? That I am unhappy with you for bearing this mark?" A devilish grin painted his face.

We stared at each other. *Where do I start? What do I say?* I thought.

"May I ask you when you noticed this?" Michael broke the awkward silence.

"This morning." My heart beat painfully in my chest.

"Why didn't you tell me?" he asked, a small hint of hurt tinting his eyes.

"I was scared." The answer was simple. "I woke up to an empty room with a mark glowing on my wrist, and I didn't know what it meant. I didn't want to lose you over something that I didn't have any control over."

Michael chuckled. "I would never leave you," he said, kissing my forehead, "but you need to trust me. This"—he traced the mark on my wrist—"does not just *happen*. It is a sign of the bond." Although Michael's words were sincere and steady, I could sense there was something that concerned him about the mark.

He drew closer to my side. Then he took my hands in his, hesitated, but lowered his head to kiss my intricately tattooed wrist. "This is called the *Statara*. The word *Statara* means blood bond. It only takes place between two vampires. It means that through an exchange of blood, you have bound yourselves to each other." Michael paused, searching to see if I understood.

"But what does this have to do with me? I haven't performed the blood exchange thing." I was thoroughly confused.

"No, *you* didn't." Michael paused as he looked away. "But I did." His heart dropped, and fear, hurt, and regret burned within him.

"Wait, what?" I asked. "No, *how*?"

Michael just shook his head. "It was an accident."

"How was it an accident?" Then, it hit me. "The night I almost died," I said softly as I sorted it all out. "Gavin stabbed me. I remember lying on the floor, and then I heard you." I stopped and closed my eyes as I tried to remember. "You ran into the house and saw me. You thought I was dead. You cradled me in your lap. You were panicking. Then, you tipped my head back…" My voice died as I realized what happened. "The drowning, the burning, the metallic taste, it was blood. Now, it all makes sense. You were trying to save me."

Michael looked shocked. "How did you know? I didn't think you were still conscious. Your heartbeat was too weak." Michael's puzzled look was understandable. I, too, was still unclear about the events that lead from the accident up to this moment.

"I saw it," I tried to explain. "But through *your* eyes. How *you* saw it, not me. I can't explain it." I pulled my hands away, embarrassed. Nothing about this was normal. I couldn't be any further away from normal if I tried. I was a half-human, half-vampire. I could feel the emotions of others, and I had visions but couldn't tell if they were useful or not. *Oh, and let's not forget that now I have a weird mark on my wrist that apparently binds me to Michael.*

Freeing my hand from his, I rubbed my face. As I folded my arms and looked away, I felt Michael get up from the couch. Barely a millisecond later, he knelt in front of me.

He took a deep breath and smiled at me. "It looks like there is more than one side effect." Michael paused to assess me. "I don't know where to begin."

163

"Neither do I. So much has changed in the last twelve hours. I feel overwhelmed." A few more tears escaped my eyes. Wiping the tears from my cheeks, he chuckled.

"You certainly know how to complicate things, don't you?" Michael asked, sitting next to me again.

"I guess I do." An awkward silence fell over us. "Can I ask you a question?" My heart skipped at the thought.

"Sure, anything."

"When I woke the first time, the doctor said something that confused me. He said I was lucky you found me when you did. That you took a great risk. What risk was he talking about?"

Michael smiled. "We are forbidden to share our blood with mortals. Our blood is poisonous. In simple terms, it will kill you within seconds."

"So, then why did you share it with me? What if it had killed me?"

Michael raised his brows and looked stumped as he considered what to say. "I was betting on the fact that you already had vampire blood in you. I was hoping that my blood would help kickstart the healing abilities within your own blood."

I thought about that for a moment. So the doctor was right. Michael did take a great risk. He risked losing me to save me. It not only worked, but I felt better now than I ever had. I could hear better, see better...even my strength was improved beyond my wildest dreams.

"May I ask *you* a question?" Michael asked hesitantly.

"Sure," I said. "It's only fair."

"What did you mean you saw it through my eyes?"

I smiled at this, then opened my mouth to speak only to close it again. "There are no words." I started, then paused, trying to find an easy way to explain it. "You know how I can feel everyone's emotions?" Michael nodded. "Well, it's kind of like that. With you, it's like hearing your thoughts. Only I can *see* them. At first, I thought they were just visions. It took a minute to figure it out, but I think I have been seeing your memories." I stopped, waited for him to call me a freak, to walk out, but Michael seemed to be in deep thought.

"Can you tell me about these visions?" he asked.

"Well, to be honest, they are more like snapshots. I can only recall a few."

"I'd love to hear them."

"There was one where a lady with auburn hair smiled as she wiped your face. She wore my same necklace?" My statement came out like a question.

"My mom." Michael's face fell. I saw the lady again, kneeling down to wipe his brow. This time, the stone walls behind her were more in focus, and I could make out a delicate green dress that spoke of some high position.

"She was the queen," Michael said, as the memory played its way through.

Then, the memory changed, and I saw arrows flying through an open window, and from the doorframe, I could see two bodies lying still in a bed with arrows sticking out from the sheets. My heart sank; this was the brutal way his parents had died. They didn't even know what happened. I wanted to cry for his loss.

"I'm sorry." The words just slipped out. It wasn't my memory to see. I felt like I was violating his thoughts.

"It was a long time ago." Michael averted his eyes and looked anywhere but at me as he tried to hide his heartache.

"Why didn't you tell me about the blood exchange thing? When I first woke up, I mean?" I asked, hoping the change in conversation would help. It did.

"The same reason you didn't tell me about the *Statara*. I

was afraid you'd leave." Looking out the window, and into the deepening night sky, Michael smiled. "It looks like we've been discussing for a while. Would you like dinner?" He went to stand, but I held his arm.

"Yes, but first, I have two more questions."

"All right, what?"

"Why was Phoenix so determined that you see the mark? How does this affect the rest of the coven? It's just a mark, and it's easily hidden."

Michael closed his eyes before gazing out the window again. "The *Statara* has always been created between two vampires. It has never appeared on a mortal before—at least not in my lifetime. Also, the mark is supposed to be blue. It is said that the mark of the true ruler will appear in red, to show the flow of true blood. It means you are supposed to bring balance in our world."

Something drew my attention to the door. Standing up, I smiled. "Enter," I said, only realizing once I'd spoken that nobody had knocked yet.

With a confused look on her face, my mom entered the room.

"My apologies, my lord, but the coven is ready."

SEVENTEEN

A s Michael and I entered the hallway, my mom stepped aside. She bowed her head to me, then to Michael. Something about her demeanor was off, even for her. She was subdued, restrained. There was something wrong.

"If I may, my lord." Mom nodded in my direction.

"Is this all right?" Michael asked me. He knew I was less than thrilled about being alone with my parents, even just one. It was odd. When Catherine had arrived, Michael had practically stamped me with a *don't touch, mine* warning. Now, it was a silent war for my loyalties and attention. I would have hoped that Michael knew that my devotion and my heart belonged to him.

"Yes, of course," I said. Michael took a wary glance at me before making his way down the hall.

"So." I shrugged. "What's up?"

My mom hesitated. "Nothing really, just walking with my daughter." She smiled, but it was weak and fragile.

"I mean, are you okay? You've been quiet and distant since you got here. You're usually open and assertive. What's wrong?"

Mom's smile widened, but only by a fraction. "I see you have come out of your shell a little. I like it." She bumped her shoulder against mine. "But, uh, you're right. Things are different between us now, aren't they? I wasn't expecting you to have changed so much."

"I know, but Mom, you have to understand, you and Dad…" I was finally ready to defend myself, but Mom interrupted before I had the chance.

"Arri, I know. You have all the right in the world to be upset with us. Your father and I were wrong to keep what you are a secret from you."

I was stunned. I'd been ready to fight, but Mom just up and surrendered. I peered at her in question as we slowly walked down the hall following Michael to the dining room. "Then why…why not tell me before I was attacked? Before Nicholas and his men had the chance to find out where I was?"

"Simple. We were hoping that if you could lie low for long enough, then Nicholas would stop looking. We were hoping that we had more time, time to teach you what you were up against." There was no emotion in her voice, like she was reciting a prewritten speech.

"You two were betting on me being hidden until you had time to teach me what I was up against. How much time were you hoping for? I'm twenty years old. You two had to have realized that it was only by chance that they didn't find me before now. So just how long were you guys expecting me to live with you?" I stared at her, waiting for an answer, but nothing. She just sat there and looked at me. Although her shoulders were back and her head was held high, projecting confidence and poise, internally, she scrambled as she with telling me the answer or hiding the truth again.

"The truth, Mom. Tell me the truth. I can feel how hard you're struggling to cover it up, but it won't work. Why?"

Mom sputtered at my frankness. "You may know what you are, but you, my dear, still have a lot to learn. Just because you live among vampires doesn't mean that you are ready to face your future." She tipped her head to the side.

"No, you're right. I still have a lot to learn. I have to learn everything that you and Dad were supposed to tell me. I have twenty years' worth of lies and deception to digest and sort out."

"We were trying to *protect* you. We were doing what we both thought was right."

"Did you think of the repercussions? What would you and Dad have told me if I'd moved out right out of high school, like most kids?"

"What would you have had me say? What would I have told you? We brought you up in the world of mortals."

"If you had brought me up with the knowledge that I was different, and that I was part of two worlds, then I would have been better prepared to defend myself. The three of us could have fought this fight together." There was a long pause as the two of us stared at each other. Not that I was going to admit it, but Mom had a point. How was she supposed to bring me up in both worlds if they were trying to hide me?

"We still can. You don't have to fight this alone. Your father and I will fight it for you."

"I don't *want* you to fight it for me!" My voice had crept up to a yell. "All I've ever wanted you to do is trust me. This isn't about Nicholas or Michael. It isn't even about what I am. It's about all the lies that you and Dad have fed me over the years." I shook my head. "You know, my whole life, I've always wondered why you and Dad were so suffocating to *me* when the two of you were so adventurous. You've been to countries I've only dreamed about. I was so jealous and angry watching the two of you stifle who I wanted to be that eventually I all but gave up the fight. But here, now, I won't allow you to suffocate me or push me into obeying you. I think it's great that you and Dad are here. I don't know your role in the coven. I don't even know mine. But while I'm here, and while I'm with Michael, I will do things as I see fit. This is not a matter of you being my parents. This is a matter of me being who I want to be, and who I need to be."

"Is this what you were trying to prove to me and your father by challenging Phoenix to a fight?"

"No. I challenged her so that she and I could start my training. Michael brought her here to teach me to fight and defend myself."

"Arri, you are still young. Why hurry to learn now when you can learn in good time? None of this has to be decided today."

"Yes it does, Mom. You may have been living with your head in the sand, but out here in the real world, we are on the brink of war. And I for one don't want to get stuck without the ability to fight my way out."

"I doubt things are as dire as you think." My mom's voice had turned dismissive, almost mocking. She was still seeing me as a five-year-old in a princess dress rather than the woman I had become.

"I'm afraid she is right." Michael's voice carried in from the hall. "With Nicholas's men knocking at my door, and the fact that your daughter has had several attempts on her life, it is indeed that dire."

"My lord." My mom bowed as Michael entered, then looked back at me and gestured to him. "So, is this where your loyalties lie?" Her question rang with emptiness, like a wide chasm, and her eyes welled up with defeated tears. I saw a woman who felt hollow and void. I thought back to the memories I had of her before I left home. She was always so strong, powerful, confident. It hurt to know that I was the reason she was no longer that way.

"Yes, but not there alone. I still love you and Dad. I'd like for us to be friends again, how we used to be. But can I count on you to tell me the truth? Can I trust that you and/or Dad won't take advantage and lie to me again?" I'd have to call a truce here. After all, they were on my side, or so my mom claimed. As I spoke, she snapped her attention from somewhere behind me.

"Yes." My dad's voice carried over my shoulder. Turning to him, I was relieved to see he was smiling. "I was wondering when you were finally going to tell us how you really felt." His tone was light but to the point.

"So you planned this?" I asked.

"No, your mom sought you out on her own. I just happened to be walking from the other room to get you and overheard it." I searched my dad, looking for any sign he was lying, but he seemed to be telling the truth. "I don't mean to cut your conversation short," he went on, "but the coven is waiting, and I feel that they may be getting restless." My dad gestured for Michael and me to come with him, but I stopped mid-step.

"Wait, I have a question for you two." My parents looked at each other with concern, but nodded. "Good," I said. "Now that we are being honest with each other, what should I call you? Roger, Emily, Steven, Ava, mom, dad?" I smiled and a chuckle escaped my lips.

"You're right." My dad laughed. "I should have known that you were bound to hear a few stories about your parents while you were here." He shot a meaningful glare at Michael, who reciprocated and growled in return.

"Well?" I asked, interrupting their power play.

"As I'm sure you already know, the name I am known as is Steven, and your mother here is Ava." My mom nodded, and a smile spread across her face.

"So, how would you like me to address you?" I asked.

"Steven and Ava." My dad answered.

"Or Mom and Dad," my mom piped up. "Either is fine." I looked at my parents. It was like I was seeing them in a new light. There was still some animosity between us, but at least we were trying. I had a feeling that I was going to need their help if I was supposed to live up to whatever it was the coven thought I was destined for.

EIGHTEEN

A s we neared the meeting, I heard a loud and hearty voice from three doors down. It sounded like Alain, but I've never seen him out of the kitchen. Michael and my dad slowed to listen. I, too, could make out what this strong and sturdy man was saying, and it caught me by surprise.

"You are not paying attention. Now, I'm sure that Michael would like to have you believe he is still strong and incomparable, but if I have my histories right, then Steven is far more forceful and powerful than Michael could ever be. I'm thinking that we should follow *his* leadership instead of Michael's." There was some muttering among the members, but one woman's voice stood out over the crowd, hushing the rest into silence. She sounded like an angry teenager. There was nothing soft and timid about her voice. This woman projected with drive rather than with the subtlety and refinement of someone like my mom and Phoenix who had mastered the art of finesse and sophistication.

"You're right. So far, Steven has never lost. His deeds prove that he is far more ruthless and deadly than any other vampire, including Nicholas. In fact, this is one of the reasons why Nicholas fears him. But you are wrong about Michael." The feminine voice grew stern and deadly.

"Am I now? Is this the same fearless leader that is

harboring a half-breed against Nicholas's rule? Surely you have all felt and seen the struggle of power and authority between Michael and Lord Steven. Is that not proof enough to show the lack of might in your heroic ruler?"

"Nicholas's rule?" The female voice was shocked and in disbelief. "Nicholas has no claim on the vampire world. He may have you believing that he is our so-called king, but I assure you, you are both wrong. You have to make a decision here and now."

"And what decision is that? A decision that will have me following a woman's wishes?" There was some rustling before I heard the familiar sound of metal scraping metal. I knew the sound like the back of my hand. Phoenix had just drawn her swords.

"You will defend yourself. If you have the audacity to support Nicholas in such company, then you must have the courage to defend your words." Unlike the last speaker, Phoenix was clearly not in the mood for games, her words forceful and stern.

Michael looked at my father and nodded. Steven squared his shoulders and strode into the dining room with my mother at his side, then stepped aside for Michael and me to pass with a low bow of confidence.

"My lord," the deep baritone greeted Michael with false loyalty. "If you please, I'm afraid that your friend here is ill of mind."

"No, I don't think she is," Michael said. "See, Phoenix here is more than a friend. She is a member of the Insidiatori. I doubt that one of their ranks would have fallen to lunacy." Michael looked at the traitor with fury.

"But my lord, her actions have no merit." The coward was backing away from Phoenix.

"I'm afraid that conspiring with Nicholas is punishable

by death." Michael nodded to Phoenix. "If you want a chance to live, you will defend yourself." He took my arm and led me to our seats.

"You will give a woman permission to do your bidding?"

At that, Michael stopped dead in his tracks.

"You told us that the girl has not changed our plans," the traitor went on. "But it is the mere presence of the child that has started this war." His words were cut short when my mom left my dad's side and appeared next to Alain.

"You may have this coven fooled that you are here as a member of Michael's coven, but it is because you were cast out of Nicholas's coven that you found yourself here. Nicholas has placed a price on your head, did he not?" My mom's voice turned wicked. "I would consider whose company you keep, because you have now found a new enemy." With that, my mom slapped his face with a loud smack that echoed throughout the large room. "That was for my daughter, and this"—she gestured to Phoenix—"is for betraying what little trust we had for you."

Phoenix glanced at Michael for permission before she swung her swords with whistling speed. Michael put his arms around me, pressing me to his chest so that my eyes and ears were covered, but the lifeless thump that resounded off the floor still told me that our chef was out of commission.

"Is there anyone else in this room, or in this coven, who wishes to declare their favoritism for Nicholas?" My dad's voice was commanding and arresting. The room quieted and stilled.

"Are you claiming leadership?" a young, stout man asked. His voice was hesitant and faltering, but he stood tall and strong.

"I am here at the request of Michael. I have no want or right to lead. Michael has my life and my loyalty." Every member turned to look at Michael. Lowering their heads, they all bowed before him and held a pledging hand over their hearts.

"I hand-picked and formed this coven's high council so that we could fight against tyranny and the domination of one ruler. I hold loyalty and authority over this coven as a leader, but I am not a dictator. I will stand up and fight against any and all members that are willing to test my devotion to keep you and your covens from becoming subject to Nicholas's oppression." Not a soul moved or blinked as everyone stared at Michael with admiration and respect.

"You have my coven's and my loyalty. I pledge our lives to you and your ruling, my lord." A dark haired woman said as she knelt and offered her troth.

"And mine," a man said, also kneeling and offering Michael his life and loyalty. As all the members knelt, one by one, a sense of honor and trust filled the room.

"And mine," my dad said, as he and my mom knelt and bowed their heads in allegiance.

The only ones left standing in the room were Michael and me. Looking out at the faithful coven, I could see how much Michael and his leadership meant to them. Even as my dad tested Michael's power and authority, he still submitted and showed Michael that he saw him as the rightful ruler.

The seconds dragged by like minutes or hours. The weight of responsibility fell over me as I realized that I had not knelt. Sneaking a glance at Michael, I saw the pride, respect, and admiration he had for his members. He looked tall and powerful as his eyes scanned the room. There were over one hundred members of the high council filling each and every inch of this room, and not a one had stood against him.

When Michael's eyes made their way to me, I offered him a light, genuine smile, and bent my knees to kneel. With a steel-like grip, Michael held me straight and pulled me up close to him.

"My mate does not bow in my presence," he whispered in my ear. As he kissed my cheek, I felt his lips turn into a smile. I blushed, surely turning bright red, and felt my own, embarrassingly big smile spread over my face.

"Thank you." Michael gestured for them all to stand. "It is because of such loyalties that I am honored to be your leader." The members all stood, and then waited for Michael and me to sit in the only two chairs at the head of the table before seating themselves. "To start this meeting, I would like to introduce two new members to our coven, Steven and Ava Stone." My parents stood and bowed.

They took their seats next to me, and a hush fell over the room the members exchanged looks of not only confusion, but of shock and disbelief as well. I could feel the fear that tightened every member's heart, and with each mistrustful emotion I felt, the individual's feelings and thoughts got stronger. An assault of visions invaded my mind, different versions of how my dad was perceived. Some saw his heartlessness as he slaughtered people, and others saw his ruthlessness as he tormented and hurt anyone in his path. The images came at me fast and hard like flashbacks from a war zone. I wasn't sure if the scenes of all their experiences were mixed into one, or if they all looked and felt the same.

The visions eventually faded, but I now saw my dad in a new light. I knew what everyone saw, what they remembered, but I also knew that those actions of his had been guided by Nicholas. As much as I saw that the coven members feared my dad for what he had done, I also saw my dad's actions through his own eyes. Paying him back for every order he didn't follow, Nicholas would torture and subject my dad's brethren, his coven, to agony and suffering. Coming back as the second wave of visions and emotions dulled, I scanned the room, everyone's emotions laid bare. I saw the sternest of women and the steeliest of men cower on the inside. I saw and felt the actual weight that followed in my dad's wake.

Slowly, each coven member's eyes turned to me. Michael gave my hand a gentle squeeze. That warmth and caring assurance brought me from my thoughts and truly back to the meeting. Yet I couldn't shake the feeling that something was wrong with me. Light gasps echoed and hushed whispers spread throughout the room. I could hear the faintest sound of wood creaking and splintering under pressure. Looking at my own hands, I saw that my grip on the table was crushing the surface. Heat arose from my core and that familiar, irresistible feel of my strength came to the surface.

"Arri…" A tentative voice caressed my senses. I followed the sound to Michael and his uncertain gaze, which softened my anger. I dropped my shoulders and calmed my rising temper. Biting my lip, I looked at the floor.

"I know that there is much to discuss," Michael addressed the coven, his eyes still locked on me, "but I would like to give our two new guests time to settle in and adjust. Because of the late hour, may I suggest we reconvene in the morning?" Despite Michael's excuse, there was no question why we were adjourning as the members stood and wandered off in small groups.

My mom offered me a smile. "I think your father and I will dine in town tonight. I hear a new steakhouse opened. I think a reversal in mortalities would be nice for a change." I know that Mom thought she was fooling everyone with her high spirits and unfaltering smile, but she knew the lingering members were waiting to speak to Michael alone. "Would you care to join us, sweetheart?"

I looked at Michael. "No, I'm good. I think I'll just turn

in for the night. Can I take a rain check? Tomorrow maybe?" A small and ever so slight hint of disappointment flitted over my mom's face. Then she grabbed my dad by the elbow and gently tugged him out of the room.

As the door clicked closed, the vultures took no time to descend on Michael. But with the raise of his hand, the crowd stilled.

"I think you had the whole room nervous there for a moment," he muttered to me in a low voice.

"Sorry, it's just…this shocking reality just blindsided me," I whispered back. "I'll be fine though."

"You really should give your parents a break, you know. All they ever wanted was to keep you safe. No one could have predicted what and when things would have happened."

"I know," I admitted. "I'm not that upset with them anymore, but I haven't forgotten what they are capable of. As long as they're honest with me, and let me be me, without directing and pushing me into what they want me to be, we'll be fine."

"All right, then. Sweet dreams, my love. I'll be up later."

After a kiss goodnight, I headed to the door. But before I left, I watched as Michael took command of the onslaught of comments on allowing my parents to join the coven, and couldn't help but be impressed at the natural way he took command. He interlaced his fingers on the table as he waited. Then, almost in unison, the members all started talking at once. All their voices blended into total cacophony until Michael raised a steady hand.

"Please, one at a time."

With that, I closed the door and headed up to bed for some much-needed rest.

NINETEEN

A s Nicholas's icy hand closed around my neck, my heart stopped. His frigid grip held me against the wall as his evil, sinister look promised pain and torture. His vile and wicked laugh tore through my strength, but I held my head up high and didn't budge. I stared him down with a might and courage I didn't fully feel. He pulled me away from the wall and held me in midair, drawing a sword that he lightly traced along my neck. The cold blade scratched my skin, but he didn't draw blood. He merely moved the blade from my neck, and gave me a smile that said he was testing my bravery. Then, he lowered me to the floor, turned me around, and pressed the tip of his sword against my back, pushing me forward with the blade tip. The dimly lit cavern showed no signs of life. I took a few steps until my toes met an edge and I came to an abrupt halt, even as the sword bit into my skin.

"It would be a lot easier if you were to just surrender." Nicholas's voice was blunt and cold. "Let's face it; you have no chance against me. My strength is far superior to yours."

"If that is so, then why have you exhausted so many resources to obtain me?"

"So naïve. You think you have it all figured out? Well, before you get too impressed with yourself, just think of all the innocent people that you have sentenced to death."

"What innocent people? Every one of the men you sent? Their deaths were on your hands, not mine."

Jamie Ripp

"Who said anything about my men? I was talking about the humans I killed to determine your whereabouts."

I was shocked. I didn't remember there being any reports of unnatural deaths.

"Puzzled, are we? You honestly didn't think that Maggie was the only one, did you?"

Instantly, I was thrown back to the night I was told that Maggie had died. Unwilling tears flooded my eyes as I tried to gather as much courage as I could. I would not let the words of one man bring me to my knees.

It was then that lights illuminated the darkened cavern. My heart stopped. My breath seized. My bones froze. The chill that filled my heart at the sight before me ran through my veins like a freight train, and the slick, black marble cavern we occupied grew cold and damp. Clenching my jaw, and fisting my hands, I tried to hold my temper. I took deep, shaky breaths and closed my eyes. The sight of a half dozen men and women I barely knew littering the floor surged before me. The image of their lifeless bodies would be permanently engraved in my mind. Opening my eyes, I saw that Nicholas had moved in front of me, studying me.

"You are hiding something, child." His mocking voice carried a hint of curiosity and wonder. *"There is something within you I cannot see."* He looked thoughtful before his features hardened.

"You always knew where I was," I said. "Now the question remains—why are you hiding in the shadows instead of coming after me yourself? Are you afraid that a simple half-breed child could beat you?" I could feel the fire within me growing. Soon, he would see and feel my strength if I couldn't keep it together. Holding onto the last bit of self-control I had, I steadied my emotions.

He picked me up by the neck and pressed his sword to my chest, the pressure of his grip increasing by the second. With every

181

breath I took, he pushed harder, until it felt like I could hold back my cries of pain no longer.

"You are pathetic," he whispered in my ear. "And to think, when I heard the scrolls that foretold my undoing, I had actually expected to fight someone worth the effort." His voice pricked the back of my neck. "Your weak and uncontrollable nature could never surpass me." Then, with one quick move, he shoved the sword through my chest and into my heart. As I begged and pleaded for the pain to stop, Nicholas's coldhearted laugh echoed and the lights went out.

The pain stopped and the laughter faded into silence.

When I woke, the breath that had been lost to Nicholas's heartless torture rushed back my lungs. I shuddered when the cool castle air feathered around my skin. My eyes burned in anger and pain. My hands clenched at my sides as my nails bit into my skin. My heart pounded as fury and agony over the deaths that I caused hit my soul.

"Hey. Nightmares?" Michael's concerned voice matched the look on his face.

"Yeah," I said, taking a deep breath and looking around the room. For a split second, I was confused by my surroundings. The windows were on the wrong side of the room, the bathroom door was in the wrong place, and the bed…and then it hit me. I was in Michael's room.

"It was just another Nicholas nightmare. That's all." The statement couldn't be further from the truth. Every dream I had was like a new clue as to Nicholas's undoing, and I could see the things that were either hid from me, or unknown to those around me.

With doubt in his eyes, Michael sat up on his side of the bed and pulled me into his arms.

"I can hear the pounding of your heart, the speed your blood pumps through your veins. You are panicked." He spoke the truth. I *was* panicked.

"With every dream, my death becomes more painful," I explained. "I know he plans on killing me on an altar, with his coven watching, but he still isn't sure he can capture me. His heart is still unsure, and his confidence fades the more I escape his attempts to capture me. His followers are growing restless. But in my dreams, his façade is fading, too. His voice is still cold, and his grip is still icy, but there is doubt behind his laugh."

I wiggled out of Michael's embrace and rubbed my face. "What if I can't do it? I've heard some of the coven members talking. I know they think I am destined to kill him, but...I don't know if I can."

Gently, Michael took my hands from my face and held them in his. I stared down at our intertwined fingers. "You will never have to fight Nicholas alone. You will always have me with you. Together, we are stronger."

I considered, and with a saddened heart, I gave him a tentative smile. "I know. It's just there is so much uncertainty. Who said it was my job, anyway?" Holding back a faint sob, I looked back down to our hands.

"Your father."

I snapped back up. "What?"

"Your father. He was the one that foretold Nicholas's death at the hands of a half-breed." Michael's voice was calm, and his expression was blank, but I could feel that he was prepared for a fight.

"You mean to say that my dad knew all along that I was supposed to kill Nicholas?" My raised voice was nothing compared to the slight vibration that carried throughout the room. The windows trembled and dust fell from the high beams as anger seeped into my system. Summoning the power within was no longer an issue. The trick was calming the roaring tide of emotions that fed into my strength.

Michael carefully reached out a steadying hand, and gripped my shoulder.

"Arri, look at me." His words were soft. As I met his emerald-green eyes, a smile spread across my face.

"Sorry, I just can't believe Dad knew. The whole time he played the boring dad and all the while he knew who and what I was?"

"There is a lot your dad knows that even I don't. The Old One entrusted him with all his wisdom. It has been said that the undoing of Nicholas would come from one with the same abilities he had."

"The Old One? I have heard of him before."

"You might have. With the prophecy so close, many will look to the scrolls for the answers." Michael led me back to the bed. "See, your father was one of the originals. He was from the same Viking clan that Nicholas destroyed. After he was turned, he sought revenge on the ones who killed his family, which turned him into a monster, feeding off the lives of others. The clan believed that eating the heart of mortals would take in their life force and that they would become immortal. The only flaw in this was that none of them was immortal, save one. The Old One was said to be a seer, and knew of Nicholas's coming and told Steven of his visions. And among those many vivid visions, he foretold of a mortal vampire. A person born of both worlds." Michael's gaze held doubt and concern.

With a deep breath, I closed my eyes. For all my dreams of an adventurous life, I never dreamed of anything like this. I looked at the man before me. He knew of my daunting future, and he knew the chances of my untimely death, and yet, he was still here, loving me. I had long since come to terms with the fact that I was not normal since the moment I found out Michael was a vampire, but with each passing day, my world got darker and more like the Twilight Zone.

"Look, there is plenty of time to go over the scrolls and the future, but for now, may I offer you a boring day of shopping and food in town? I promise, there is no agenda." Sensing my heavy heart, Michael gathered me in his arms and carried me to the bathroom, where he deposited me on a bench before turning on the shower and opening a drawer full of my clothes.

"I take it you want me to get ready?" I joked, blowing a few unruly strands of hair out of my face.

"I'll be waiting for you in the dining room." He kissed me on the forehead and closed the bathroom door behind him.

With the excitement of a visit to town, and the thrill of a meal that didn't include a hundred or so glasses of thick red wine, I was dressed and ready before I knew it.

Looking in the mirror, I paused before I applied the small amount of makeup I normally wore. The reflection that stared back at me didn't look like my own. My rounder face had slimmed, and my complexion had softened and perfected. Were it not for my hair, I would have almost thought I was looking at a younger version of my mom.

The changes in me over the last several months as I'd lived among the vampires had been subtle, but now that I knew what I was, I could see the changes for what they were. Slowly, I had been tapping into my vampire side. As I traced the lines of my cheeks, the shining, glittering mark on my wrist caught my attention. The mark was a reminder of a curse and a blessing. Shaking my head, I pulled the sleeve of my light sweater down to cover the scrolled design. Taking one last look of myself in the mirror, I smiled again, knowing we were leaving the castle.

Several of Michael's coven members lowered their heads as I passed them in the hallway. Some waved or bowed, but the majority smiled and wished me a good morning. As I entered the foyer, I overheard thirty or so members talking among themselves. The topic was a common one these days: the loyalties of my dad. Their hearts didn't trust him. Looking in my direction, a man with a hearty voice and kind eyes smiled and held out a hand to me.

"Miss Arri, if you will."

Taking his out stretched hand, I followed him back to the group.

"So, what have you, where does your heart lie?" The man's voice was light but sincere.

"I'm afraid I don't understand." I shook my head, and a smile spread across his face.

"Your father. You know him better than any. Where does his loyalty truly lie?" As the faces looked to me for a respond, I thought of my dad. Even with all the lies he'd told, he'd done nothing but protect me. The answer was simple.

"I believe he is loyal to Michael. His ties with Nicholas have long been broken. I believe when he hid me, he made an enemy of Nicholas." I felt that was enough. In most cases, I tried to stay out of their conversations. In what world would I have anything to say that they have not already heard or considered?

A man beside me patted me firmly on the shoulder. "Your words are wise. I believe you have brought us to a consensus." With that, the group nodded in agreement. What the agreement was, I wasn't sure, but hopefully I had come to my dad's aid, instead of his downfall.

TWENTY

A fter leaving the crowd, I entered the dining room. The remains of the coven's breakfast were scattered in glasses on the table.

Nana and Michael were in deep conversation at one end of the table. The concern marring Michael's brow was apparent, and the sadness that suffused Nana's sickly face broke my heart. Phoenix was talking to my parents and Catherine at the opposite end. They smiled, and even laughed a time or two. Then, the conversation lightened. Catherine's and my parents' disbelieving looks made me chuckle. As Phoenix's story became more elaborate, her hands gestured wildly and her animated expressions almost had me rolling. I noticed several dawdlers by the doors, but only a scant few, and they bowed their heads immediately at my presence, then backed out of the room and closed the door behind them. It was odd, really. For the last several days, the coven members had seemed to be a little more respectful than usual. Not that they weren't normally, but this was different. I wondered if it was because of my parents' presence, or because they could sense the same dormant power I sensed in myself. Either way, it was almost as if they revered me.

As I waited until Nana and Michael were done, Phoenix spotted me.

"Arri!" She waved her hand in the air, as though I

couldn't see her through the nonexistent crowd.

"Hey guys," I said as I approached them. Michael's eyes darted toward me as I took a seat and a light smile touched his lips.

"Wow, you are up early!" Catherine said brightly.

"Oh, really? What time is it?" I looked around the room for a clock, and as I did, the window caught my attention. The drapes were pulled back, and a beautiful view of the pre-dawn sky stared back at me. The sun was still below the mountains and the world was cast in purples and blues.

"So, are you up for another sparring round?" Phoenix sounded excited at the chance. "There is no way I'd ever let you beat me again." She wiggled in her seat. But I must have looked shocked, because her voice turned to a whine. "Oh come on, It'll be good practice."

My mom and Catherine practically choked on their drinks.

"You lost?" They said in unison.

"My losing was a temporary lapse in concentration. It won't happen again." Phoenix defended herself with a tone that was both bitter and resentful.

"And what caused the great and powerful Phoenix to lose her concentration?" My mom said jokingly.

"Well, if you must know..." Phoenix sat up tall, squared her shoulders, and raised her chin. "You." She gave a pointed look at my dad.

"Fair enough. I was rather harsh," Dad admitted.

"So, how *do* you feel about round two, Arri?" Her whimsical voice rang with eagerness. It took me a moment to answer. Wait—she said she was distracted by my dad, and that caused her to lose. It just dawned on me that I may not have actually beat Phoenix in the last scrimmage. Looking back and forth between Phoenix, Catherine, and my parents,

I felt the twinge of expectation. What if she beat me again as she had the first time? I would hate to disappoint. As I looked at Michael, he met my gaze, and a simple nod told me to try. Feeling Michael's faith and confidence in me, I accepted her invitation.

"Yay!" she squealed. Jumping up from her chair, she skipped to the door, then paused and turned back. "Aren't you coming?" she asked, looking confused.

"Yeah, but I need to eat first."

Cocking her head, Phoenix frowned. Then, as if just remembering that I was part human, she laughed.

"Oops, okay. You eat and I'll set up." She squealed again, then left the room.

"What are you hungry for, dear?" Mom asked, getting up from the table.

"It's okay, Mom. I'll have the new cook make me something."

My mom gave me a sad smile, but took her seat. I glanced back at Michael, who touched a button on the table, summoning the new cook out of what seemed like thin air. Michael nodded toward me, and then went back to talking with Nana.

"May I take your order, Miss?" the new cook asked. Her features were flawless—as was the case for all vampires—yet she was not as breathtaking as most. She looked worn and tired. Her hair was falling out of its perfect bun, and her eyes had a faint sadness to them.

"Yes, just some French toast, and a glass of chocolate milk, please."

She nodded and looked to my parents and Catherine.

"No, nothing, thank you," Mom answered for everyone. As the woman turned and left, my mom sighed.

"I don't think she'll make it." A shadow of doubt crossed my mom's features.

"Oh, really? Why would you say that?" It seemed rather odd to conclude that the new cook wouldn't last, since she'd barely been here a day.

"Did you see her? It is obvious she is struggling. Maybe there is another place in Michael's coven that would better suit her. I'll talk to her and see if there is anything she would rather be doing."

Mom was a sucker when it came time to place something or someone where they should be. It was one of her best attributes.

"Right, well, now that my breakfast is being made, tell me—what have you three been up to while you were away?"

My mom let out a sigh of relief and settled down into her chair, clearly realizing I didn't ask her to cook so we could talk.

We talked for a few minutes until my meal came, and as I ate, my parents told me a small bit of their adventures in Egypt. I wasn't surprised to find out that their trip was a planned ambush, but I was heartened to find that it blew up in Nicholas's face. They were sent there so that they would have no choice but to take me along. Nicholas was betting on the fact that his men had just made an attempt on my life and that my parents would never have left me behind. When they found out I was alone, he sent another assassin.

Moreover, I learned that Nicholas's men had been steadily making their way into Egypt and most of the remaining countries that had not completely sworn their loyalty to Michael. The covens that were there were either afraid to talk or dead. Nicholas had been working his way through the world, placing his men at the head of the covens, making it seem like he was the ultimate force and therefore unbeatable. Bullying his way to the top, in other words.

As my mom told me their story, my dad's emotions

waved and roared. He was hiding something. Whatever it was, he was proud of it. A small but unmistakable smirk curved his lips. With his telling look, and his confident and omniscient smile, Dad was up to something. He was aware I knew there was something up, but what?

"So how did you eventually get out?" I asked, still following my mom's story.

"Well, as always, we flew."

"You flew? I thought you were trapped there?"

"What did you expect us to do? Run?"

I cocked my head and *tsk*ed light-heartedly at her sarcastic remark.

"We flew," she said again. "One of the dignitaries heard that there was a plan to capture our daughter and created a distraction for us. Catherine had it a little easier. There was only one of her, and she is not dangerous." Mom gave Dad a *sorry, but it's true* look. "Nonetheless, the distraction worked." Mom's cat-ate-the-canary look made me laugh, but there was still that word. *Dangerous.* I must have been frowning, because Dad and Mom were staring at me.

"Go ahead, hun," Dad encouraged, seemingly knowing what I was going to ask.

"You know, it's been a day or two since you've arrived, but after Michael announced your attendance in the coven, a few of the members asked me if you could be trusted." I paused for a moment as my mom and dad exchanged an uneasy look. "I said yes."

Another sigh of relief came from my mom, but my dad was waiting for the other shoe to drop. I kept going. "I figured the day you hid me from Nicholas, you made yourself an enemy. Please tell me I didn't lie to the coven?" I waited for the brush off, but to my surprise, it never came.

"There is much that fell into place the moment you were

born, but you didn't lie. Your mother and I are in fact members of Michael's coven, and we have vowed our lives to protect it." Still, I knew there was something he wasn't telling me, something that felt so important that his answer seemed almost hollow.

"And?" I pressed.

There was a long pause as my dad seemed to assessed the many different ways to tell me.

"I have been planning for your arrival since The Old One died. Things, men, and plans have been in place for hundreds and hundreds of years. I just didn't plan on the new power being my daughter. I expected to have to seek you out, not have you born to me." My dad bowed his head.

"I knew exactly who and what Nicholas was the moment he wandered into our camp. I knew because I had created him. Nicholas was not the first to rise from near death. His creation was planned and calculated, and although I knew of the many ways he would advance the vampire world, I had underestimated the vengeance, hate, and fury that inflamed his heart. The moment I saw his hatred, I should have stopped him, but Bork knew Nicholas was coming. By this time, Nicholas had already started to win the loyalty of the clan. If I had known then that the new power was to be my daughter, I would have sacrificed our growth, but as fate has had it, you are the new power that is destined to bring the vampire world into balance."

"My fate isn't your fault," I told him. "I have a feeling that I would have been chosen regardless of your plans or circumstances."

"Still, it is my mistake."

The doors slammed open.

"Are you coming, or are you going to waste more time?" Phoenix looked testy but still in good spirits. Then, as if realizing how loudly she'd interrupted, she backpedaled. "Oh, I'm sorry, Monsieur Steven. I wasn't aware," she stammered. In reality, I was a little bummed she interrupted. I was hoping to hear more.

Phoenix bowed her head, obviously frightened that she'd offended my dad, and waited to be excused.

"It is all right, Phoenix. We were just trading stories. Please continue." His booming voice was intimidating.

"Actually," Michael interrupted, getting up and making his way to the four of us, patting Nana on the shoulder as she passed us. "I would like to have a word with Arri and her parents alone, if you wouldn't mind." He glanced between Phoenix, and Catherine.

"Oh, yes, of course." Catherine got up from the table, and she and Phoenix left the room together.

Michael led me by the hand to the other side of the table so that he and I could face my parents.

"They need to know," Michael said as his thumb rubbed the scroll design beneath my sweater.

Part of me knew he was right, but the other part had no problem hiding the mark under sweaters and long-sleeved shirts for the rest of my life.

"Steven, Ava..." Michael started.

The room was so quiet it seemed the echo the sound of my breathing as the four of us exchanged glances. My dad interlaced his fingers on the table, and Michael tightened his hand around mine, and then rested it on the table where both he and my parents could see it.

"Well?" My dad asked, clearly trying to be patient.

As I cast around for a way to broach the situation, Michael finally broke the awkward silence.

"A few days ago, Arri had a bout with one of Nicholas's men named Gavin. During their struggle, Arri was stabbed, and—"

"Yes, we know," my mother interrupted. "We have heard the stories of what had happened."

"Yes," Michael continued as he looked down at our intertwined hands, "but what you didn't hear was that I walked in when Arri's heart was weak and barely beating. Her hands were cold, and she had lost a lot of blood. In that moment, I did the only thing I knew to do." He sharpened his gaze at my parents. "I love your daughter with all my heart. I had intended to ask her permission first, but because of the circumstances, I offered Arri my blood, hoping it would save her life."

My parents looked momentarily confused.

"Your blood?" My dad asked.

"Yes."

"And does she bear the mark?" My dad's voice was laced with anger.

"Yes."

"How long have you two been hiding this from us?"

"I didn't see it until yesterday when I met with you and Michael in the library," I spoke up.

"So that's why you asked to speak with him alone." My mom said. She must have remembered how adamant Phoenix had been about seeing Michael.

I nodded and looked away.

"Are you okay with this, Arri honey?" My mom asked keeping the conversation going as my dad and Michael remained quiet.

My dad's inner battle was clearly fierce. He now knew that the blood had saved my life, but he also realized that Michael had bound me to him without my permission.

"Yes," I said without hesitation.

"Do you bear the mark?" my dad asked Michael with a glare.

"No."

My dad pounded the table with his fist and I jumped at the sound. I knew he was angry, but I didn't know why. I hadn't betrayed him. I hadn't done anything wrong, and neither had Michael.

"Wait, she's human. They can't bond with us," my dad said as if he had just realized a loophole. "How?"

"Well, I'm still part vampire, and that side of me is only getting stronger."

"Yes, but you were at death's door. You didn't know what you were doing. The exchange has to be mutual; you have to accept it wholeheartedly."

"And I did," I said evenly. "In my final moments, I thought I felt Michael, and in that time, I had accepted him completely, hoping to hold onto his memory as long as I could. Apparently, it was enough to initiate the bond."

"Will you show the mark?" My dad folded his arms in front of him.

"Sure." There was nothing he could do about it now that it was done.

As Michael pulled my sleeve up, my parents gasped.

"The Divination," my dad said in a hushed and reverend tone. "I was positive that you were the prodigy, the chosen one foretold by The Old One, but this..." He lightly touched the marking as though it were a sacred relic. "This proves it."

"Proves what?" I asked, furrowing my brow.

"It proves that you are the chosen one. The prophecy foretells of a child born of two worlds, bearing the mark of the divination, or the prophesized pure blood. There is only one other one that bore this mark as well. Bork, the Old One." My dad looked back and forth between the two of us.

"But I am half-human. I'm not a pureblood." I shook my head.

"It doesn't mean pureblood, per se; it means that you are destined to purify our blood from evil, as foretold by the Old One."

"Oh, that's right. I'm supposed to kill Nicholas," I said with a snort of disbelief.

"You mock the prophecy?" my dad asked as he leaned forward.

"Yes, I know that you guys live by the rules and beliefs set forth by the Old One, but how does the Old One expect me to kill Nicholas? I'm just *me*. I'm not special by any means."

"But you are wrong," my dad said. "Those abilities you hold within you are not just any. You were destined to receive great abilities, abilities that even I do not possess."

"Does the prophecy foretell of a beginners manual to defeating vampire dictators?"

The room fell quiet, as though the three of them didn't know how to answer.

"Seriously, I don't know if I can do this," I said. "Last year I found out that vampires and werewolves existed, now I find out that I am only half-human and destined to defeat a vampire who has reigned in terror throughout the vampire world, and you guys *still* think that I'm qualified to do it? I'm not ready to fight a vampire, especially one as terrifying as Nicholas." I stood up, shaking my head, and smiled down at everyone.

"I'm glad you believe in me, but I don't. I'm sorry."

It was too much to place on my shoulders. It was the weight of the world.

"If you'll excuse me, I'd better go meet Phoenix. I did promise." With one last glance at my dad, I headed to the door.

As I left the dining room, I could just make out my dad and Michael talking, but I'd heard enough.

Blindly, I walked through the house and ended up in the

courtyard. A slight blur of motion whipped past me as Phoenix disappeared and reappeared in front of me about ten feet away.

She brought her hands from behind her back, and in her delicate grasp she held two antique-looking swords. My breath froze and my heart stopped. She twirled the swords around her, making it look so easy. Playing with them was clearly second nature to her. I felt my intimidation mount as she tossed and turned the swords around with ease. With a snap of her wrist, she flipped one of the swords into the air. It flew with perfect accuracy and landed between my feet, pegged deep into the soil and swaying slightly.

"Well, don't just stare at it! It won't bite. Or at least the handle won't."

"I thought we were just playing? Where are the wooden swords?" I said, pulling the sword out of the ground with all my strength. It was heavier than it looked. The handle was slick and had hardly any grip left. The weapon had obviously been used at least a time or two.

Phoenix continued to talk as if I had said nothing. "Obviously the idea here is to show the strike, not to actually follow through with the impact, okay?" There was something deadly and intimidating about the way she walked as she came to my side, determination and purpose in every step, confidence radiating off her in waves.

"No, no, no, no. I had agreed to *practice* with you, not to challenge you to an actual sword fight. You don't actually expect me to really fight you, do you?"

Ignoring my complaints, she walked behind me, and put her arms around me. Placing her hands on the sword with mine, she helped me pick up the sword, showing me the right way to hold it.

"See? Now, isn't that better?" Phoenix asked, then

released me and walked back to her previous position. "The sword is like an extension of your arm. It takes more energy to swing and miss than to swing and hit. And, if you miss, you give your opponent an opening to strike." As if that explained the sum total of techniques for sword fighting, she playfully swung her own sword around and readied herself.

"Are you serious?" I asked, only to be ignored again. Phoenix advanced slowly, then came at me with a steady swing—not a threatening one, but still. "You're crazy, you know that? I can't sword fight with you. These are real. You'll kill me!" I yelled, backing up and away from the clearly crazy person.

The blade of metal swung right for my head. I lifted my sword just enough to block the hit and dance out of the way, but stumbled in time for Phoenix to aim another swing at my feet. Jumping this time, my heart raced and my breath was shaky. I was scared out of my mind. This lunatic, deranged vampire thought I could actually fight back and was attacking me with a genuine vengeance. Still, I matched each advancing swing as I ducked, dodged, and danced out of the way. Staying alive was my only thought, and Phoenix was not making it easy.

"You are not supposed to run! You are supposed to defend yourself, then, hit me back." Phoenix said as she swung another set of hits toward me, which I managed to block and dodge in the same manner.

"Yeah, easier said than done. Except, you don't have a sharp medal blade flying at your head. I already told you, this is ridiculous." The image of my still body lying on the ground dead kept popping up in my head, so I was having a hard time focusing on the never-ending swings coming at me. The blade stirred the air, and with every swing there was whistle, a whoosh, or a whir as it passed my ear.

"You have at *least* mastered the art of dancing and dodging," she taunted me. Now, granted, this was mere child's play for Phoenix, she was in fact, a vampire with superhuman strength. Still, she made it seem like she was playing with straws rather than the deadly weapons she wielded. Our swing-dodge-banter routine went on for almost a half an hour, and we were starting to gather a small crowd. My parents and Catherine were front and center before the crowd filled in. Initially, the other coven members were just waiting to see who would prevail, sitting on the grass with their wine like I would watch a baseball game with a bag of popcorn. But gradually, the energy from the growing crowd intensified. Finally, there was a set of swings where I think I actually hit metal, but it was hard to tell; I was so panicked that we were using real swords. The wooden play swords were much less daunting.

Suddenly, Phoenix stopped, and fear lit up her eyes. The murmuring crowd fell silent and the energy turned anxious and almost instinctive. The spectators were standing up; their faces matched hers. Some of them took a few steps forward but were quickly halted by a simple raise of Phoenix's hand. Even my mom and dad stopped in their tracks, but the look that marred my dad's face promised retribution. Confused by his reaction, I walked toward Phoenix.

"Arri, I am so sorry. It was only an accident," she said. I could feel the crowd's instincts surfacing like a slow growing fire, and their reverence turned into shock and hope.

Phoenix yelled for Michael, and then pried her eyes off mine and down to my arm.

As I followed to where she was looking scared and shocked, I noticed a small droplet of blood finding its way down my arm. Within seconds Michael entered the courtyard. When he saw the wound and real swords in our hands, he was angry and enraged then started wrapping my wound.

Phoenix drew blood. Realization rushed into my mind. My arm burned, and the cut stung, but it was the fact that my beautifully scored crimson mark was now in full view for all to see that pained me the most. The fear that had been lodged in my heart, the fear that normally followed my panic, was now melting into anger and rage. I knew Phoenix hadn't meant to actually nick me, and the injury alone would have almost been fine. But to show something I wished to hide bit into my heart. When Michael was done dressing my cut, he glared at Phoenix.

"I will deal with you in my office. *Now.*"

With that, Phoenix lowered her blade and bowed.

"Let's get you into the house." Michael had also seen the exposed mark and I could feel his pride and concern for me.

"No, I want to finish this." I grabbed Phoenix by the arm as she passed us. Looking at my arm, I smiled. "It was getting too hot for a sweater anyway."

Michael's stern and unforgiving look in Phoenix's direction was more of a warning.

"Besides, I have a score to settle," I said, smiling.

Michael looked and cocked his head to the side as he considered letting me fight. After giving me a full-fledged kiss that stamped me as his in front of the entire coven, Michael retreated to the sidelines to watch the fight.

Giving Phoenix a wry smile, I shed the sweater and readied myself.

The coven gasped and low murmuring rumbled throughout the crowd. Of all emotion among them, my dad's internal battle was the strongest. On the one hand, his fury and rage at the idea of what has happened, and the fact that Michael didn't bear the same mark, only made him angrier. On the other hand, he saw that his scrolls were right. The red scoring showed proof. I was what he already knew I was, the one he foretold would bring Nicholas's reign to an end. But first, I needed to focus.

Phoenix had drawn blood, intentionally or not, and I wasn't about to let her get away with it. My heart raced and the rush of adrenaline spread to every corner of my body.

"Are we playing for blood?" I asked with a smirk.

"Are you sure you're ready?" There was some concern in her voice, but she didn't miss the chance to raise her sword and ready herself for an attack.

"Yep. You ready to see what I'm really made of?" I wasn't hiding the challenge, and she didn't miss the invitation in my voice. The other vampires remained back and sat in the grass. It was like we were the showstopping number in a Broadway musical, center stage and all eyes on us.

She posed, waiting to spar. Her expression was playful, but her excitement was menacing. With a leap forward, she made the first strike. This time, her moves were more strategic and artful, as though in slow motion, creeping below her general super speed. I easily blocked her thrust, but as soon as I did, she came at me with another, then another. She never swung and missed, but I met her blow for blow, metal on metal, sparks flickering.

Fear, tension, and apprehension filled the air as the crowd stirred with excitement. The wine was no longer in their hands. They were squirming as they encouraged and cheered on their favorite: Phoenix—who in my opinion was the better bet—or me. For the coven, this was like a sport.

Shockingly, I was able to see it all and still manage to concentrate on the fight. Everything was clear and detailed, the looks in the crowd were expectant and engaged, and just as surprised that I was doing so well against the coveted Phoenix as I was.

Feral instincts flared through my body; my power

warmed me from the inside. I narrowed my gaze, and I was out for blood. I was superwoman: stronger, faster, and almost completely inhuman. The swings kept on coming, but I was picking up speed, and oddly enough, the fight became fun. Phoenix made a thrust at my legs and without warning or planning, I jumped backward in a full flip—upside down, then right-side up—and landed in a battle-ready squat, sword in hand. Realization stunned me only a moment: I had just managed a complete backflip and landed like a Jedi knight. Then Phoenix flew through the air, straight at me, and reality and reflexes kicked in. I was airborne again, eyes closed, sensing her very presence in the field. I swung midair, in the midst of an aerial over Phoenix and managed to catch her off guard. It was only for a second, but just enough to throw her off balance. The longer we fought, the more I felt like a host in my own body. Another force was at play, and I was just its puppet. The moves and the thrills of the fight ran deep. I felt alive and free, drawn out by an ancient momentum that felt unstoppable. A hint of aggression in my core was trying to release itself bit by bit, and with all my jumps and turns, I landed on my feet like a cat, poised for combat. My surprise at her actually hitting me gave way to close attention to her swordplay as I studied her form between the swings and blocks. I was learning fast. Her technique felt more and more familiar as I recalled a few from our last fight. Like the way she made more swings and favored her left sword over her right, or how she did backflips, trying to level the playing field or throwing off her opponent. She seemed erratic at first, but as I analyzed her method and skill, I could see it was art.

I could feel her excitement, the thrill of the game. As I concentrated on the vibrant emotions of the crowd around me, I fed into them and allowed them to power me. When she just about had me, the crowd would gasp and wince, but just as they thought I was done for, I was back on top. Even with Phoenix's enthusiasm, I could tell she was trying to take it semi-easy on me. She was better at this than I was, but I was not going make it easy for her to win. Foreign instincts kicked in I circled her, looking for an opening. Just as Phoenix and I were about to go another round, Michael stepped between us, hand raised to signal the end of the fight.

"Tie?" I panted.

"Tie." Phoenix was exhilarated. I could sense as her heart leaped; she was in wonderment. As we bowed to each other and placed our swords on the ground, the crowd quieted.

"Phoenix?" I asked. But she just looked past me with astonishment.

I turned to see what Phoenix was so focused on, but froze.

The coven had all fell to their knees. They'd pledged themselves to me. I looked back to Phoenix, but she too was kneeling, a hand over her heart.

"Do you still think you are not ready, that the prophecy made a mistake?" Michael asked as he gestured to the coven he had assembled under his roof. When they had bowed to me, they displayed their loyalty and the promise of liberty and freedom their prophecy said I would deliver.

Then, I remembered something Phoenix had said. *Vampires hold respect to be the utmost form of loyalty. To disrespect is to show that one places no value on your life.* Seeing everyone down on one knee was more than a pledge. Their display of respect was showing that they valued my life, that I was no longer merely half-human. I was a member of their coven. For me, that was the highest form of respect that they could have demonstrated.

It was overwhelming as I stared out over the coven, bowing to me. But as Michael had asked me…was I ready?

With a nod, I accepted their pledge, but I wasn't sure

what I was going to do after that. It was too late to back out now. When the mark was exposed, I made the intentional effort to claim and reveal the full symbol and what it meant for me to bare it to the entire coven, showing them I accepted my role as the ancient scrolls had predicted. I just hoped that I could live up to their expectations.

As each member got to their feet, they drew close to Phoenix and me.

"Well done, Arri. Well done," Phoenix said enthusiastically. "You proved an excellent adversary." She reached out her hand, which I took with a disbelieving smile.

"Is that after you tried to kill me, or because you were taking it easy on me?" I couldn't resist a little humor.

The approving crowed applauded and shouted out in excitement.

Phoenix cocked her head as she watched the crowd. "It looks like you have the approval of your audience."

I looked at the crowd gathered around us and knew the significance of this moment. What it meant for them to offer their acceptance, and how they celebrated me as the light of a new hope.

Michael was front and center, with a close and watchful eye on me. His pride for me beamed throughout him, and his smile was broad and wide.

"And who said I was taking it easy on you?" Phoenix said. "I treated you like every other fighting companion. I was just having fun. I never would have hit you intentionally, though, if that is what you mean by trying to kill you." I could tell she was asking for forgiveness, but her joking tone betrayed her concern.

With that, Phoenix took off her fingerless gloves, and then picked up my sword from the ground. I was exhausted. I stretched out my hands as I extended and flexed my fingers repetitively. My hands felt tight, and my arms felt weak. My legs were wobbly, but oddly enough, I was exhilarated.

"Well, to set the record straight." I playfully narrowed my eyes at her. "You did in fact nick me. If you want proof, there is a small gash in my arm." I gestured to the bandage. There was no longer any pain. In fact, I was sure I was already healed.

As my dad and mom parted their way through the thinning crowd and came to stand beside Phoenix, Michael, and me. My dad and Michael talked about me training with real swords, but both admitted they was genuinely impressed with my ability to defend myself, and that I handled it so well When Michael first came to the courtyard and saw me bleeding he was scared and angry, but as I started to fight back with the same ferocity and bite as Phoenix, Michael's concern faded fast and was replaced by amazement and awe.

My dad started to talk to Michael about the divination, but my mom and Phoenix caught my attention.

"So, when's the next fight?" My mom asked Phoenix as she wiggled in excitement.

"What next fight?" I turned my head toward Phoenix who grinned.

"Let's give her a few days to recover before we train again."

"Let's not. I'm good for a while." I playfully glared at the two women planning my immediate future. I was preoccupied when they mentioned the fight that I missed the rest of the conversation with Michael and my dad.

"Come on, let's get you cleaned up." Phoenix said pointing to my arm then started to escort me back to the manor.

My mom hung back and walked with my dad and Michael as they followed us and continued talking. Phoenix and I walked arm in arm as she told me about the training she did, and how when she first started to learn, she was the worst, but as she learned the craft, she also learned that confidence was half the battle. In me, she saw the same potential. She had hoped that if I could at least block a few hits, my confidence would soar, but as it turned out, my anger and my ability to let go proved to be my secret. It hadn't been until Phoenix nicked me that I finally allowed myself to really fight back. Somehow, the touch of the blade was my inner demon's invitation, and instead of tamping it down like I normally did, I allowed it to peek out its head and see what was going on. As we spoke, I absently rubbed my mark. It wasn't going anywhere, but for some reason, I felt oddly embarrassed about it.

"Do you want to tell me why you went quiet?" I asked.

"Yeah. I was just thinking…" She gave me a curious look, then looked at Michael as something he said caught her attention. With a raised brow, she looked back at me, then down to my arm as if something just dawned on her. "Curious that only you bear the mark. Why aren't you ready to be sealed as one of us?" As we walked through the front doors of the manor and into the foyer we lingered by the staircase as we talked.

"I thought I became one of you the moment Nicholas chose to pursue me?" It had been at that moment that Nicholas laid out my future. He made me into the heroine he feared would overthrow him.

"I meant *that*." Phoenix gestured toward my arm. "Michael doesn't bear it, meaning it isn't complete."

I looked at the mark, then back to Michael. A full smile spread across my face as I realized that although it meant one thing to the coven, for me it also meant that I had sealed myself to him. It was there because Michael willingly shared his blood. The bonding process was only half complete, but I would rather be bound to him for life than go through life without his claim on me.

"No, he doesn't, and to be honest, I think I have always been a member but to finish the process is not up to me. All it takes is one question. But he hasn't asked yet, and I won't push," I said, and Phoenix pulled me into a hug.

As Michael walked up behind me, Phoenix gave him a questioning look. We both laughed at his curious expression.

"So, how did I do?" I asked, before he had a chance to wonder what we were talking about.

Michael gave me a knowing look and then smiled.

"You did great." He drew me into a deep, passionate kiss, like no one was looking. "I will think twice before upsetting you again," he teased.

"I didn't know I had it in me. It was kind of fun, actually."

Michael chuckled as he walked me inside the house. "Are you ready?" he asked.

"For what?"

"For our bloodless, meeting-less dinner?" he asked, caressing my arm where I was branded.

"Mmhm." I smiled as tingles and waves of excitement wound their way through me, making my stomach do backflips like a butterfly dancing.

As my parents and Catherine finally made their way through the foyer, still filled with members talking about Phoenix's and my bout, Michael wrapped his arm around my waist and took me upstairs to get cleaned up and replace my shirt. Phoenix had managed to cut the sleeve off of this one.

TWENTY-ONE

A s I sat on the edge of the bed, buckling my boots, I thought back to what Phoenix said. *Are you ready to become one of us?* Of course, I *was* one of them. At least I thought I was…well, mostly. There was no way I could fix the fact that I was part human, not without killing my human side, which I didn't think was an option.

The thought kept repeating itself until I finally gave up. I looked down at the mark on my wrist and tried to convince myself that I was okay, that only I bore the mark and Michael didn't, but I couldn't do it. Wasn't it every girl's dream to be married? Didn't we start planning our weddings, or at least envisioning them, as children? Now I was bound to Michael, but Michael was not bound to me. The difference between marriage and being bound was subtle, but still distinct. Still, I held them with the same regard. Marriage may be for life, but the bond is for eternity.

As I tried to clear my mind, I was startled as someone placed a hand on my shoulder. I let out a slight squeal as every muscle in my body tightened. I looked up and saw the one man I would always love. As my heart slowed to its regular pace, Michael cocked his head.

"Sorry, I didn't hear you come in. You startled me," I said as he took a seat next to me.

"Is everything okay? You have been up here for a while."

Michael's voice may have been playful, but his expression showed concern.

"I'm good. I just don't have your superhuman speed quite yet." I smiled, then shook my head. "I'm kidding. I'm just cinching up my boots." I shrugged like everything was fine.

"So, what's on your mind?" Michael asked. It was obvious I wasn't fooling him, but this was something I had to keep to myself. The decision had to be his. I didn't want him to feel obligated.

"What makes you think something is wrong?" I asked, avoiding his eyes.

"The fact that I startled you is proof enough that your mind is elsewhere."

"Sorry, I just..." Michael still didn't look convinced.

"You're keeping something from me." He gave me a cockeyed grin as I faked a shocked look. "You buckled your boots wrong." He gestured to the buckle I was fighting with and chuckled. Moving my hands, he started to undo and redo the many straps. When he finished, he offered me his hand to help me up. As I smoothed out the wrinkles in my blouse, Michael narrowed his eyes. "Besides your trembling touch"—Michael covered both my hands with his and drew to his chest—"I can see it in your eyes. The natural way your eyes glimmer with wonder and curiosity has dimmed, and a shadow of uncertainty clouds them. They're also gray." A small smile creased his face. "Something is bothering you."

I mustered a passing laugh as I swallowed my uncertainty and tried to cover my worries.

"For now, I'm fine. Nothing a trip to town won't fix."

As he looked down at my attire, he froze, and a genuine smile replaced his pacifying look of understanding.

"No long sleeves?" With wide eyes and his eyes set on my arm, his shock was apparent.

"Nope."

"What changed?" There was a little bit of hope behind his words.

"There really isn't a point in hiding it now, not after everyone has already seen it." I shrugged, then looked down.

"Why did you hide it in the first place? Why did you think I'd leave?" Although he tried to conceal it, I could feel the pain he tried not to feel.

"It seemed right at the time," I said. "I didn't know what it was, and with my luck, it was a brand that said you needed to kill me. I was, and still am, a little scared. Humans don't bear such marks. Humans have tattoos, but they put them there on purpose, they just don't show up glowing and glittering like a beacon." My voice shook as my breath trembled. Michael took my arm and lightly traced his brand.

"Curious, though."

"What?"

"The fact that you bear this mark. One is usually..." Michael's voice faded.

"Usually what?" My heart tightened in fear.

"One is usually bound willingly." Michael looked up and met my eyes. My confused look must have shown through my panic. "Usually during the bonding ceremony, we must both be completely willing. We must want and trust wholeheartedly, without doubt, without falter, and without reluctance. When I shared my blood with you, you were unconscious. How could you have known?" I could feel that he was baffled, warring within himself, asking himself if this is what I truly wanted.

"But I did." Michael's eyes snapped to mine, and his heart gave a hopeful leap. "The moment I felt you, the moment I thought you were there, I gave myself to you. I trusted you even if you were to only be there with me while I died. With you, it's never been a matter of whether I did or didn't love you. My love for you has always been undying and unconditional. Whether I was conscious or not wouldn't have mattered. You already had my heart and my trust." As embarrassment seeped through my confession at the thought that he may not have felt the same, my heart tightened, and my breathing became shallow.

"You know, I am very proud of this mark"—a small smile curved his lips—"but I don't want you to be uncomfortable wearing it. There is no way to reverse the past, but you are not obligated to finish the bond." He bowed his head as a shadow of regret crossed his features. "I heard what Phoenix said. She asked if you were ready to be one of us. I'm afraid I didn't get to hear the answer, but whether you finish the bond or not, I consider you mine." He closed his eyes briefly, then looked back at me, attempting to erase the look of pain from his face once again.

"I said I thought I was, and I was only waiting to be asked." A single tear fell down my cheek. Michael shook his head and pulled me close, whispering in my ear.

"You never fail to underestimate your hold on me." I could feel him smiling against my cheek. "Bonded or not, I will always be yours and you mine." As he kissed me as if it were the last time he would ever kiss me, I knew I was his. When we ended the kiss, my knees were weak and a giddy smile had spread across my face. He took me by the hand and spun me around in front of him.

"Where did you get those clothes?"

"In my closet. I thought you put them there." I smiled, looking at myself in front of the floor-length mirror. I was not a vain person in general, but even I had to admit that the clothes brought out my sassy side. The outfit was a little outside of my comfort zone: tight-legged black pants and a classic red chemisette cinched with a black front-lacing leather corset. It looked a little bold and brazen, and a little racy for my normal attire, but I liked how it hugged my figure and added definition.

"Why? Do you not like them?" At the shocked look on his face, I panicked and started back to the closet. My confidence was shaken as I realized he didn't like my new look. Fortunately, there were some new clothes in my closet. I liked my old clothes all right, but they weren't mine. They were what Nana had dressed me in.

"No, they're fine." His voice was weak and gruff. "I like them." He grabbed me by the arm as his eyes darkened, like he was fighting a carnal instinct. His pupils dilated, and his hand clenched at his side. Taking a deep breath, he steadied himself. His knowing grin turned into one of instinct and need as his narrowed eyes focused on me.

"Should I go change? I know this is not my usual style, but I thought...well..." I stammered as Michael stepped forward shaking his head.

"I wouldn't change a thing." He pulled me close, leaned forward, and stamped his mouth to mine. His tongue carefully traced my lips as his hands gripped and pulled at the back of my shirt. The leather corset tightened as we continued our kiss and his hands pulled at the leather. But he stopped abruptly, his nose flared. "We'd better go, before..." he said through panting breaths before he snapped his mouth shut and clenched his teeth. His want and need were strong, but I could feel him pulling himself back into control.

I was about to object, but Michael saw the fight and put a finger to my lips.

"I promise you. It will be done, but not now, not whilst your parents await our attendance downstairs."

Smiling, and surely blushing, I gave a deep sigh then

nodded. As Michael pulled my chin up, I met his gaze. Easing his way back into my arms, he leaned forward and gave me one last passionate kiss. As he pulled away, he leaned his forehead against mine.

"We really need to go. It is getting hard to keep my control." Michael chuckled as he pushed himself away from me and headed to the door. "Are you coming?" he asked as he held the door open for me.

Taking one last look in the mirror, I nodded and followed him out.

"No worries. You really do look great," Michael whispered in my ear. I had started fidget when I saw a rather large group of the coven. As we passed, there were murmurings among them.

"Good afternoon, Arri," one of the members greeted me. "You look rather well this afternoon." I smiled and he bowed with a surprising look of approval. His smile met his eyes as he watched me carefully.

"Excuse me, my lady," another member greeted me. Michael and I stopped, and he bowed his head. His eyes flashed to my marking, which was on obvious display, then to Michael, and a puzzled look marred his face. His gaze bounced between the two of us before he took a step back.

"Good work. I just thought you ought to know. The sword fight was quite the show." He was obviously covering his real reason for stopping me. His curiosity about the mark was written on his face, as it was for all the others in the group. One by one, they all began to notice the crimson scrollwork, and one by one, their feelings of confusion and interest overwhelmed me until it felt like a tidal wave. I trembled.

"Is there a problem?" Michael inquired as the man started at us.

"No sir," the man stammered as he took a few more steps

back. "I was only admiring her bond mark. Curious that it is red." He bowed his head.

"Does it surprise you?" Although he hadn't said anything explicitly, there was a challenge in Michael's voice. He was daring them to contest him. His demeanor was calm, but his look promised retribution if any chose to rise up against him.

"Have you no thought as to why the color?" Michael asked. The man shook his head. "Ignorance," Michael said through a growl. "Have you no knowledge of the scrolls?" The man shook his head again. "Then may I suggest you glance at the scrolls once more."

"You mean for us to believe that Arri, a half-breed, is to be the chosen one?" Anton's voice was soft but defiant. Michael growled, and I could see he was losing his temper. With a small squeeze of reassurance, I let go of his hand and placed myself between them.

"Before you question the validity on things you do not yet understand, maybe you should first know what it is you have neglected," I said. "To know where one is going, one must first know where you come from." I stood tall and unyielding, gave a curt nod, and let a smile curve my lips. "Good day, sir," I said as I tugged lightly at Michael's hand once again. His reluctance to follow me was obvious as he gave the men a sinister glare, but with another tug, Michael followed me along the banister and down the winding staircase.

My heart fluttered as I realized I had just confronted Michael's men over not only the basis and meaning of my existence, but also their knowledge of the prophecy. My breath was quick and rushed. I felt light-headed, and a sense of power and control rushed through me. My uncertainty and confusion were gone, replaced with confidence and fortitude.

"Are you feeling okay? You're trembling." Michael's sweet voice wafted over me and brought me back to reality.

"Yes, thank you. I'm fine." Worry seeped through my defenses. "I'm sorry about what happened back there. It won't happen again." I lowered my head and waited for Michael's reprimand.

Michael laughed as we approached my parents.

"What is so funny?" my mother asked, taking my chin and tilting it up. A sad look briefly crossed her features before she cleared her expression.

"Your daughter," Michael said as he kissed me on the temple. "Now, who is ready for town?"

My heart jumped with excitement. Although trouble usually found me in town, I had my parents, Catherine, and Phoenix, to protect me. Add Ash, Phoenix's mate, to protect me. I was golden.

Ash had only arrived a few days ago from the northern front. From rumor alone, he was as good as Michael. Phoenix and Ash were experts in the battlefield. Even though Ash and I haven't really gotten to know each other since he got here, he felt like one of the group. Phoenix spoke of him nonstop and if he is as good as everyone says, what could go wrong?

As Michael and I left the driveway, my attention was quickly drawn to the trees.

"See something?" Michael asked.

"No, I was just thinking. I haven't seen Alex and the wolves for a while." My heart filled with sadness.

"No worries. It took a while for Alex to get over Sara, then he and Jonathan conducted a thorough investigation on the rest of the pack. I was relieved to hear that there were no more traitors among them." Michael's voice was distant and professional.

"I'm not one of your members, Michael. This is *me* you're talking to."

Michael shot me a look. "Yes, you are, but you are right.

Alex is just as much your friend as he is mine, but he has been rather distant lately. He has taken the treachery of one of his pack a little harder this time."

"You mean this has happened before?"

"Yes. It is rare that a werewolf has the ability to not only betray their leader, but also lie to them. See, a wolf's bond to his or her leader is as strong as our bond to each other. There is no hiding or lying. There is nothing that could be hidden from the Alpha. When you join the pack, the wolf mind is bound through blood, giving the Alpha full and complete control of his pack. But Sara, she was different. She fought his command from day one."

"How?"

"We don't know. That is the mystery." Concern and question burned in Michael's heart. There was something he felt eluded him, but he couldn't place just what it was.

A blur sped through the trees as we entered the freeway. Looking to Michael, I could tell he'd seen it too. He took out his phone and called one of his Ravens.

"Yes, Lyle, could be shadows, but keep a general sweep around us until we meet the others. If there is someone out here, I'd rather face them on the ground." There was a pause. "Good." He hung up.

"Is it possible it was one of the pack?" I was hoping it was. I didn't want any issues today.

"No. They are in town awaiting our arrival." His stern and no-nonsense expression gave me chills.

As Michael stepped on the gas, we accelerated until the speedometer could no longer track our speed. After that, it was only minutes before we slowed down and entered town by a back road.

The usual stream of people crowded the sidewalks. With school starting in a few weeks, back-to-school sales lined the sides of the streets. Like many of the shoppers, we pulled up to one of the shops and parallel parked.

Although I had been surrounded by hundreds of Michael's bloodsucking members with all the time in the world, I was more scared of the people on the street. I had been separated from humans for so long that now they felt like scurrying mice. While they busied themselves, and worried over things outside their control, their nervous and excited energy made me jumpy.

"Ready?" Michael asked as he took my arm and escorted me through the endless crowd. Onlookers gossiped and stared, but Michael ignored them and continued walking.

"Why are they all acting weird?"

"You've changed."

I looked at my clothes, then realized that while the vampires dressed as they saw fit, whether it be in tights or white-powdered wigs, here in town, my look might not have been appropriate.

"It's not in the way you dress; it is in your persona and demeanor. You are not a little girl anymore. You are one of us, flawless and perfect." His words hit me just as I saw a few of the girls I used to work with. Their faces fell as they recognized me.

"Arri, is that you?" Jenna asked. Her long red hair had been cut since I last saw her and now swung just above her shoulders. Her disbelieving look grew as she drew near. Jenna and I had never been friends. When Mary was plotting and manipulating the girls against me, Jenna had been the first to fall in line.

"Friend of yours?" Michael asked, ready to defend me.

"No, just someone I used to work with," I answered under my breath.

"Oh my, look at you. You've gone *alternative* on us."

Jenna's voice was mocking. I wanted to retaliate with a snide remark, but it would have been useless, and without missing a beat, she squealed and bounced up and down. "Oh, and guess what?" She squared her shoulders and stuck her nose in the air. "I've been made the new branch manager." Her prideful smile made me laugh. Michael, sensing my oncoming hysterics, jumped in.

"Well, congratulations," Michael said. Jenna smiled at Michael for acknowledging her promotion, then glared at me. "It's a tough position to keep."

Her smile faded as she folded her arms, her expression affronted and insulted. "Yes, well, I'm sure I can handle it," she replied as she pushed her hair behind her ear and pouted.

"I'm sure you can," I said, "and congratulations." I tried to sound sincere, but her boasting made it difficult. Still, Michael was right. It *was* a hard position to keep. If you looked at the last few managers, they'd all ended up dead— Anna, Mary, and Susan. Unfortunately, I didn't have a chance to meet Susan before my vision showed her dead at Nicholas's feet. With that thought, I actually felt bad. Jenna had no idea what she was walking into when she accepted the position, and I couldn't help but wonder what the managerial position had to do with Nicholas.

"Thank you." She furrowed her eyebrows and cocked her head. "And what brings you two to town? It is not often we see you."

"Dinner. We have reservations at the Sage Grill." Michael was quick to answer. "Now, if you'll excuse us, I've promised to spoil Arri here." A seductive smile spread across his face as he leaned down and kissed me, then whispered in my ear, "and more of these clothes." An embarrassing laugh escaped my lips as I blushed. Shock and scandal crossed Jenna's features as Michael hooked his arm around my waist and escorted me to the little diner in the center of town. Michael walked me around the hostess station and up a set of stairs. At the top, there was a yellow door. Without knocking, Michael turned the brass knob and entered a small studio apartment.

"Here," Michael helped me up onto a six-inch platform that seemed to be just wide enough for me and one other person, then sat down at a small wire garden table for two.

"I thought you said we had reservations?"

"We do, but first—"

I started to step off the platform, when a lady, with speed only a vampire could possess, circled me to take measurements.

"I needed these taken." There was a smug look on his face as his heart jumped excitedly.

After a cup of tea, and a brief chat with the woman, Michael and I left through the deserted back alley.

I could smell theater popcorn permeating the air as we passed the back entrance to the small theater.

"Movie?" Michael asked. Looking at the display of the only three movies playing, and the only four time slots, I shook my head.

"No thanks. I'm happy just being with you."

When I glanced past Michael, I spotted Seth. As pedestrians hurried by on the sidewalk, Seth remained still and seemed to stand out. Something about him still made me uncomfortable, like the way it did when he used to ask me out at the credit union, or when I saw him in the corner of the Chinese restaurant when Michael took me to lunch. Right now he was talking to Jenna. Whatever they were discussing, he wasn't happy about it. Everything, from the way he towered over her, to the scowling expression on his face, screamed he was up to no good. Because he was one of the richest men in town, he constantly tried to use his money to bully people. In short, he was a weasel and a mealy little man.

As Michael followed my gaze, he laughed and pushed me into the shadows. We were well hidden as the sun slid behind the mountains, and the shadows darkened.

"They are of no concern to us," Michael said with a wolfish grin.

As a few people passed us, Michael leaned in slowly. His lips were only centimeters from mine. I could feel the warmth radiating off his mouth. He placed both his hands flush against the wall behind me, on either side of my face, and held himself there, teasing me. His taunting smile tempted and coaxed me. I licked my lips and leaned my forehead against him in invitation.

"You are very alluring," Michael whispered, gently grabbing my waist.

"Then why fight it?" I asked as I put my hands on his cheeks.

"Tempt me not, luv; bonding is hard enough without seduction." With a kiss that made my legs tremble, he pulled me close to him. His hands clung to me as he pressed me against the wall. Then, just as fast as it started, it ended, as a young teenage couple turned the corner. Michael gave me a devilish grin, then took me by the hand as we walked past the couple and down the street.

"Did we miss our reservations?" Making a full circle around the block, I noted the many people that still littered the sidewalks before Michael helped me into the car. With dusk falling, and the streetlights coming on, I was worried we were late.

"No, but it is not exactly within walking distance."

Closing the car door behind me, Michael paused when he saw my dad across the street. He was talking to a young man with golden hair, a real pretty boy. His vampire status was obvious to me, but to the passersby, he was just eye candy. His tall, muscular physique, his flawless posture, and the way he radiated power—all was a dead giveaway.

As he and my dad talked, the pretty boy's features creased, and his heart was tinged with fear. The man pledged something as he bowed his head, and placed his hand over his heart. The conversation, although I couldn't hear it, seemed important. The man handed my dad a manila envelope, a car passed, and my dad and the golden-haired man were gone.

Michael stood tall and unmoving as he watched the scene before us. With a sigh of apparent relief, my dad acknowledged Michael with a brief nod and a flash of the envelope. Then, as if he was never there, my dad disappeared from sight.

TWENTY-TWO

"Who was that?" I asked as Michael got in the car. "He is of no concern right now. Your dad is handling the situation."

"What situation?" I asked, but Michael wasn't paying attention. His concentration had shifted, and he became quiet and withdrawn. I could almost feel his panic and nervousness as if it were my own. The closer we got to the restaurant, the quieter he got.

As we turned on a small side road, a well-hidden, well-designed parking lot appeared, tucked behind a gray, moderately kept old building. There were quite a few vehicles already parked between the only streetlamp, and the warehouse.

Michael exited the car, then, within the space of a heartbeat, he opened my door, offered his hand, and helped me out. As he kissed my hand, I saw uncertainty in his eyes. Michael was always so fluid and poised, but now, although his external self-projected composure and dignity, I could feel that just below the surface, his anxiety soared.

As we neared the entrance, I expected for the doors to show the name of an industrial company, but instead, I was shocked to see the words *Sage Grill* etched into the frosted, double-paned glass doors. Michael held the door for me as we entered.

"Good evening. Do you have a reservation?" a deep voice asked. Standing up tall, Michael nodded to the host. The man looked impressive, from his spiked brown hair, tailored black suit, and black-soled dress shoes,. Usually, in small towns like these, you didn't often see a restaurant that catered to a crowd beyond families.

When we first neared the building, it looked like a general warehouse used for machinery or farm equipment, but it was nothing of the sort. The interior was extraordinary. Some of the original, rustic brick walls remained untouched, left with their authentic, almost primitive wear and tear. Earth-yellow and fall-colored paint covered the newer interior walls. The front foyer was separated from the dining area with a gently flowing waterfall. Its tranquil melody added to the quaint and urban-rustic ambiance. The tables were designed for privacy and solitude. All in all, it was a well-designed, upscale restaurant.

"Yes, the name is London, Michael London." Michael's confident voice made the man stammer.

"L-London?" he asked as he checked the reservation book. As the reality of who Michael was kicked in, the man's nervousness level jumped through the roof.

"Yes, sir. I'm sorry, sir. This way, please." The host took two menus from the stand with shaking hands, his breathing coming in nervous sputters. "Your table, monsieur," the man said as he escorted us through the crowded restaurant toward the mid-back of the dining room. As we passed a few of the couples, I felt oddly underdressed. Looking down at my tight black pants, knee-high boots, and modern spin on the pirate look, I felt like I might as well have been dressed in jeans, a tank top, and old sandals.

"You're fidgeting," Michael remarked as we stopped at our table.

Michael gestured for me to slide into the bench seat first before sliding in beside me.

"Your waiter will be James this evening. He will be by shortly to take your orders," the host asked.

"Sorry, I feel out of place. Everyone here is dressed up, and I'm not." I looked down. "I guess this afternoon when I was getting dressed, I didn't realize we would be coming to a place this upscale."

"This"—Michael waved his hand around—"is not upscale. This is merely a restaurant that isn't concerned with serving kids and young families." Michael gave me a crooked smile. "It also has its advantages." He leaned forward and kissed me.

Our passionate embrace intensified, his hands gripping my shoulders. Kissing Michael was always a pleasure, but ever since I was bound to him, it had only gotten better. The more he showed me his affection, the more I craved it. I fed off his desire, which made him even more intoxicating. Our kiss continued, and with each passing second, it was even more proof that I would always be his, bound or not.

Michael closed his eyes as he tenderly pushed me away by the shoulders to break our breathtaking kiss. He fought for control, clenching his teeth and swallowing hard.

"I definitely like the advantages," I said with an innocent smile. "It does make dinner more entertaining." Although Michael kept his features passive, I could feel his internal instincts and his fight for restraint rage within him.

"You test my control, *mon amour*," Michael said as he kissed the back of my hand.

"I hope so." I grinned as I leaned in and nuzzled his neck. My touch sent his emotions skyrocketing, and Michael held his breath. With careful ease, he backed out of my grip. he looked nervous for a second, before he erased his anxious expression and replaced it with one of love and adoration.

He took my left wrist, turning it over so that my crimson marking was visible. With careful, steady hands, Michael traced his mark, and a satisfied smile brushed his lips.

"When you first presented this mark to me, I could see fear in your eyes." His smile faded a bit, replaced with a look of genuine esteem. "I saw confusion, unhappiness, and discomfort. I feared that you were going to reject me for what I had done to you." Michael looked so crestfallen as he remembered the look on my face that evening. The fear he saw in my eyes meant something different to the two of us. I feared I was cursed. He feared I was troubled and disappointed at the thought of being bound to him.

I wanted to tell him he thought wrongly, that I could never be happier than to be with him, but his encouraging and hopeful eyes turned to me. I saw his understanding. He knew how I felt. A hunger and want burned within him in that look. In that look, I saw his past. I saw his trials, his childhood, and even saw the moment of his mortality's end. His emotions were strong, and his love for me ran deep. Michael loved me. Half-vampire, half-mortal, didn't matter. I could see and feel his undying devotion to me.

"I know I am undeserving of such a wondrous possession. To me, you are more than a means to fulfill the prophecy. You are strong, smart, and understanding. You have a heart capable of untold love and compassion, and you are more than I could have hoped for." Michael closed his eyes for a brief second to gather his courage. With his most secret fear of my rejection tainting his heart, Michael regarded me anew with affection and warmth. "To see this mark on your arm has always been a dream, but I too wish for your brand to mark me. Our bond is yet to be completed, but I ask of thee will me bind me to you." Michael waited patiently as I came to my answer.

"Yes," I whispered. My voice got caught in my throat. My pants came out in sporadic sweeps, and my heart pounded excitedly.

Michael let out a withheld breath. A tentative, and then wide smile spread across his face as he pulled me into his arms. I could feel his heart leap with relief and excitement. His arms wrapped around me and held me tightly, and with fast and growing passion, Michael kissed his way from my ear to my lips. As we deepened that kiss, our desire and love melded. In that moment we were one. I could feel his thoughts, see his life through his eyes, and see what he knew we would be, together.

The moment was perfect. Just as Michael wiped away my joyful tears, he kissed my cheeks.

"Thank you," he said with heartfelt words as he leaned his forehead against mine. My heart melted.

When Michael reluctantly let me go, he reached into his coat's side pocket. Pulling out a closed fist, he took my left hand in his. "In my day, it was arranged as to who would be wed to whom. I know that my time's tradition is no longer honored, but I have asked your father's blessing, and he has granted it." Then, opening his fist, he dropped a small something in my hand.

To be honest, I didn't know what to expect. I knew that the scrolling was the vampire version of a wedding band, so I wouldn't think a ring would hold value to him.

"My mother wore this as a symbol of my father's everlasting love." A shadow of sorrow crossed his face with the thought of his parents. "I would be honored if you would wear this as a symbol of mine." Opening my hand, my eyes fell upon the smallest and daintiest silver ensign. The thin silver wire made an infinity symbol with a small diamond placed in the center where the sign crossed.

"Oh, Michael. It's lovely. I will wear it always."

"Here." Michael reached behind me and unlatched the simple, elegant necklace he'd given to me a year ago. As he took off the amber gem, where the thin scrolling held the amber in place, the infinity symbol latched to the opposite side, creating balanced lacing around the entire gem. After replacing the necklace, Michael leaned back and admired it carefully.

"It looks just as I remembered it." He touched the gem in remembrance of his long-lost parents. Then, with a warm and comforting smile, he kissed my cheek.

"Good evening. My name is James and I will be your server for the evening." James was a tall, young man with windswept hair; dark, eager eyes; and a broad, white smile. His outfit was similar to the host's, with the addition of a black apron. Pulling out his order pad, James concentrated only on the paper in front of him.

"Can I get you something to drink while you look at the menu?" he asked.

"Yes, thank you, but we are ready to order as well" Michael answered, never looking at the man or the menu, but only at me.

"Wonderful, sir, and what would you like to order?"

"The lady will have a Coke with the chicken Parmesan, and I will have the dark red wine from your special label preferred stock, and the spaghetti and meatballs."

"Yes, sir." James left our table with a bow of his head and without further question. As our dinner was being prepared, James returned to deliver our drinks. He handed me my Coke with a bashful smile, then carefully placed Michael's drink before him. As Michael swirled the thick wine and took in its aroma, the waiter's face turned pale and almost green. With a choked grimace, he excused himself and ran to the kitchen.

"So, I see you have managed to return from your worldwide traveling." A slick, greasy voice pronounced as he approached the table. Seth, the selfish, money-grubbing bully, stood tall and pompous. "And here I thought you were never to return," he sneered.

"And who or what gave you that insane idea?" I asked, cocking my head.

"I thought I heard a few of the girls whisper about your disappearance."

"I'm so sorry to have disappointed you," I said through a plainly fake smile.

"Yes, well, just you remember who the real power in this town is. I fund this town with all of its needs. You stay out of my way." As Seth pointed his greedy little finger in my direction and scowled, Michael rose to meet him. Seth wasn't tall by any standards. He *tried* to look tall as he puffed out his chest, and stuck his nose in the air, but he really was no taller than five foot five. Michael towered over Seth with a deadly glare.

"I would take care how you address my fiancée." Michael's indignant response and the miffed tone in his voice sent chills through the air. Although Seth's bravery and courage faltered and fell, he still attempted to retain his valor.

"And who might you be?" he asked, almost shaking.

"Michael London. And who, might I ask, has the audacity to so rudely interrupt us this evening? I'm afraid I haven't had the displeasure." As Michael's name left his mouth and realization hit, Seth's narrow face scrunched. "Oh, you've heard of me," Michael said as he casually took his seat.

"Uh…yes. A-although I can't quite think of from where." Seth was lying through his teeth. His heart palpitated as he struggled to answer.

"Well, I suggest you try to remember. It might remind

you why my name is so important." Michael's tone was demeaning and coarse. "Now, if you will excuse us, we were about to enjoy our meal." Michael motioned to the man standing behind Seth. Moving out of James's way, Seth headed to the door and left. James placed our meals in front of us and left in a hurry. Just like my dad, Michael possessed a power of intimidation that made people nervous.

"Wow," I said, shaking my head.

"What?"

"I don't remember Seth being a vampire." My heart skipped a few beats as I thought of how relentless he'd been about dating me. I remember him almost cornering me, pushing me to say yes, but back then, he felt like less of a threat than he did now.

"There is more to that man than meets the eye." Michael looked deep in thought. His expression hardened, furrows creasing his forehead as his eyes narrowed.

As I picked up my fork to eat, Michael excused himself for a moment, but not before I saw him dial my dad's number as he left the table. A few minutes later, he returned with a look of concern marring his brow.

"Is everything all right?" I asked when he sat down.

"Yes, I think," Michael said absently.

"Enough with the cryptic answers. Please just tell me what's up. I think I've earned the truth." The hint of warning in my voice told him I was serious. Michael's mouth dropped open.

"I wasn't trying to be elusive. I'm just trying to protect you."

"You can't protect me from this. Whether I like it or not—whether *you* like it or not—this is my life now. Every fight, every threat, every attempt on my life, is mine. I can't hide from it. I can't disguise it. It is what it is, and I have to face it. So please, tell me: what's going on?" My hands were shaking. I'd always known that this was my fight, and although Michael and my parents stood beside me, in the end, it was going to be Nicholas against me.

"You're right. I'm sorry. I don't want you to have to face any of this. You're not ready. You may have the blood mark, and you may be the prodigy, but I'm still going to be here for you. Bonded or not, you are mine, and I will sacrifice my life to protect you." He spoke from the heart. His words were not full of fluff and frills to cater to my tenderhearted nature. There was a sense of pride and responsibility behind them. He grabbed my hand, flipped it over, and stared at the marking. "You are my special girl, and I will always protect you."

"I know. Thank you." I closed my eyes as he kissed my forehead, and for a brief moment, the world disappeared. Time stood still, and we were the only two to exist.

As the world gradually returned, and time continued, so did the people in the world. Then, as if from nowhere, five new additions joined our table.

"Mom? Dad? What are you doing here?" I asked as Catherine helped herself to my chicken. Michael slapped her hand, but she just shook her head and chuckled.

"Ooh, so protective." She shrugged and winked. Catherine's playful and nonchalant side was fun to see. She and my parents were always so serious, and it was entertaining to see their *less* serious side.

"You called?" My dad said just as Michael showed his teeth. They pushed each other's buttons just like two teenagers would test each other's limits.

"Yes. Seth. Do you know of him?" Michael's and my dinner was now over and the meeting had begun.

"Yes, he is confōrmāre. His forma is unknown." The same concerned look tainted both their eyes.

"Confōrmāre? Forma? What are those?" I interrupted. My dad simply looked at me as if appalled with my behavior, but it was Michael who answered.

"A confōrmāre is a newly created vampire. They are usually rash and quick to act, but what they lack in discipline, they make up for in bravery. They are willing to prove their valor, but they are easily outsmarted. A forma is their creator. A vampire can only be created with their last breath. When a confōrmāre wakes, they are usually in great pain. To breathe life back into a lifeless body is not an affair to be taken lightly. It is only done with purpose and intent. There has to be a reason Seth was created."

"Jenna," I said under my breath, shaking my head. She either has no idea what Seth is, or she *did* know, and that is why she was so scared when he was towering over her.

"I beg your pardon—what was that?" My dad's look was stern and worried.

"Jenna, the new manager at the bank. She was talking to Seth earlier. I assumed they were dating, but whatever the case is, I don't think she knows what he is."

"How do you know Jenna?" My dad's voice rose with each question he asked.

"She was one of the girls who worked under me at the bank. I know she was hoping to get my position, but when I arrived and Mary started to spin her web, Jenna was one of the first to fall in line behind her."

"Is she a vampire now?" There was obvious anticipation in my dad's voice.

"No," Michael spoke up. "We saw her today. I can verify she is not one of us."

"Why? What would that have to do with anything?" I knew there was something I was missing.

"Only a vampire can manage this particular credit union.

It was created and formed remotely for us. Vampires are its founding fathers. To place so much money in a mortal financial institution would raise question and suspicion. A human is too easily subject to a vampire's thrall and can be manipulated and coerced into revealing our identities." Michael's voice was forlorn and empty, as though he were reciting a speech.

"Yes, I see." We fell quiet, contemplating.

"Seth said that he was the boss of this town," I said. "He had to have been approached. His sole goal was to be mayor. This puts the mayor in the palm of his hand. In exchange for information, he was given power. Now what?"

Everyone stared at me.

"Excuse me." James stood at the edge of the table with a nervous look on his face.

"Yes?" Michael's voice held restraint even though he looked agitated.

"I'm sorry…" James looked at the newer additions to our table, confused and distracted from whatever he'd arrived to say. "Will the rest of the table like to place orders?"

"No, thank you," Michael answered, but James didn't leave.

"Yes? Is there anything else?" Michael brought his attention back to the matter at hand.

"Yes…right," the waiter said. "There is a young man claiming to be meeting you this evening, Mr. London. Would you like me to send him back?" Michael glanced at the host station, then nodded.

I was surprised to see that it was the slick-haired coward I'd fought. His clothing had changed, and his demeanor was pompous and smug, as opposed to the nervous and fear-hearted man who'd left me for dead.

"It looks like we have some unwelcome company."

Michael sneered as he rose to greet our unwanted guest. "Gavin." His name fell from Michael's lips with exaggerated sarcasm.

"*Michael.*" Gavin reciprocated with equal contempt.

"Do tell—to what we owe to your unfortunate visit?"

Gavin let out a barking laugh that made my skin crawl. "I didn't come for you." Gavin looked past Michael and directly at me, his assessing stare wandering over me with hate and detest. All eyes were on me before returning back to Gavin.

"Please, may I sit?" Gavin gestured to the chair at the head of the table.

"No," Michael said. "You won't be staying long enough to get comfortable".

"Talk, Gavin. What is your purpose here?" Michael's low voice was almost a growl.

"As I said, I didn't come for you. I came to seek an audience with Arri." He looked pointedly at me. Judging me. His lips curled into a knowing grin, and his fingers twitched as he awaited my response.

"If I were to grant your request, what would the subject of our discussion be?" I tried to sound secure in my answer. Gavin merely cocked his head.

"To negotiate your surrender, of course."

ASCENDANCE, BOOK THREE IN THE PARADOX TRILOGY

In the final days of the vampire war, masters will be betrayed, friendships will be splintered, and allies gained.
Knowing what will befall everyone if Nicholas possesses absolute control, the unthinkable may be Arri's only choice.

But will she be strong enough to end this for good?

Pick up your copy of Ascendance here.

As Arri waits for her destiny to reveal itself, she finds a piece of the past that helps her discover her origins and the myth behind the ill-fated and infamous word, vampire.

Here is an excerpt from Forgotten Journal.

***

FALL

I've written down my thoughts and experiences as a matter of record. The best way to do this is to start from the beginning.

When I was younger, I didn't crave the thick crimson blood of others. I never abandoned my loyalties or shirked responsibilities like some of my fellows. No, I worked hard for what I got and did more than my fair share, and I never would have done what I was about to do.

The day started like any other. The sun was trying to make an appearance as the moon dominated the predawn sky. I lit the lamps before I got dressed and left. The marketplace had been busier than usual, so I wanted to get there before the sun rose, and I had hoped before the crowd. I was glad I wasn't a slave, being born from an upper-class man. Walking around the main square, I passed many shopping for their masters. I felt terrible for their working, but as my father's father had been before him, most of our ancestors began as slaves. It was a hard reality and truth, one I learned early on. They taught me to be grateful for the place I held and not to snub anyone below my status. As I picked up my supplies, I greeted the merchant and noticed a slight drain in his color. He seemed paler than usual, and the bags under his eyes confirmed his ill status.

"Sir?" I asked as I picked up my purchase. "Are you feeling well?"

His sunken gaze already told me the answer.

"I'll fetch the apothecary."

"No," the man said as he reached out his hand and grabbed my shirt. "Go. Run. Save yourself." His words slurred together and his voice was gruff, as if he were speaking through sandpaper. "Please. Pl—"

His final plea fell short as his eyes rolled back and his heavily rounded body thudded to the ground.

"Young man!" a hearty voice thundered as I cradled the merchant's head in my lap.

"Gruth! Gruth!" I called out to the merchant as he laid there, unconscious and limp.

"What have you done?"

I tried to tell him as I shook my head as stunned tears

streaked my cheeks. "He told me to run and save myself, sir. What did he mean?"

"I know treachery when I see it, young man." He grabbed my arm and yanked me from the ground.

"Leave him, good man. It wasn't him," the apothecary said as he approached with a bag in his hand.

"Sir, I did nothing, I purchased my goods then realized he looked sickly. Please help him," I begged as he came to sit beside me.

"I know you did nothing. I have been seeing Gruth."

Like everyone else my age, I had hopes, dreams, and aspirations to become more than I was. I had responsibilities, and I was well on my way to becoming someone, but something happened that night that had changed my life forever. Something I will never forget no matter how long I live.

After the sun sank behind the mountains and darkness crept into the valley, my skin burned, and my heart pounded. I felt feverish, and hot chills left beads of sweat on my skin. My ears rang, and I knew. This is what Gruth had warned me of, but how? Had he known something I hadn't?

Then it hit me: the apothecary.

I ran from my bed and pounded on Romud's door. Squinting into the darkness until he saw me, he cracked it open, then pulled me in and locked the door shut behind me.

The apothecary eyed me carefully. "Did he cut or scratch you?"

I tried to think. "No, sir, not that I know of."

"Here," Romud said before pulling on my arms and lifting my shirt off over my head. Yelling in triumph, he poked at my back.

"See, here!" he said, poking again at the tender spot on my back.

"What?" I gasped for breath.

"Gruth scratched you, and now you are ill. I knew it. I knew it would work." The apothecary seemed elated by his discovery, but I did not understand why. I felt like I was dying, and he was happy?

"What worked? What have you done to me?" I accused him, but he seemed to ignore me and was writing in a book. "What have you done?" I yelled through labored breaths as I pounded my hand on his writing.

"The merchant was ill because of what I gave him when he came in with a burning heart. Maybe you will survive."

"What?" I cried as the room went black. I hit the ground. My body aches vanished, and my thundering heart stilled. Even my fever abated, but after that, I couldn't move or open my eyes. I was trapped in my body with no control. Soon after that, I heard the apothecary speaking to someone.

"Did he have someone at home?"

"No, he was the son of Mazleous."

Then that was it. After that, I remember nothing. I felt nothing, heard nothing, thought nothing. Everything was blank and black. I don't know how I came back into this world. I suppose I could hallucinate that I might have been someone of importance for this to happen, or that I am just a man down on his luck, but in all honesty, I don't have a clue. That's when it all started. I remember the excruciating pain of burning from the inside out and how no matter what I did, I couldn't escape it. I felt the torture of death drowned me in agonizing torment. Every move I tried to make felt like red hot daggers stabbing into my sides. Breathing became horrifyingly excruciating, and my eyelids felt like molten branding irons piercing my retinas. When I awoke from my painful death, this terrifying hell, I felt an inextinguishable burning along the lining of my throat every time I fought for air. I wished for the sweet release that only death could bring, but my prayers were unanswered as I fought for either life or death.

***

I hope you enjoyed your sneak peak of Forgotten Journal. To read the rest of the exclusive bonus chapter download *Forgotten Journal* at jamieripp.com.

For updates on new releases join me on Facebook or at Jamieripp.com!

DEAR READER

Hello Readers,

Thank you for reading Revelation, it means a lot to me that
you read the second book in the Paradox Trilogy.

I'd love to hear from you.
If you enjoyed Revelation, please consider leaving a review.
Every review helps, even if it's only a sentence or two. You
know us author types, we just love that sort of thing!

For reviews!
Amazon
Goodreads

For new release updates and to follow me:
Facebook
jamieripp.com

Thank You and Happy Reading,
    Jamie Ripp

ABOUT THE AUTHOR

Jamie Ripp is the author behind the Paradox Trilogy. She has lived a full and adventurous life as a hostage negotiator, a referee, and a monster slayer. Jamie is the main character of her own personal safari as she fights off mountain lions, has standoffs with bears, and contains flightless aviaries and herds of hoofed wildlife. She has studied battle strategy, visited the rainforest, battled vampires, demons, and courted death with nothing more than a pen and caffeine.

Actually, while living in the mountains of Montana, Jamie has come face to face with a mountain lion, slept in a tent alongside a bear, and enjoys feeding her chickens and deer while trekking through three feet of snow. As for a referee and monster slayer, well, she is married and the mother of three.

While Jamie has never been in a hostage situation, she has been part of a group chat and has been a prisoner of war within the battalion of three teenagers.

While writing, Jamie has played the part of writer and character. She has defeated coven masters, found love among the trees, and courted the Grimm Reaper.

In short, she is Super Woman with an imagination, also known as an author and a mother.

BOOKS BY JAMIE:

PARADOX TRILOGY:

Paradox
Revelation
Ascendance

EXCLUSIVE BONUS CHAPTER:

Forgotten Journal

www.ingramcontent.com/pod-product-compliance
Lightning Source LLC
Chambersburg PA
CBHW022004170626
46808CB00001B/274